Dear Reader,

There's been a Chisholm running the Double Diamond Ranch since the first homestead was deeded to my great-grandfather in the late 1800s. It's a lot bigger than it was back then—more land, more cattle, more work. But this land is more than rangeland and wide-open spaces—it's about a way of life and family. It's mostly about roots, I guess. And in spite of the hard work and worry, there's nothing I'd change, except maybe for the fact that my kids are growing up without a mother. Mostly we manage, and I try not to think about it. But every now and then something happens that stops you dead in your tracks and makes you wonder.

The other day I caught a glimpse of my oldest daughter curled up in front of the fireplace, reading a book, and for a split second I thought it was a stranger sitting there. Somewhere along the line, she'd turned into a young lady. My four kids are growing up, and I hadn't really noticed. It was as if I'd blinked once, and years had slipped by. And as I stood there watching her, I wondered if I'd done a proper job of raising them. When I'm old and gray, will I be able to look back without regret? I hope I can, because my kids are what keep me going. Without them, none of this would really matter. Not the ranch. Not the land. Not the generations that have lived here before us. Those kids are the reason I get up every morning. I hope somewhere down the road they understand that. And I hope they know how damned much I love them—because that's what life is all about.

Jason Chisolm

Ranch Rogues

1. *Betrayed by Love*
   Diana Palmer
2. *Blue Sage*
   Anne Stuart
3. *Chase the Clouds*
   Lindsay McKenna
4. *Mustang Man*
   Lee Magner
5. *Painted Sunsets*
   Rebecca Flanders
6. *Carved in Stone*
   Kathleen Eagle

Hitched in Haste

7. *A Marriage of Convenience*
   Doreen Owens Malek
8. *Where Angels Fear*
   Ginna Gray
9. *Inheritance*
   Joleen Daniels
10. *The Hawk and the Honey*
    Dixie Browning
11. *Wild Horse Canyon*
    Elizabeth August
12. *Someone Waiting*
    Joan Hohl

Ranchin' Dads

13. *Rancher's Wife*
    Anne Marie Winston
14. *His and Hers*
    Pamela Bauer
15. *The Best Things in Life*
    Rita Clay Estrada
16. *All That Matters*
    Judith Duncan
17. *One Man's Folly*
    Cathy Gillen Thacker
18. *Sagebrush and Sunshine*
    Margot Dalton

Denim & Diamonds

19. *Moonbeams Aplenty*
    Mary Lynn Baxter
20. *A Home on the Range*
    Judith Bowen
21. *The Fairy Tale Girl*
    Ann Major
22. *Snow Bird*
    Lass Small
23. *The Countess and the Cowboy*
    Linda Randall Wisdom
24. *Heart of Ice*
    Diana Palmer

Kids & Kin

25. *Fools Rush In*
    Ginna Gray
26. *Wellspring*
    Curtiss Ann Matlock
27. *Live-In Mom*
    Laurie Paige
28. *Kids, Critters and Cupid*
    Ruth Jean Dale
29. *With No Regrets*
    Lisa Jackson
30. *Family Affair*
    Cathy Gillen Thacker

Reunited Hearts

31. *Yesterday's Lies*
    Lisa Jackson
32. *The Texas Way*
    Jan Freed
33. *Wild Lady*
    Ann Major
34. *Cody Daniels' Return*
    Marilyn Pappano
35. *All Things Considered*
    Debbie Macomber
36. *Return to Yesterday*
    Annette Broadrick

Reckless Renegades

37. *Ambushed*
    Patricia Rosemoor
38. *West of the Sun*
    Lynn Erickson
39. *Bittersweet*
    DeLoras Scott
40. *A Deadly Breed*
    Caroline Burnes
41. *Desperado*
    Helen Conrad
42. *Heart of the Eagle*
    Lindsay McKenna

Once A Cowboy...

43. *Rancho Diablo*
    Anne Stuart
44. *Big Sky Country*
    Jackie Merritt
45. *A Family to Cherish*
    Cathy Gillen Thacker
46. *Texas Wildcat*
    Lindsay McKenna
47. *Not Part of the Bargain*
    Susan Fox
48. *Destiny's Child*
    Ann Major

Please address questions and book requests to: Harlequin Reader Service
U.S.: 3010 Walden Ave., P.O. Box 1325, Buffalo, NY 14269
Canadian: P.O. Box 609, Fort Erie, Ont. L2A 5X3

WESTERN *Lovers*™

JUDITH DUNCAN

ALL THAT MATTERS

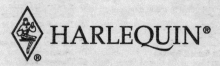

HARLEQUIN®

TORONTO • NEW YORK • LONDON
AMSTERDAM • PARIS • SYDNEY • HAMBURG
STOCKHOLM • ATHENS • TOKYO • MILAN • MADRID
PRAGUE • WARSAW • BUDAPEST • AUCKLAND

HARLEQUIN BOOKS
225 Duncan Mill Road, Don Mills,
Ontario, Canada M3B 3K9

ISBN 0-373-30164-2

ALL THAT MATTERS

CHAPTER ONE

THE SENSE OF SPACE was almost overwhelming. For years, she'd heard her boss refer to it as "blue sky country," but she'd assumed it was just another catchphrase from the west, like "beautiful British Columbia" or "sunny Alberta." But this one was true. She'd never seen sky line like this in her entire life.

Squinting against the glare of sunlight off the hood of her car, Susan Lynton's expression became thoughtful. This drive across Canada had certainly been an eye-opener for her. It was during the long journey that she finally realized what a narrow textbook concept she had of her native land. Having lived in Ontario all her life, Susan was fairly knowledgeable about the heavily populated and industrialized central part of Canada, but it wasn't until these past few days that she realized how little she knew about the rest of the country.

The forsaken wilderness of northern Ontario had filled her with a feeling of solitary awe. The miles and miles of forest was punctuated with craggy outcrops and countless crystal-clear lakes. There was a raw, wild beauty about it, but there was also a haunting aura of isolation. The silence of the uninhabited wilderness was eerie, almost smothering in its intensity, and Susan had never experienced such an overwhelming sense of loneliness.

The great plains of Manitoba and Saskatchewan had seemed like freedom, and the tabletop flatness and the sense of never-ending space had invigorated her until the monotony of the arrow-straight highway encased her in boredom.

The towering grain elevators that crowded against the railroad in every town appeared like immobilized Goliaths, giants that dominated the fertile sweeping fields, subsisting on enormous quantities of grain. And she'd felt almost intimidated by it all.

Now, as she traveled south from Calgary, the prairie plains heaved and buckled into the treeless bleak foothills of cattle country, and Susan experienced an uncomfortable feeling that she'd been royally conned. Her boss in Ottawa had inundated her with propaganda on the wonders of Alberta, thundering from his soapbox of enthusiasm, ''It has everything, Susan—the prairies, the foothills, the mountains. It has wheat fields and forests. You travel Alberta, Susan, and you'll see for yourself. It's God's land.'' Susan grinned to herself. Clayton Chisholm was probably the most articulate salesman, the most fervent evangelist for the west in all of Ottawa.

Her smile faded as she adjusted her sunglasses, and a slight frown appeared. One of these days, though, she was going to regret her tendency to get swept into situations by other people's enthusiasm. And she had a nagging suspicion it was going to be much sooner than she expected.

When Clayton Chisholm had first suggested that she take an extended holiday from her very demanding job as his executive assistant, she had shrugged it off. But when he offered her a job on the ranch he and his nephew owned in the Alberta foothills, her interest had been sparked. Now that she was rapidly approaching her destination, she was beginning to wonder if her decision had been a wise one, especially when it had been so strongly colored by his enthusiasm, her own curiosity and an unfulfilled fantasy.

The curiosity was aroused by Clayton Chisholm himself. Even before she went to work for him seven years ago, Susan had been well aware of his impressive record as an elected member of Parliament. He had tirelessly served his southern Alberta constituency, and when his party, which had sat in opposition for many years, had enjoyed a sweeping victory in a recent federal election, he had been appointed minister of a very major portfolio.

Susan knew everything there was to know about his public life. But she knew very little about his private one. For all his affability, there was a certain reserve about the man. Many listed him among their most trusted and valued friends, but no one knew who was closest to Clayton Chisholm. Even though he had just turned sixty, he was still an Ottawa hostess's dream come true—a man who was eligible, successful and financially secure. He possessed a natural charm, an unquestionable masculinity, and it was no secret that the honorable member had more than one Ottawa socialite in determined pursuit. Over the years a multitude of idle, unfounded rumors had surfaced about his private life, but he'd never even bothered to acknowledge them. Clayton Chisholm's private life was exactly that: private.

No one had ever been allowed any personal glimpses. No one, except Susan.

It had happened six winters ago, shortly after she started to work for him as a junior researcher. A government scandal had been uncovered involving a senior party member who had been a colleague of Clayton's for many years. When accusations were shouted across the floor of the House of Commons that the honorable member, Clayton Chisholm, who held such an influential post in the opposition's shadow cabinet, had known what was going on, the public outcry was heard right across the country. The members of the governing party and the press gallery had a field day demanding his resignation. No one, except Susan, ever knew how close they came to getting it.

It had been right at the peak of the crisis, after days of unpleasant publicity and parliamentary mudslinging, that Susan saw a side of her boss that she intuitively knew no one in Ottawa had seen before. She had gone back to his offices at the parliament buildings one night to try to document a certain sequence of events that would clear his name. It had been very late and she was exhausted, but she'd continued to go through box after box of old files, looking for the information she needed.

She was seated at a table in Clayton Chisholm's office, cartons filled with thick file folders stacked around her, a nearly hopeless task ahead. The futility of what she was doing, combined with fatigue, finally wore her down, and in a fit of frustration, she'd thrown a file across the room, then buried her head in her arms and wept.

She hadn't heard him come into the office and wasn't even aware of his presence until he patted her reassuringly on the shoulder and commented wryly, "Don't despair, Susan. Nothing is ever so bad that it can't get worse."

The dryness in his tone struck her funny and she found her shoulders shaking with a mixture of tears and unexpected laughter. Wiping her face, she sat back in her chair and with a deep sigh, looked up at him. "Thanks a lot," she said, her tone as dry as his own. "I really needed to hear that."

His famous smile was a little ragged as he patted her shoulder again then went to his desk and wearily slouched into the chair behind it. "I'm beginning to think that anyone who gets involved in the machinations of bureaucracy is either the village idiot or totally insane."

Susan propped her chin on her hand, her previous sense of hopelessness giving way to amusement. "May I quote you on that?"

He laughed as he leaned back and laced his fingers behind his head. "The headhunters would wet themselves in utter delight if you did." His expression grew solemn as he stared off into space, his face lined with fatigue. After a moment of silence he turned his gaze to Susan. "Have you been able to nail down those dates?"

She shook her head, a defeated sag to her shoulders. "Not yet. I'm afraid it's going to take a while."

He pursed his lips and nodded, a frown furrowing his brow. Again he gazed off into space, then inhaling deeply, he leaned forward and rested his arms on top of his desk.

He solemnly studied her for a second, then spoke, determination in his voice. "We're wasting our time. I've decided I'm going to hand in my resignation."

Susan couldn't have been caught more off guard, and she stared at him in disbelief. Finally she found her voice and stammered, "B-but you can't."

"Why not?"

The thought of his resigning left her speechless, and it took her a moment to gather her thoughts. "Because you know the allegations are unfounded, and given enough time, we can prove it."

He gave her a warped smile, and for the first time since she started working for him, Clayton Chisholm looked his age. "I'm not a young man anymore, my dear, and I'm getting tired."

She had found it impossible to meet his unwavering gaze, and she dropped her eyes and began to fiddle with the papers scattered before her. "I can understand that. But don't quit now. You have to see it through." He made no response but continued to stare at her. She had begun to think she'd overstepped her bounds, then she saw a tiny hint of humor gleaming in his eyes. She flashed him a smile and pushed the issue. "And besides, if you quit, I'll be out of a job."

He gave her an amused look as he tipped his head toward the boxes of files. "With that ahead of you, I'm surprised you still want it."

She'd left her chair and was kneeling on the floor, picking up the papers that had scattered from the file when she'd thrown it across the room. Tucking her hair behind her ear, Susan looked up at him and grinned. "Since I've started working, I've developed a habit of eating regularly and the novelty hasn't worn off yet."

Clayton Chisholm chuckled and nodded.

There was more fact than fiction in that statement, Susan silently acknowledged as she stuffed old letters into the file folder. She had gone to work for him as soon as she'd graduated from university with a B.A. in public relations, and a regular paycheck had been heaven. But the real truth was that she absolutely loved her job.

She stuck the last sheet in the folder and stood up. A feeling of apprehension settled on her as she quietly studied him. He was hunched over his desk, a preoccupied expression on his face as he slowly rolled a pen between his fingers.

With her voice muted by uncertainty she asked, ''Have you already tendered your resignation?''

The lines on his face seemed to be more deeply etched when he raised his head and looked at her. Without breaking the silence, he reached into the breast pocket of his jacket, withdrew a single folded piece of paper and handed it to her. Her spirits sank when she unfolded the heavy white bond and saw the familiar silver and blue insignia on the letterhead.

''I was on my way to hand deliver it, but I saw the light on in here.''

As she stood there staring at Clayton Chisholm's letter of resignation, the only coherent thought that surfaced was *I can't let him do this.* But when she finally looked at him, she saw him with clearer vision, her belief in his invincibility no longer distorting her view. The man was exhausted, both mentally and physically, and right then he looked old, very old—and very alone.

Her tone was gentle. ''Will you hang on to this,'' she asked, indicating his letter, ''and give me until the weekend to dig through this mess?''

''You may never find the documentation we need, you know,'' he responded, quietly preparing her for defeat.

''Yes, I will.''

Clayton Chisholm watched her for the longest time, then said quietly, ''I hope your father is damned proud of you.''

A rueful smile appeared as she refolded his letter. ''He wavers between pride and exasperation.''

He responded with a snort of amusement and Susan looked at him. Her face sobered as she scrutinized his expression for some clue to what he was thinking. "Do I have until the weekend?"

He dragged his hand across his face and sighed. "Yes, you have until the weekend." He lowered his eyes and stared at his clasped hands, his face suddenly haggard.

She gazed at him, concern darkening her eyes. "What is it?" she asked softly.

There was a long silence, and when he finally spoke, his voice had a sad, reminiscent timbre to it. "There are times when I wonder why I've kept on going." There was something in his tone that made her realize there was a specific reason why he drove himself so hard, a reason why he had never married. And for Clayton Chisholm, it was a very private reason.

After that night, after gaining an unexpected insight into the man, Susan's compassion was aroused. And when Susan's compassion was aroused, she mothered with unrelenting dedication. Instead of looking upon him as her boss, she began viewing him as a favorite uncle. Not only did she find the documents they needed to clear his name, she also uncovered some unexpected information that placed the integrity of Clayton's most vocal accuser on the line. Eventually the storm blew itself out, but from then on, Susan did everything she could to take the pressure off, to anticipate problems, to be one step ahead of his needs.

At first he had viewed her actions with a certain amount of amusement, but he began to depend on her more and more. In time, she became his confidante, and she was responsible for everything from approving his itinerary to editing his speeches to keeping him informed on even the smallest matter that might impact his department. An alliance of mutual trust and respect developed between them, and after working so closely together for so long, they'd reached a point where they could read each other perfectly.

They shared a solid rapport, and Susan knew she was closer to him than anyone else was in Ottawa, yet there was still that private part of his life she knew nothing about.

She'd catch him in an unguarded moment, a haunted look in his eyes, an expression of such loneliness carved in his face that it would make her want to cry. The reason, she suspected, would be found here in the place he still considered home.

Susan's wandering thoughts were dragged back to the present when a white road sign with the wild rose emblem on it flashed past. She pulled onto the shoulder of the road and stopped, then extracted a road map from the narrow space between the emergency brake and the bucket seat. Pushing her sunglasses on top of her head, Susan refolded the map to isolate the last leg of her journey. Assured that this was the right turnoff, she slid the map back in the slot, replaced her glasses, and after checking for traffic turned west on the secondary highway.

The foothills rose before her, blocking out the distant panorama of the mountains. As she continued due west, she was surrounded by nothing but bleak, rolling hills. There was a quality of desolation about this part of the country that she hadn't expected. It seemed so barren, so empty, not at all how she had pictured it from Clayton's descriptions. Her doubts became even more unsettling. She didn't know if she could stand all this vastness, this *nothingness* for three months.

And she was, unfortunately, committed to three months. Clayton had arranged a two-month's leave of absence for her while the house was in summer recess, and she had taken a month's holidays. But she was committed for other reasons. His sister-in-law had had a stretch of very poor health, and her doctor had warned that she had to take it easy for a while. Clayton was concerned that unless he stepped in, Mattie Chisholm would simply ignore doctor's orders and carry on. He felt that the summer work load was simply too much for a woman her age, and was convinced his executive assistant was the one and only candidate for the job.

He talked to Susan about hiring on as cook then let her

think about it, and the longer she thought about it the more she wanted to go. Ever since she was a kid, Susan had harbored a love affair with the west, and the idea of spending time on a working ranch held enormous appeal. So with her judgment colored by Clayton's enthusiasm, Susan took his word that the job would be a piece of cake.

Susan grinned to herself. Some cook. She could organize a banquet for four hundred without blinking an eye, but she was beginning to wonder if she'd be able to slap three big meals a day on the table for a crew of men. She had grown up on a tobacco farm in southwestern Ontario, which didn't really mean much under the circumstances, but a favorite uncle owned a large mixed farming operation in Manitoba, and until she started working during her high school years, Susan had spent a part of every summer vacation there. Even as a kid, who had more important things on her mind, like jumping out of the hayloft or chasing gophers, she was vaguely aware that her aunt spent most of her day preparing meals and doing dishes. Well, at least all those summer vacations would stand her in good stead now. She could tell one end of a cow from the other.

Suddenly, her few small doubts became very large ones. What did she *really* know about these people, anyway? Clayton often talked about his family and she felt as though she knew them, but actually they were still strangers. Susan knew from bits and pieces of conversation that Clayton's parents had been dead a long time, that his brother had been killed many years ago in a riding accident and that it was that brother's son who was now managing the ranch. She knew that the nephew's name was Jason, and that he was the father of four children who ranged in ages from thirteen to six. She knew he was divorced and in his middle forties, and she knew that his mother, who had done considerable traveling, had moved back to the ranch at the time of his divorce to help him raise the kids. And she also knew, with sudden absolute certainty, that she had made a very big mistake.

The narrow highway became more twisting and Susan blocked off her glum thoughts to focus her full attention on her driving. Cut into a steep bank, the road wound its way down into a deep ravine that had been carved by centuries of erosion. The drone of the engine changed pitch as Susan shifted into a lower gear while she navigated the sharp curve at the bottom of the gully. The sound of her passage echoed hollowly as she crossed a narrow wooden bridge that spanned a small stream, which lost itself in the random growth of wild berry bushes and stunted willows. A long incline zigzagged out of the ravine, and she geared down again when the engine protested the long, steep climb.

As she approached the crest of the hill, Susan experienced the same feeling she had from time to time when she was small: that she had reached the edge of the world and there was nothing on the other side.

But there was. And it was so breathtaking it was beyond description. She pulled over on the gravel shoulder and switched off the ignition, overwhelmed by the vista that was spread out before her. The ridge of bleak hills formed the natural rim of a valley that opened up to the most spectacular view she'd ever seen.

Off in the distance, the snowcapped Rocky Mountains loomed up in majestic splendor, creating an impregnable barrier that thrust jaggedly into the clear blue May sky, their imposing fortresses shaded in hues of blue, purple and gray. A high range of hills, densely covered by coniferous forest, rose against the base of the mountains and added a misty dimension of distance to the diorama. Here the range was no longer treeless, and coppices of poplar and aspen were scattered across the landscape, their crowns brushed with soft wisps of green from the first buds of spring. Sturdy sentinels of fir and spruce towered above the newly budding trees, their dark green boughs accentuated by the delicate shades of new growth.

The sky, blue and endless, encompassed it all. The colors were magnificent. From the purples, blues and grays of the mountains, to the variegated greens of the forests, to the rusts, ambers and golds of the rolling grassland—it was an artist's palette, and she absorbed every nuance of it.

Susan had no idea how long she sat there, entranced by the beauty before her, but when she finally stirred and reluctantly started the car, she felt as though she had just been given a long, cool drink after a very tiring journey.

Maybe she hadn't made a mistake, after all. The feeling of expectation grew as she covered the final miles, her host of doubts no longer badgering her. It was the strangest sensation, but she suddenly felt as if she were coming home.

And that feeling became even stronger as she crested a small rise and saw a group of buildings off to the right. It all seemed so familiar. "The buildings are set off to the north in a little hollow that's a fair distance from the main road," Clayton had told her when he gave her directions. "The first thing you'll see is a windbreak of spruce trees along the drive and the big white arena where Jason trains his horses. There's a typical ranch gate, a pole arch with the Double Diamond brand carved into the crossbar. You can't miss it."

As Susan slowed to turn into the gate, she glanced up at the impressive row of gigantic spruce that lined the far side of the drive. Their roots went deep into this Chisholm land, as did Clayton's. Why, she wondered, did he ever leave, feeling the way he did about this place?

The lane curved down into a sheltered hollow, and Susan felt a rush of warmth as the house and buildings came clearly into view. Several acres of land adjacent to the road had been left untouched, and thick stands of poplar and pine were scattered across the rolling terrain. The driveway, which angled sharply across the yard, separated the raw untouched land from the lawn surrounding the Chisholm home.

The huge old-fashioned house, which faced the gravel driveway, looked like it had been recently painted, its black trim standing out sharply against the sparkling white. A ve-

randa stretched across the front of the building, the still-bare
branches of vines tangled profusely along the spindled rail
and up the pillars at the corners.

A high hedge of lilacs, which was just beginning to show
the first touch of spring, bordered the east side of the yard.
Through the bare branches, Susan could see flashes of sunlight off the metal roof of the arena she had first seen from
the road. Another windbreak of trees was located a fair distance behind the house, which, she suspected, hid the rest
of the farm buildings and corrals from view. The setting
was picture-book perfect.

She followed the driveway around to the back of the
house where the road continued on, disappearing into the
trees. Susan parked her aging Volkswagen beside a row of
caraganas, and as she switched off the ignition, her uncer-
tainties came marching back in full force. Taking off her
sunglasses and hanging them on the sun visor, Susan
combed her fingers through her shoulder-length, curly hair,
then mentally squaring her shoulders, she climbed out of the
car.

She was just passing through the broad opening in the
hedge when the screen door opened and a woman with snow
white hair came out. She was attractive and of medium
height with a surprisingly good figure, and as she came
down the steps, she brushed her navy slacks, which had
smudges of flour across the front of them.

This was not exactly a grandma of the first order. Not the
kind that spent her winter evenings knitting mitts or mend-
ing socks, Susan was willing to bet. This was a woman who
liked to be where the action was, who liked to face new
challenges. But her face had compassion and humor written
into it with every line, and her blue eyes held a warmth and
understanding put there by years of laughter. And as she
came toward Susan, her face wrinkled with a huge smile as
she stretched out her arms in a gesture of unaffected welcome. It was as though she'd known the younger woman
all her life, and Susan felt suddenly very much at ease.

"You have to be Clayton's Susan," Mattie Chisholm said warmly as she clasped Susan in an enveloping hug. "He's told us so much about you, I think I'd know you anywhere."

Clayton Chisholm's sister-in-law released her and, Susan who was several inches taller, smiled down at the older woman. "I am. And you must be Mrs. Chisholm."

"Mattie, dear. Mattie," she corrected firmly. "Don't make me feel any older than I already do." A large tan-and-black curly haired dog, the obvious product of wildly indiscriminate breeding, came bounding around the house, his stubby tail wagging furiously. He rollicked around in front of Mattie in a delirium of excitement, and she pushed him aside as he jumped up against her. "Down, Dudley! Down," she commanded sternly. "Don't get so wrought up."

Susan's eyes lit up and she laughed. For some reason, his name seemed oddly appropriate. At the sound of her laughter, he stopped his bouncing and perked his ears in her direction. He inquisitively tipped his head to one side as he studied her with bright eyes, then pushed his head roughly against her thigh, blatantly begging for attention. Susan stopped to stroke his glossy coat. "Well, hello Dudley," she said as the dog crowded against her legs, wagging his tail so hard he looked as if he were hinged in the middle. "Aren't you gorgeous."

From behind her came a light jingling and the sound of shod hooves on gravel, then the unmistakable creak of a saddle. "Gorgeous is stretching it a bit, don't you think?"

Straightening up, Susan turned around. A man mounted on a magnificent horse was silhouetted against the sun, the blinding brilliance radiating behind him in a fiery corona. Feeling strangely breathless, she shrugged, her expression still animated. "That's a matter of opinion. I think he's wonderful."

"I suspect the feeling is mutual."

The tone of his voice flustered her and she groped for something to say. Mattie unwittingly came to her rescue.

"This is my son, Jason. And Jason, this is Clayton's Susan."

There was a slight hesitation, then Jason Chisholm signaled his mount with a light touch of his heel, and the horse moved forward out of the masking brightness of the direct sunlight. The animal, who tossed his head with a nervous arrogance, was a mahogany bay Appaloosa stallion. Susan didn't know much about horses, but she *did* know enough to realize that this was a superb specimen of horseflesh. She glanced up at the rider and a strange flutter unfurled in her midriff. Jason Chisholm wasn't so bad, either.

With him astride the restless animal, it was hard to judge how tall he was, but everything else about him registered with startling clarity. The impact he had on her was staggering. This man literally radiated an aura of strength and masculinity. He was powerfully built with heavily muscled shoulders, but beneath his unquestionable virility, beneath his physical toughness, there was something…some indefinable quality that drew her. She wondered what kind of person *really* lay beneath the macho image.

And Jason Chisholm did have a macho image. He looked as if he had just ridden off a western set for a highly successful beer commercial. He was dressed in faded blue jeans and a dark blue plaid western-style shirt that fit him like a second skin. Threaded through the loops of his jeans was a wide hand-tooled belt that sported an engraved silver buckle, and on his feet he wore a pair of scuffed lizard skin cowboy boots. His face was heavily shadowed by the broad brim of his gray Stetson, but even that couldn't conceal the strong jawline. He was, in every sense, a man's man.

It was Jason Chisholm who finally fragmented her thoughts. Resting one arm on the saddle horn, he leaned forward and extended his other hand toward her. "Welcome to the Double Diamond."

Susan felt vaguely suspended as she met his steady gaze. Placing her hand in his, she was bombarded by disturbing new impressions. Handsome? No, not exactly, but there was a compelling attractiveness about him, an attractiveness that was unfeigned and indestructible. His eyes were hazel, flecked with gold and amber, and the thick long lashes accentuated their hypnotic intensity. His dark bushy eyebrows were heavily sprinkled with white, and the stubble of beard along his jaw showed silver in the sun.

There was something very intriguing about his face, something that touched her in the most profound way. It revealed a depth of character, an inner strength, but it also revealed an imperviousness that had been carved by disillusionment. It was the face of a man who had forged on alone, a man whose sensuous mouth had been hardened by grim determination. And Susan felt an immediate affinity for him that she had never felt for another human being. Her keen awareness of him as a man had an immobilizing effect on her, and she was conscious of nothing except the warmth of his touch and his unwavering gaze.

"I just made a fresh pot of coffee," Mattie said, breaking the spell. "Why don't you take a rest, Jason?"

Susan was unwilling to break physical contact with this man, and she reluctantly withdrew her hand from his grasp.

The change in him was immediate. It was as if some vital link had been broken, and his expression was suddenly shuttered as he scrutinized her. He stared at her a second longer, then glanced at his mother. "I can't right now. Duffy and I are heading over to the south pasture to cut out the yearlings from that herd." Shifting his weight in the saddle, he gathered the reins and cued the stallion with a barely perceptible movement. As the horse and rider turned, Jason glanced down at Susan and touched the brim of his hat in a gesture that was as old and as traditional as the west itself. "Hope you enjoy your stay here," he said stiffly.

It was obvious that he had, for some reason, withdrawn behind a wall of cool politeness, and that bothered Susan more than she liked to admit. Her voice was uneven when she responded, "Thank you. I'm sure I will."

Their eyes connected, and for a split second his guard

was down, and Susan experienced a sudden galvanizing rush that set her heart hammering wildly against her ribs. But beneath that electric undercurrent of sexual chemistry there was another, less pleasant feeling. Whatever initial attraction there was between them, it would go no farther. Jason Chisholm would see to that. He gave her another salute, and with an undetected signal the powerful bay snorted and arched his neck, then pivoted on his hind legs, fighting the restraint of the rider. But the rider's discipline was relentless. No one—not man or beast—would ever breach this man's control.

CHAPTER TWO

"THAT MAN WORRIES ME," Mattie said, an anxious frown appearing as she watched horse and rider disappear into the trees.

Susan glanced down at her companion. "Why?"

Mattie sighed and shook her head. "He drives himself too hard. If it wasn't for his horses, Jason would have absolutely nothing for himself."

"Clayton says he breeds championship quarter horses."

"He does, and he loves it. But he has so little time for it." She turned to face Susan and sighed, then gave her a wry smile. "Forgive me, Susan. You didn't come all the way out here to listen to me froth off about my son." She patted the younger woman's arm then motioned toward the house. "Come in. We'll have a coffee than I'll show you around."

Susan studied her as they walked up the worn path, silently marveling at the snowy whiteness and thickness of the woman's wavy hair. But as they stepped into the harsh sunlight, Susan could see signs of poor health. Mattie's breathing was labored and her pulse, which was plainly visible in her neck, was very rapid. She looked utterly exhausted.

They climbed the steps and as Mattie opened the screen door, Susan caught the distinctive fragrance of cinnamon and lavender, and suddenly she felt homesick for her own grandmother—maybe *all* grandmothers smelled of cinnamon and lavender.

The porch was part of a large addition that had been built

onto the entire back of the house. From it, doorways led to the left and to the right, the one on the right obviously leading into the main house.

Mattie indicated the space with a wave of her hand. "We added this part about thirty years ago. We needed a kitchen for the men and some sort of living quarters for the cook, when we had one." She pointed toward the door on the left. "I'll take you on a quick tour to show you your room."

Susan followed her, absorbing every detail as they entered the enormous kitchen. There was a large U-shaped work area with fairly new white Arborite-covered cupboards. Above the sinks, there was a large window facing west, offering a spectacular view of the mountains and foothills, and Susan mentally acknowledged that no job could possibly be tedious with a view like that.

Adjacent to the work area was the eating area, which was furnished with a massive table that would easily seat a dozen people. Along the north side of the kitchen there were four more windows that overlooked the backyard and the windbreak of trees beyond.

Although the walls could do with a fresh coat of paint and the whole place looked as though it could stand a thorough scrubbing, the room had a certain homeyness about it that Susan found very appealing. All the woodwork around the windows and doors was oak, the color darkened to a deep mahogany shade by repeated varnishings. The window ledges were wide and old-fashioned and held several pots of flourishing red geraniums. The floor was covered with old red and gray inlaid tile that showed faint trails of wear and spatterings of paint. None of the wooden chairs around the huge solidly built table matched, and the stove, which was enormous, looked like an old converted wood burner.

"Your room's in here," Mattie said as she led Susan around a corner to a short hallway that had two doors on either side and another door at the far end. The door on the right led into a small bathroom that housed a big old tub with clawed feet, and even from the doorway, Susan could detect the weird, wavy flaw in the mirror that covered the ancient medicine chest.

The door to the left led into a spacious bed-sitting-room. And stepping into it was like stepping back in time. The furniture was old and a little worn, but that didn't detract from the ageless beauty of it. Susan ran her hand appreciatively over the rich wood of the massive burl walnut dresser, which was still graced by the original beveled mirror set into a hand-carved frame.

The bed was metal, its most recent coat of paint being white. It was a marvelous old filigreed thing with a wild variety of curlicues, doodads and baubles twisted and turned into the elaborate design. It was amply covered by a hand-made patchwork quilt of various prints and ginghams. The once-intense colors had faded with age and countless washings, but the intricate design was still distinct.

There were two well-worn armchairs, which were upholstered in a deep maroon embossed velour, standing on either side of an old lamp table that was, Susan was sure, made out of solid cherry wood. Two colorful hand-braided rag rugs lay on the dark wood floor, one beside the bed and one covering the floor beneath the two chairs. The three long narrow windows on the far wall were covered by old-fashioned fringed blinds and lace curtains. And in Susan's eyes, even with the signs of age and wear, this room was perfect.

"It's all a little old-fashioned, I'm afraid," Mattie said. "But on a ranch, new furniture is never a priority."

Susan grinned knowingly. "You can't convince me that you'd ever part with a single piece of this gorgeous old furniture."

Mattie shrugged, her smile a little sheepish. "Well, no I wouldn't, but sometimes young people don't understand that."

"Well, I certainly do. I'll enjoy every minute I spend in this room, believe me."

"I hope so." She smiled warmly at Susan and motioned

toward the door. "Now I'm sure you're more than ready for that coffee."

Having left the bedroom, Susan turned to leave the way they'd come, but Mattie pointed toward the door to the left. "No, we can go into the main house this way. This door was here when we added on, so we just left it."

She opened it and entered another short hall. Again, there was a bathroom on the right and another door on the left, which was closed. Mattie motioned to it. "This is Jason's room. When I came to live with him, he insisted I move back upstairs into the master bedroom. It has a smaller room off it that used to be a nursery, so he fixed it up as a little sitting room. He thought that I might need a quiet place of my own now and again."

Susan only caught a glimpse of the enormous living room as she turned and followed Mattie down another wide corridor toward the other smaller kitchen, but it was enough to comprehend just how large the Chisholm home was.

The rooms had high ceilings, which added to the spaciousness, but in spite of the size, there was still a special charm and warmth about the place that only came with age. Instead of being heavy and oppressive, the extensive ornate woodwork gave each room an air of durability and quality, and the beautiful antique furniture, which had obviously been in the Chisholm family for decades, reinforced the sense of solidness, of permanence, of unbroken continuation. It would be a very secure place to grow up in, Susan reflected, knowing that generations had gone before and generations would probably follow. She thought of the man with the steady hazel eyes, who was the product of those many generations. Perhaps that's why he was so solemn— the weight of that responsibility would not sit lightly on his shoulders.

The timer on the oven pinged, and picking up a pair of pot holders that were laying on the counter, Mattie opened the oven door. The mouth-watering aroma of hot cinnamon buns came wafting out, and Susan's empty stomach responded.

"I hope you aren't one of those women who's constantly dieting," Mattie said as she slid the cookie sheet onto a rack on the counter.

Susan laughed and shook her head. "Not me, Mattie. I tried it once and hated it."

"I'm glad to hear it. I'm afraid this preoccupation with thinness is not doing the younger generation much good."

Using tongs, Mattie broke off four of the enormous rolls and put them in a basket, then brought them to the table. They looked and smelled delicious, and Susan eyed them with relish as the older woman bustled around getting coffee, napkins and the cream and sugar.

Placing a side plate in front of Susan, Mattie glanced at the clock above the cupboards. "We made it just in time. The children will be home from school soon and if we hadn't already had ours by the time they get here, we'd be lucky to get even a nibble."

Slowly stirring the cream into her coffee, Susan smiled with fond recollection. "I can remember when we were kids how we'd tear home on the days Mom baked. I don't know why it was, but there was always something very reassuring and comforting about the smell of freshly baked peanut butter cookies when you'd had a lousy day."

Mattie smiled and nodded her head in agreement. "I know. That's exactly why I still do it."

Once again Susan was struck by how totally drained this woman looked, and she was trying to think of some tactful way of asking about Mattie's health when the older woman spoke. "You have brothers and sisters, Susan?"

Susan grimaced. "I most certainly do. There are seven of us—five boys and two girls."

"Goodness—seven! Were you the eldest?"

"No, I have two older brothers." She grinned and shook her head. "Looking back, I honestly don't know how Mom and Dad survived. We were such a bunch of little hellions."

A look of relief crossed Mattie's face. "I'm so glad you're used to children. These four can be a handful at times, and I was worried they'd bother you."

"They won't bother me, Mattie," Susan said reassuringly. "Kids and I usually get along pretty well."

Mattie studied the younger woman for a moment, then tipped her head and smiled, an astute gleam in her eyes. "Yes, I'm sure you do. I suspect there aren't many you can't handle."

Susan laughed. "Well, no, not many. But let's face it, I've had my share of practice."

"Well, I can assure you these four will give you some more. Patricia and Lucy aren't too bad, but those two boys are a handful." A look of weariness crossed her face. "There are times when they wear me right out."

That was apparent. After glancing around, Susan could see that *everything* was wearing her out. The rooms were tidy but there were signs everywhere that the house was simply too big for Mattie to handle: the windows needed to be washed, the kitchen floor desperately needed a scrubbing, and dust and fingerprints covered the furniture.

Coming from such a large family, Susan knew how much work was involved. But she had been raised in a home where the chores were shared, and even the boys had to help with housework. She had a sneaking hunch that was not the case here. Which meant that either Mattie was simply too tired to organize household tasks, or these kids were also a bunch of little hellions.

Susan found out a short time later about the Chisholm children. The two boys came boiling in the back door like dual tornadoes with jean jackets, lunch kits and school papers caught up in their momentum.

The first tornado turned into a stationary bundle of energy who was, unquestionably, all boy. He greeted his grandmother with open affection. "Hi, Grandma! Watcha making? Hey, cinnamon buns!" He turned and looked at Susan with unveiled curiosity. "Are you gonna be our new cook?"

There was an undertone of amusement in her voice as she nodded. "Yes, I am."

Mattie came forward and ruffled his hair affectionately. "This is Michael. He just turned ten." She smiled at the other boy who'd come to stand beside her. "And this is Todd. He's eleven and a half."

Todd met her eyes with the same steady hazel gaze as his father's, then flashed her a smile that was pure charm. "Uncle Clayton sure can pick 'em," he said, his grin deepening to reveal a big dimple in his left cheek.

Mattie gave him a stern look and opened her mouth to scold him, but Susan intervened. "You're much too young to be a flirt," she said, somehow managing not to laugh.

There was a contrived innocence about him that hinted of irrepressible mischief when he answered gravely, "Just covering my bases, ma'am."

Susan knew by the gleam in his eyes that she was faced with an inveterate tease, and she fell in love with the kid right there and then. "Covering your bases is one thing, Mr. Chisholm, but just don't try stealing any!"

Her response sent him into a fit of laughter, and she watched as he doubled over. A movement at the door caught her eye and she glanced over.

Two girls had entered and were standing in the doorway. The older one, who Susan knew was thirteen, was firmly holding the smaller girl's hand as she gravely watched her brother's performance. She wore her long, curly hair pulled back in a ponytail, the style accentuating her solemn eyes. *There,* thought Susan with sudden circumspection, *is a desperately unhappy child.* Seeing the girl brought back some not-so-happy memories of her own. She had gone through a period of a year or so when she had been really chubby, and she had hated every pound. Fortunately it was a stage she had eventually outgrown.

This girl, she suspected, would not be so lucky. The conversation with Mattie about dieting came to mind, and she had a feeling that this child was the reason for the woman's

concern. Susan smiled at the girl who shyly smiled back,
and she experienced a rush of sympathy. Adolescence could
be such a rotten, lonely period, and from the expression in
this girl's eyes, Susan guessed she was having a more difficult time than most.

The younger one was a different ball of wax altogether.
She was all cute and bubbly and had a dimpled smile that
would turn granite to mush. Her red-and-white dress was
liberally trimmed with ruffles and lace, and there was a big
red bow tied in her tumble of dark curls. She looked as if
she had just tap-danced her way out of a Shirley Temple
movie. She was a doll, and Susan suspected that this little
Miss Chisholm certainly knew it.

"This is Patricia," Mattie said, indicating the older girl.
"And this is Lucy," she added as she smoothed down the
little one's curls. "Girls, this is Susan Lynton."

Both girls smiled their welcome, then went over to the
counter and laid down the things they were carrying. For a
moment, all four Chisholm children were grouped together,
and Susan couldn't help but notice the strong resemblance
Todd, Patricia and Lucy shared with their father. They had
the same almond-shaped hazel eyes, the same straight nose,
the same full mouth, and even though Jason hadn't smiled,
she'd bet the farm he had a big dimple in his left cheek.

All four of them had brown curly hair, but Michael's was
several shades lighter and had deep auburn highlights. It
was, in fact, practically identical to Susan's. There was no
question that the children were brothers and sisters, but Michael did not possess the unquestionable Chisholm likeness.
She studied the boy a little closer and wondered why he
seemed to be strangely familiar.

Just then, Michael lifted his head and looked directly at
her. Susan experienced an eerie start of recognition, and an
odd sensation fluttered in her stomach when she realized it
was more than the same hair coloring they shared. Susan's
eyes were an unusual shade of deep blue—delphinium blue,
her grandfather used to say—and Michael's were the exact

same shade. His wide eyes and dark arched brows dominated his oval face, and thick sweeping lashes accentuated his slanted cheekbones. His resemblance to her was so strong, so definite, he could have easily been her son.

A funny feeling unfolded in her that she tried to ignore. It was her maternal instinct rearing its head again, and that always got her into some sort of trouble. Susan smiled as she watched him worm a second cinnamon bun out of his grandmother; he might not have the Chisholm looks, but he certainly had the Chisholm charm.

THE NEXT TWO DAYS were fairly hectic for Susan, but once she found out where everything was, and was able to arrange a tenuous truce with the monstrosity of a stove, she settled into a comfortable routine. Except for suppers, she usually just had the four men to feed. There were the two hired hands, Duffy and Len, who lived in the big bunkhouse behind the garage, and Walter, a cousin of Clayton's, who had his own small house back in the trees. He'd been away helping a neighbor, and so far had only been home for two meals. And there was Jason.

She came to the conclusion that her first impression of him had been a figment of her imagination. He was not as he seemed; he was remote and abrupt, and after she'd been around him for a while, she could not for the life of her figure out why he had affected her so strongly.

By the fourth day, Susan had everything under control and was beginning to find time heavy on her hands. She liked being busy, the there wasn't really that much to do, and the boredom was starting to get to her.

But as soon as the men left after dinner, she started eyeing the kitchen floor. It was a mess. It had such a thick buildup of wax some of it had to be ten years old. There were also spatters from previous paint jobs in a rainbow of colors, and there were so many black scuff marks that it looked like an entire army had marched through. She really couldn't stand to live with *that* for three months.

Rummaging around in the huge closet in the porch, Susan discovered a gallon can of Varsol and a very old floor polisher. When she had cleaned out the cupboard under the sink, she had found two full cans of liquid wax, so she had all she needed to do a thorough job. And really, what was the harm, she rationalized as she stacked the chairs on top of the table, especially when she'd be done in plenty of time to fix supper.

In less than an hour, she had nearly half the huge area stripped. It was going much faster than she expected, and the results were certainly amazing. Susan hummed to herself, feeling smugly satisfied with her efforts. She honestly didn't mind housework when she could see the results of her labor, and she could certainly see what she was accomplishing here.

She was using the floor polisher to scrub off the dissolved wax and the howl from the motor masked all other sounds. She did not hear the back door slam. What she did hear was somebody swear, and she whirled around just as Jason yanked the plug out of the wall. "What's going on here?" he demanded curtly.

He'd caught her so by surprise that all she could do was stand there and stare at him with her mouth hanging open. His curly salt-and-pepper hair was clinging damply to his temples, and he looked hot and cranky. He stared at her stonily. "You were hired to do the cooking. That's all. Nothing more."

Susan couldn't really see what the problem was, but his attitude was beginning to ruffle her feathers. It was almost as though he resented her being there, and that nettled her; it wasn't as if she was falling down on the job. But in spite of her annoyance, she managed to keep her voice relaxed as she answered, "I didn't have anything else to do so I thought I'd clean the floor."

"That is not what you were hired to do," he snapped, his chin stuck out a mile.

Okay, Susan, she inwardly steamed, *you won't lose your*

temper. Aloud she said, "I realize that, but it needs to be done and I don't mind—"

"This is not your job," he retorted stubbornly.

Susan was beginning to see red, and she placed her hands on her hips, her own chin taking on a tenacious set. "This is totally ridiculous. While we're standing here arguing over whether I should or should not scrub the damned floor, the solvent is probably dissolving the glue." She stomped over and picked up the cord and under her breath, she muttered, "And I'll do as I damned well please."

The expression on his face was thunderous, but she ignored it and reached past him to plug the floor polisher back in. His arm shot out and he roughly caught her wrist and twisted her hand over. The skin, irritated by the harsh solvent, was red and slightly abraded, and Susan had the feeling he was just itching to give her supreme hell.

Just then, Duffy stuck his head in the door. "We've got the horses loaded and we're ready to roll, Jase."

Jason dropped her hand and glared at her, then he turned, and giving Duffy a slicing look, slammed his hat on his head and strode out the door. Duffy raised his eyebrows in a baffled expression but Susan only shrugged, feeling more than a little baffled herself. It didn't make much sense. He was acting as though he'd caught her starving the kids, instead of doing a monotonous household chore that most men didn't even know existed.

For the remainder of the afternoon, Susan alternated between a slow burn and teeth-clenching vexation. She had the distinct feeling she'd been unjustly castigated simply because, as her grandmother would put it, "he felt like kicking the dog." Consequently, her mood bounced through everything from anger to feeling hard done by, but eventually a niggling little feeling wormed its way into her indignation. She had a tough time acknowledging it, but she finally had to admit that she was beginning to feel like an idiot for reacting the way she had.

Once she went that far, she also had to admit that her

female ego had suffered a bruising the past few days, thanks
to Jason's aloofness, and it was further bruised when he had
jumped on her that afternoon. And somewhere between
waxing the floor and washing the windows, it dawned on
her that maybe Jason had never wanted her there in the first
place, that maybe Clayton had rammed her down his throat.
The more she thought about it, the more troubled she became, and the more troubled she became, the more she immersed herself in hard work. By the time five o'clock rolled
around, she had cleaned every square inch of the kitchen
and anything that could be scoured, scrubbed, waxed or polished had been. But as she surveyed the results of her efforts, she didn't feel the usual satisfaction from a job well
done. Instead, she felt oddly discouraged.

After trying to shed her gray mood in a long hot shower,
Susan put on a bright pink blouse that tied at the midriff,
glumly hoping that the vivid color would pick up her spirits.
Slipping into a new pair of blue jeans, she felt some satisfaction. For once, the length was adequate. She was tall,
nearly five foot eleven, and it was nearly impossible to buy
anything that was long enough in the legs. She had discovered at a very early age that if she wanted something decent
to wear, she was going to have to make it herself. She
smiled as she retied the blouse. Clayton had always kidded
her that the only reason he hired her was because she was
a "snappy" dresser and had enough class not to eat with
her feet.

She put on a pair of leather thongs, then went out to the
kitchen and got the vegetables she was going to prepare for
supper out of the fridge. Filling the sink, Susan immersed a
head of cauliflower and bunch of broccoli in the ice-cold
water and grimaced when the wetness stung her raw,
chapped hands.

As she reached for a paring knife, she glanced out the
window. Lucy was standing on the rope swing that hung
from a thick branch of an enormous poplar, pumping away
as she sang at the top of her voice, her face contorting with

outrageously affected expressions. She was obviously lost in some world of her own, and Susan grinned as she watched her. If this kid didn't end up an actress, there was no justice in the world.

Susan finished the vegetables and put them on the stove to steam, then started fixing the salad. Michael and Todd came around the garage with their ball gloves, a bat and a baseball. There was a loud argument about who would do what: Michael wanted to pitch to Todd, Todd wanted to bat flies for Michael to catch, and the whole time they argued, Dudley romped back and forth between them, wagging his tail in anticipation.

Susan stopped working, and bracing her hip against the counter, stuck her hands in the back pockets of her jeans. She'd quickly discovered that the Chisholm boys loved baseball. But then, so did she. The brother who was a year younger than she pitched for a major league team, and while they were growing up, Susan was always the one Peter either conned or bullied into catching for him. Over the years, she had become somewhat of a pitching expert—and a damned good catcher.

Michael won the argument, and Todd moved back and crouched in a catcher's squat. With a knowing eye, Susan watched his windup and delivery. The pitch was high and outside, but for a boy his size, he had tremendous speed. She narrowed her eyes contemplatively as she watched him, but the vegetables boiled over and she was forced to turn her attention to the stove.

Supper, which was always at six sharp, turned out to be a strained affair. When the two boys came in to wash up they were unusually subdued, and Susan gathered by the murmured comments that they'd caught hell from their father for horsing around in the barn when they were supposed to be helping with chores. Lucy was sitting at her place at the table swinging her feet, animatedly engrossed in a whispered conversation with some imaginary friends, while Patricia sat cross-legged on another chair, her nose buried in a book.

When Susan heard the back door slam and masculine voices in the porch, she started carrying the steaming serving dishes to the table. Setting the basket of fresh buns at one end, she glanced at Patricia. "Tricia, would you please go tell your grandmother supper's ready?"

"Sure, Susan." Marking her place, she closed the book, laid it on a window ledge and left the room. Feeling very uncomfortable about their earlier clash of wills, Susan deliberately avoided looking at Jase as the men came in and sat down. She suspected that there wasn't much he missed, and it would only take a quick glance to see that not only had she defied him and finished the floor, but she had done considerably more. And she really didn't want another confrontation, especially in front of a bunch of people.

She put the last of the food on the table and had just taken her place when Patricia returned. "Grandma says she won't be in for supper, Susan. She's not feeling well."

Something made Susan glance at Jase, and she experienced a twinge of guilt when she saw how tired he looked. Dragging her attention away from him, she helped Lucy fill her plate. She'd slip in to check on Mattie later, she decided silently, and make sure there was nothing seriously wrong.

"I checked that south pasture today, Jase," said Duffy as he reached for a bun. "If we don't get some rain pretty soon, we're going to have to move that herd. Them cows have damn near grazed that grass down to dirt, and that creek'll be bone dry in a week."

Len nodded in agreement. "It's bad, that's a fact. I was talking to Cliff Seward yesterday. He says he's going to have to start culling his herd if he don't get a soaking pretty soon. Course, he was already in pretty bad shape last fall."

Susan poured some gravy on Lucy's potatoes, then looked at Len. "I thought most of the streams around here were mountain fed."

"Well, ma'am, they are. But we had a light snowfall last

year and we just ain't had the runoff we usually get. There wasn't even that much snow in the mountains so them streams are pretty scant.''

"We had a real dry summer and fall last year," explained Duffy. "So that ground's bone dry. It ain't going to grow nothin' but thistles. I doubt if there's a green blade of grass within a hundred miles, and you can't keep a herd alive on wishful thinkin'.''

Susan digested that. No wonder Jason was so quick to fly off the handle when he was faced with a major drought. And her right-minded conscience piled more guilt upon her head. Okay, she'd apologize the first chance she got. *You'd better make it good,* niggled her conscience, *since he likely didn't want you here in the first place.* Wonderful. Now she really felt lousy.

"Hey, Dad, we have a baseball game in town tomorrow night. We play that High River team that beat us before.'' Todd put some dressing on his salad, then looked at his father. "I told Mr. Wilson you'd help, okay? He said he needed a base coach.''

"What time?'' They were the first words Jason had spoken since he'd come in, and the weariness in his voice made Susan inwardly wince.

"Six-thirty. Mikey's going to be the starting pitcher and Mr. Wilson's moving me to shortstop.''

Jason rested his arms on the table and gazed at his eldest son. "Todd, I'd really like to help, but I likely won't make it back until after seven.''

Michael broke in. "You mean you won't even be there to watch? It's going to be the first time I get to pitch, Dad, and you aren't even going to be there?'' His voice rose sharply, and it was very apparent that he was upset. Susan could understand how he felt. His big chance to prove himself, and it was only natural that he wanted his dad there. But Susan could tell by the look in Jason Chisholm's eyes that the very last thing he needed today was this.

"You've never missed a game before," Todd said accusingly.

There was a strained silence as Todd and Michael fastened their eyes on their father. Susan had been a kid once; she knew exactly what they were trying to do. Only she wasn't going to let them get away with it. "I'll be a base coach for your team, Todd."

That god a response from the boys, and they stared at her as if she'd just waded through the mashed potatoes. "What do *you* know about baseball?" Todd said in a tone that was as close to a sneer as he dared in front of his father.

She stared right back. "I know enough to tell you that you miss most grounders that come at you from the right side, that you hardly ever miss a line drive and that you can really connect with a pitch that's a little high and outside." She gave him a superior smile then looked at Michael. "I know that you have a good fast ball, but you have a tendency to lose control when you throw sliders, which you shouldn't be throwing in the first place. And I strongly suspect that you like to steal bases."

There was another silence as they stared at her with dumbfounded looks on their faces. Susan managed to keep her face expressionless as she let everything sink into their devious little minds. Her facade of indifference was nearly shot to pieces when she glanced up and found Jase watching her. He had leaned back in his chair and was absently stroking his bottom lip with his thumb. There was a glint of amusement in his eyes and a hint of a smile around his mouth. As her gaze locked with his, Susan felt a warm flush color her cheeks, and she quickly looked away. She'd have given anything to know what was going through his mind right then.

"How do you *know* all that?" Michael finally stammered, his eyes still wide with amazement.

"Do you know Peter Lynton?"

"You mean the pitcher for the Blue Jays?"

Susan nodded. "I used to catch for him."

Michael's eyes looked as if they were going to pop right out of his head. "You *know* Pete Lynton?"

"He's my brother."

"Brother! Your brother!" If there was such a thing as seventh heaven, Michael had found it and he was squirming in his chair in an orgy of ecstasy. "Can you get me his autograph? Can you, Susan? I'd do anything to get his autograph! Just tell me what I have to do to get his autograph!"

"How about shoveling a trail through your room?" she responded dryly.

Jason cleared his throat, and Susan shot a quick look at him. For a split second she thought he was going to laugh, but he kept a straight face.

Patricia had been around baseball-crazy brothers long enough to know who Pete Lynton was. "Did you really catch for him?" she asked, her tone nearly as disbelieving as her brothers'.

"I did, and sprained every finger on both hands doing it." Realizing she'd managed to temporarily derail the two boys, Susan told them a bit about Peter and his career, deliberately steering Michael and Todd away from the topic of their upcoming baseball game. With a bit of luck she managed to get through the rest of the meal without giving them the chance to think about it.

The children remained at the table after the men left, indulging themselves in second helpings of Susan's rice pudding. Lucy was once again immersed in some imaginary drama, and Patricia had gone to see if her grandmother wanted anything to eat. For all intents and purposes Susan had the boys on their own. She knew that she was, as her grandmother would say, "sticking her oar in" where she had no business sticking it in, but she felt duty bound to say something.

Standing at the counter, she placed the leftover buns in a plastic bag before turning to face the boys. "Your dad has a lot on his mind right now, guys. And I don't think you were being very fair about your baseball game," she said quietly. Michael and Todd exchanged a quick glance, then as if caught in a conspiracy, they abruptly fixed their eyes on the table. But they did have the decency to look a little shamefaced as they suddenly became engrossed in cleaning every bit of pudding out of their dishes.

Susan went back to the table and started stacking dirty plates. "I don't think he'd miss one of your games unless he had to. You made him feel really bad about it, you know."

Todd shrugged uncomfortably. "Yeah, I know, but we like him to come."

"I know you do, Todd. All kids like their parents to go to things like that. But do you really think it was fair of you guys to lay a guilt trip on him the one time he can't?"

There was a short silence before Todd finally mumbled remorsefully, "No, I guess it wasn't." He looked at Susan and made a grimace of regret. "We didn't mean to make him feel bad. We were just trying—"

"Trying to apply enough pressure to get him to give in," she said with a lopsided smile. "I know. I was a kid once."

"Will you really come to our game, Susan?" Michael asked hopefully.

"Sure. I'd love to."

"And will you really help me with my pitching?"

"I will when I have time." Resting her hands on her hips, she gave them her best no-nonsense look. "Now, have either of you got homework tonight?"

"Yeah," they said in woeful unison.

"Well, you'd better get at it, okay?"

With a total lack of enthusiasm, they groaned as they slowly got up from the table and started dragging reluctant feet toward the door. As the boys disappeared into the porch, she turned and lifted Lucy off the chair then set her down on her feet. "Would you go see where Patricia is, please? I need to know what Grandma would like for supper before I put everything away."

"What Grandma wants for supper," Lucy parroted as she skipped out of the room. Susan picked up the stack of dishes and turned toward the cupboards. She nearly dropped the whole pile when somebody spoke behind her.

"Mattie's asleep so I told Tricia not to wake her."

Her heart was pounding wildly and her hands weren't quite steady as Susan set the dishes down. She turned to face the unexpected visitor, who was standing in the doorway of the hall leading to the other entrance. His shoulder was braced against the doorframe, and Jase had his thumbs hooked in the pockets of his faded jeans, the stance pulling the fabric of his plaid shirt tautly across his chest. As he shifted his weight slightly, his altered position accentuated the strong contours of his jaw and the muscled thickness of his neck, and Susan was suddenly keenly aware of his powerful build.

In the diffused light from the hall, his hair had the same sheen as polished pewter, the silver shade contrasting sharply with his weathered tan and the dark fabric of his shirt. He was watching her with an intentness that Susan found unsettling, making her even more conscious of him as a man. Everything about him was disturbingly masculine: his looks, his size, his strength, even the way he moved. He possessed the same animal grace, the same energy as the magnificent stallion he rode, only Jase Chisholm's sexuality was rigidly contained behind a wall of cool reserve. And Susan found herself wondering what would happen if that wall was ever breached.

That line of suggestive thinking got her into deep and dangerous waters as vivid images took shape in her mind, and Susan suddenly found it difficult to breathe. The sensation intensified as Jase straightened and with the characteristic loose-hipped gait of a horseman, sauntered toward her.

There was something in his eyes, some vague expression touching on gratitude that was a dead giveaway, and Susan

knew he had overheard what she had said to Michael and
Todd. She prayed he wouldn't bring it up.

He didn't. Instead he recycled something that was nearly
as awkward. "I owe you an apology for this afternoon," he
said quietly.

She raised her shoulders in a gesture of embarrassment
as she responded, "Couldn't we just forget it?"

Jase was standing very close to her, and Susan was transfixed by the intensity of his gaze as he shook his head. "No,
we can't. I have a low boiling point at the best of times,
but I had no right to jump you the way I did."

Something was happening between them that Susan
couldn't quite define, but whatever it was, it was something
she did not want to jeopardize. Her voice was oddly husky
when she said, "My boiling point isn't much higher than
yours. We're bound to strike sparks off each other."

The tiny lines around his eyes crinkled as he nearly
smiled, and Susan felt her knees go weak. She caught the
full force of the Chisholm charm as he added very softly,
"Of one sort or another."

For a breathless moment, they stood staring at each other,
then Jase broke the spell. Looking down, he gently caught
one of her hands and inspected it, slowly caressing the red,
chapped skin with his thumb.

His touch did strange things to both her equilibrium and
her pulse rate, and Susan somehow managed to control the
nearly irresistible urge to lace her fingers through his. His
voice was strained when he said, "You'd better get some
cream on them." He released her hand and went over to the
small fridge where he kept his veterinarian supplies. He took
out a white tube, and still refusing to meet her gaze he came
back to the counter and squeezed a liberal amount into her
palm. "It's Vitamin E cream. It should help."

There was a strange tightness in her chest as she watched
him return to the fridge and replace the tube. Absently
smoothing the cream into her hands, she studied his face for
some clue as to what was going through his mind. His full

mouth was pulled into an unyielding line, and there was an unusual tenseness about him that she found particularly distressing. He seemed so isolated, and Susan had a sudden need to comfort him. And for her that was a dangerous feeling. She knew she had a strong maternal instinct, but when she started feeling that way about a man who was as sexually attractive, as compelling as Jason Chisholm was, she was in very big trouble.

She found that her voice was treacherously unsteady when she suddenly found the courage to broach a topic that had been troubling her. "Clayton pushed the issue over me, didn't he? You didn't want me here, did you?"

There was a bleak look in Jason's eyes as he turned to face her. He stared at her for a moment, then answered in a strained tone. "No, I didn't." As if drawn against his will, he came over to her, and as though he were fighting a losing battle with himself, he trailed his knuckles along her jaw, his touch gentle. "I still don't think it's a good idea," he said, his voice low. "But for entirely different reasons, now."

CHAPTER THREE

SUSAN SPENT MOST of that night staring at the ceiling, trying to sort through some disturbing thoughts and even more disturbing feelings. But she hadn't come to grips with anything. Except that she was strongly attracted to Jason Chisholm. And that didn't solve anything, either, though it certainly did ruin any chances she might have had of falling asleep. She felt as if she'd been flattened by a ten-ton truck when her alarm finally forced her out of bed the next morning.

She managed the routine of breakfast out of sheer habit, but it wasn't until she'd had four cups of coffee and a cold shower that she felt more alive than dead. She finished tidying up the kitchen, made a batch of muffins and a stew for dinner and did the crossword in a two-week-old *Calgary Herald* before she gave in to her restlessness.

If she was going to put him and what he'd said out of her mind, she was going to have to find something physical to do, something where she could put her body in gear and her thoughts in neutral. What she needed, she thought wryly, was a load of gravel to shovel.

She finally went outside and found a beautiful sunny spring day waiting for her; the fresh mountain breeze helped to clear away her mental cobwebs. She watched two Stellar jays at the bird feeder for a while, then wandered toward the back of the house. She paused when she rounded the hedge. Walter was digging up the flower beds in the backyard, and as she stood watching him, Susan's expression became unusually solemn.

Clayton had told her the whole story, how at the age of ten Walter had been kicked in the head by a horse, the injury causing irreversible brain damage. Susan wasn't too sure how to deal with his disability. A physical handicap was one thing; she could face that with absolute composure. But a mentally disabled person was something else altogether. It wasn't that his condition repulsed her, but it did bother her. She felt an almost unreasonable compassion for anyone who, for whatever medical or genetic reasons, had been cheated out of a normal existence. And Walter was certainly one of those.

But even though she had been warned, she had not been fully prepared. The first time she saw him with his slow, shuffling gait and listened to his laborious efforts to speak, she had been hit with an unexpected wave of sadness. Sometimes life was so damned unfair.

The main reason she was reluctant to face him on her own was that he communicated in a kind of verbal shorthand, and she wasn't sure she'd be able to grasp his meaning. Susan decided the wisest thing to do was to leave, and she was just about to go back into the house when he turned and saw her. He smiled at her with a mixture of shyness and uncertainty, and feeling as if she were damned no matter what she did, Susan returned his smile. Then, with her heart in her shoes, she walked across the lawn to where he was working.

Dudley came bounding around the corner of the house, exuberant about having some new company. He would have jumped up on Susan, but Walter caught him by the collar and gave him a firm command to sit. That was, to Susan's way of thinking, like asking an elephant to tap dance, but Dudley surprised her and plopped down on his haunches. He tipped his head and looked at her with bright eyes, silently begging to be petted. She grinned at him as she buried her hand in his thick coat and scratched him behind his ears. Walter was watching her, and he shook his head as Dudley sagged against her legs. "He likes you," he said haltingly.

She laughed as she ruffled the dog's fur. "He should, the way I feed him." Giving the dog another pat, she turned her attention to the flower bed where Walter was working. The freshly turned earth revealed a host of new shoots that were just pushing their way through the soil. One love Susan had inherited from her grandmother was the love of gardening, and she surveyed the beds with interest. None of the plants were up far enough to really be distinguishable, and forgetting all about her former reluctance, she began questioning Walter. "What are those shoots along there?"

He stepped back into the bed and placed the garden fork by one clump. "Columbine." He moved the fork to another. "Trollius." He indicated another. "Bachelor buttons." Slowly he worked his way back down the bed, indicating every group of shoots and marking some that weren't even up yet. By the time they'd reached the other end, Susan had a mental picture of what this flower bed would look like at the peak of the season. It would be spectacular. From the time the first daffodils bloomed in the spring until the chrysanthemums froze in the fall, there would be a colorful array of flowers in bloom.

At the far end of the garden, there was a shallow hole with a long-handled spade stuck in it, and she pointed to it. "What are you going to put there?"

Walter shrugged and slowly shook his head. "I don't know. Maybe lythrum there…something that blooms later."

Susan nodded. "That would work. Then if you do that, why don't you move this bunch of columbine over there and put a clump of daisies here?"

There was no mistaking the twinkle in his eye as he grasped the spade, pulled it free and handed it to Susan. "Sounds fine," he said with a slow grin.

Susan stared at him for a split second then grinned back as she took the shovel. "That's not fair. Don't you know you aren't supposed to let just anybody plow around in your garden?''

"Not just anybody," he said, the twinkle intensifying. "*You*, Susan."

Susan slanted an amused, if somewhat skeptical look at him. "I think you bear watching, Walter Chisholm. I have the distinct feeling I've just been had."

He chuckled and pointed to a clump of shoots. "There's the daisies."

She shot him a knowing look. "I get the message."

He was still shaking his head and smiling as he grasped the handles of the wheelbarrow and disappeared through the hedge.

The two of them spent the next hour digging and rearranging, sometimes talking, sometimes sharing long comfortable silences. Walter wheeled in several loads of compost from an old manure pile and worked it into the soil. Susan had finished moving what they had decided to move, then dug up a huge clump of irises that needed separating. She was kneeling at the end of the garden, her hands and the knees of her jeans caked with dirt, humming to herself as she broke apart the tuberous roots.

"Don't tell me. I suppose you're going to do the fencing next."

Susan froze and swore softly under her breath, feeling suddenly cornered. There was no mistaking the undercurrent of sarcasm in Jason Chisholm's voice, and sighing in resignation, she turned to face him. "Look, Jase, I like gardening. So don't make a big deal out of something that isn't."

He was standing a short distance behind her, a familiar set to his jaw, the rest of his face obscured in the shadow of his Stetson. "You're not expected to do anything around here but cook. I thought I made that perfectly clear."

She stared at him for a moment, a hint of irritation flashing in her eyes. "Don't be a bore. What am I supposed to do between meals—crochet doilies?''

She thought she saw his mouth twitch, but his face remained expressionless. "If that's what you want to do with your free time, fine."

Her irritation escalated. "For Pete's sake, do I look like the type who gets a big thrill out of sitting in a rocking chair day after day, turning out pink-and-yellow pot holders for the church bazaar?"

"I don't know. Are you?"

She suspected he was baiting her, and ignoring his question, she pushed on. "What's wrong with my helping Walter with the gardening?"

He stared at her, his eyes narrowing. "Nothing...*if* you left it at that. But seeing the way you operate, I suspect I could end up with hollyhocks planted around the barn."

Walter appeared and set the wheelbarrow down. He glanced at Jason, then gave Susan a sly wink and said solemnly, "That would look nice, wouldn't it, Susan?"

His subtle and unexpected alliance delighted Susan and she grinned up at him, her eyes sparkling. "I think it's a great idea. We could transplant the ones behind the garage, and we could put a few clumps of delphiniums along the corrals."

Walter chuckled and nodded, and Jason riveted his full attention on him, as if he weren't quite sure if Walter was serious or not. But Walter's face was as innocent as a baby's as he disappeared around the corner of the house, and Jase glanced back at Susan. He scrutinized her intently, his contemplative tone tinged with an undercurrent of amusement as he said softly, "Why do I have this uncomfortable feeling that the two of you are turning out to be bad news?"

Still grinning, Susan stood up and dusted off the dirt that was clinging to her jeans. "Maybe it's just your suspicious nature."

His amusement grew. "Like hell."

Her gaze connected with his, and Susan experienced a galvanizing flutter as she fell victim to the laughter in his eyes. She had a sudden and nearly overpowering urge to reach out and touch him, but she drew a slow, measured breath and deliberately hooked her thumbs in the pockets of her jeans. Her voice was only slightly uneven as she said, "Walter must be ready for a coffee break. How about you?"

He was watching her with an unsettling steadiness that made her knees go weak, and Susan made herself take another deep breath. He stared at her for a second longer, then the laugh lines around his eyes crinkled in a disarming smile. "I don't suppose there's a piece of cake left to go with it?"

"Leftover cake? With this gang? You have to be kidding."

He picked up the spade and stuck it in the loosened earth then grinned and shrugged. "I thought I might get lucky."

She laughed and started toward the house. "You still might. There are fresh muffins—or at least there were."

He fell into step beside her and flashed the irresistible Chisholm dimple. "Then maybe we ought to walk faster."

Susan went into the house, and Jason went to find Walter and tell him they were stopping for coffee. By the time Jason came in and washed up, she had a fresh pot of coffee brewing and the oatmeal muffins arranged in a large basket. She had just finished setting the table and was at the fridge when he finally came into the kitchen. He dropped his Stetson on the counter by the door, and raking his hand through his thick curls, came to the table.

Her eyes were dancing as she glanced up at him. "You'd better eat fast. I think I just heard Duffy and Len ride in. If they get to the table first, you'll be out of luck."

He chuckled as he pulled out a chair and sat down. "It'll take them at least twenty minutes to get here. We're trailering the horses to where we'll be working today, and they'll have to load theirs."

Susan caught the fridge door with her elbow and swung it shut, then came to the table and set down the cream, butter and two jars of jam. "Mom used to swear that we could inhale four hours of cooking in ten seconds flat, but I think this bunch has us beat by a mile.''

The spark of humor in his eyes faded, and he stared at the table, a heavily retrospective look settled on his face. He leaned back, allowing Susan to set a cup of steaming coffee in front of him, an underlying weariness in his voice as he spoke. ''It shouldn't have taken a doctor to see that cooking for this crew was too much for Mattie. I should have hired someone long ago.''

Susan's own expression became solemn as she recognized the self-reproach in his tone. It would have been a perfect opportunity to point out to him that there was more than just the cooking that was too much for Mattie, but she refrained and steered the conversation in a different direction. ''How come you call her Mattie?''

Jason didn't answer for a moment, then sighing heavily, he looked up and gave her a wry grin. ''Being the only child, that was all I ever heard her called. She never bothered to make an issue of it, and I have a sneaking suspicion that both she and Dad thought it was something to encourage. She even tried to get my kids to call her Mattie.''

Susan smiled and shook her head. ''She's quite a lady.''

His voice grew solemn as he said quietly, ''Yes, she is. I don't know what I would have done without her.''

Susan realized that the situation could get very awkward if she asked any of the questions that comment opened up, so she addressed an issue she knew she was going to have to deal with sooner or later. ''I feel very badly over this deal with Clayton, Jason. I, of all people, know what he's like when he gets an idea in his head. I should have realized that me taking this job was something he'd simply bulldozed through, regardless of how you felt about it.'' Grimacing sheepishly, she gave him a warped smile. ''He can be very…tenacious…very formidable, when anyone or anything gets in his way.''

Jason studied her for a second, then leaned forward and rested his arms on the table as he absently picked at an imperfection on the mug. A warped grin appeared, and there was a touch of wry humor in his voice. "I think you really mean ornery and bullheaded—it's a Chisholm trait, I'm afraid. Clayton and I don't often lock horns, but we sure in hell did over that." He hesitated, the met her gaze directly, and she experienced a weird sensation in the pit of her stomach. His voice had a peculiar huskiness to it as he continued, "I didn't want you out here because I figured you'd expect the Double Diamond to be some sort of glitzy dude ranch, and quite frankly, I didn't think you could handle the job."

Suppressing a smile, she said quietly, "So you thought I'd be an albatross around your neck. Is that why you bit my head off when you caught me cleaning the floor?"

He gave her a twisted grin, then looked down as he continued to toy with his cup. "Yeah, something like that."

Susan leaned forward and folded her arms on the table, her expression suddenly earnest. "I came out here expecting to work, Jason, not to have an extended vacation. I know I'm here as a cook and nothing more, but I still need to be busy. I can't stand sitting around with nothing to do, and I honestly don't mind taking over some of the work that Mattie can't handle. But I don't want to face a battle with you every time I do something other than peel potatoes."

He raised his head and stared at her, a flicker of amusement lighting his eyes. "Why do I have this feeling if I give you an inch, you'll take a mile?"

She met his gaze with a hint of defiance. "I won't."

The sparkle intensified. "You will, Susan."

"I won't."

He gave a derisive snort as he shot her a disbelieving look, then pursing back a smile, he reached for a muffin. "Don't try that innocent look on me. You know damned well the minute my back's turned, you'll be up to your neck in some project or another."

"I won't do anything without checking with you first."

"Do you really expect me to believe that?"

She stared at him, a slightly tenacious set to her chin, and he raised his eyebrows in a knowing see-what-I-mean expression. Realizing that he had her cornered, and that she'd get nowhere trying to argue her way out of it, she yielded with a grin and tipped her head in unwilling agreement. "Okay, so maybe I do get a little carried away, but you don't have to be so sensitive about it."

He buttered his muffin and reached for the apricot jam, his own jaw taking on a stubborn set. "You're here to cook, not to launch a wide scale beautification program or—" he paused for emphasis "—to prove a point."

She didn't say anything as she tried to assess her best line of attack. An idea popped into her head and she finally spoke, a devious gleam in her eye. "How about if we make a deal. I'll give Mattie some extra help, and you'll give me some riding lessons."

"I'll give you lessons anyway."

"Not unless we make a fair exchange," she said stubbornly, trying to contain her satisfaction in effectively setting him up.

He looked at her, his eyes narrowing. "I think you've been around politicians too long."

"Is it a deal?"

His mouth twitched. "We'll see."

Deciding she'd better quit while she was ahead, Susan placed a muffin on her plate and reached for the butter. They fell into a comfortable silence and Susan felt strangely content, as though she had just discovered something that filled her with a vitalizing energy. And she knew, with wry humor, that this feeling of well-being wasn't from the food she was eating.

Jason interrupted her musings. "Have you ever ridden?"

She gave him a halfhearted grin. "Some."

He nearly smiled as he responded, "Define 'some.'"

"Well," she answered with a kind of perverse candor, "I can ride into a strong wind without falling off, if that tells you anything."

He tipped his head back and laughed, and Susan experienced a sudden fizzling sensation that made her catch her breath. It was the first time she'd heard him really laugh, and the transformation in him was amazing. There was a lighthearted buoyancy that stripped years off him, and Susan was mesmerized. So, she thought dazedly, beneath the sober demeanor, beneath the solemn weight of responsibility, there was another Jason Chisholm, one who was even more appealing. And the fizzle turned into an intoxicating rush.

She drew in a deep breath, and trying to ignore the excitement shooting through her, she struggled to keep her voice steady. "It isn't that funny, Jase," she said, her tone chastising as she bit back a smile.

Leaning back in his chair, he shook his head and expelled the last of his laughter on a deep sigh, his eyes still dancing as he grinned at her. "When you put it that way, maybe you do need a few lessons."

Sensing she had an advantage, she pressed him. "Then it's a deal?"

With his elbow resting on the table, he raised his cup, intently watching her over the rim. Finally he spoke. "Okay, it's a deal. But," he added emphatically, a tone of warning in his voice, "you aren't to try to do it all. Taking care of this whole house is not your responsibility. As soon as I have time, I'm going to see about lining up a housekeeper."

Susan opened her mouth to argue with him about that, then thought better of it and decided to quit while she was ahead. He was leaning back with his arms folded across his chest, his chair balanced on its back legs as he watched her through narrowed eyes.

Susan experienced an odd flustered feeling when he gave her a knowing half smile, as if he knew exactly what had been going on in her head. He studied her a moment longer then let the chair rock forward and land with a sharp thud, his mouth twitching. "You really had to bite your tongue on that one, didn't you?" he said his voice tinged with humor.

She lifted her chin and gave him a prim smile. "If you want to hire a housekeeper, that's your business."

"Then why," he asked softly, "do you suddenly have that determined set to your chin?"

She cast him a quick glance. "I don't," she retorted.

"Yes, you do."

"It always sticks out that way."

The Chisholm dimple appeared. "Then heaven help us," he said in a reverent tone of voice.

Voices drifted in from the open window and the screen door slammed as the other men entered the porch. Susan made an impudent face at Jason as she pushed her chair back, and he was still grinning at her when the men came into the kitchen. There was something disturbingly intimate about the look in his eyes, and a heady warmth spread through her as she stood motionless, transfixed by an indefinable spell. The magic lasted for an electrifying moment, then Duffy and Walter sat down at the table, and Susan forced herself to sever the connection. She tried to draw a breath past the sudden tightness in her chest as she struggled to collect her composure. If she thought she was heading for big trouble before, she thought wryly, it was nothing compared to where she was right now.

Taking another deep breath to try to calm herself, she picked up the coffeepot and went back to the table. She deliberately avoided looking at Jason as she filled Walter's and Duffy's mugs, but she was so keenly aware of his nearness that she went through the motions in a kind of daze. She refilled his cup and abruptly rammed her free hand in the back pocket of her jeans when she caught herself about to let it rest on his shoulder. His silvery hair, with its perfect blending of black and white, was a disorder of sort curls. She longed to smooth it down, but she shoved her hand deeper into her pocket instead.

Len came in as she was topping Walter's cup, and he shook his head in a gesture of approval as he shoved his mug across the table for her to fill. "This grub looks like it oughta plug a few holes. It was beginning to feel like a hell of a long time till dinner.'' He took a bite of muffin then reached for the butter, his eyes sparkling with sheer devilry as he grinned at her. ''You're one hell of a cook, Susan. Why don't you marry me and put some fat on these scrawny bones.''

She laughed as she placed the jam in front of him. ''You'd better think that offer through before you make it final. I may fatten you up, but have you any idea how much I'll thin down your bank account?''

He shook his head and chuckled. ''Don't seem quite sportin' that an old bronc buster should have to make that kind of trade-off.''

''Susan likes to negotiate, Len,'' Jason offered dryly.

Susan shot him a tart look, and her stomach did a crazy flip-flop when she realized how intently he was watching her. His eyes were gleaming with an amused challenge, as though he were silently daring her to debate the issue in front of everybody. She narrowed her eyes at him.

The corners of his mouth lifted and he looked away, the fabric of his plaid shirt pulling tautly across his shoulders as he leaned forward and rested his elbows on the table. Walter glanced from Jason to Susan then back to Jason, a glitter of comprehension in his eyes. He sat stroking his chin, nodding as he muttered to himself, ''Real interesting.''

Susan turned, riveting her full attention on him. He gave her a guileless smile and shrugged sheepishly. ''These are good muffins, Susan.''

Knowing exactly what was going on his mind, she stared at him, her hand on her hip as she said warningly, ''Watch it, Walter, or I'll dig up your peonies.''

The others had been talking and so had missed his quiet aside, and there was a sudden lull as the three men quickly turned their attention to the conversation between Susan and Walter. Unaware of their scrutiny, Walter shook his head and chuckled. ''Then you can plant them around the barn,'' he retorted haltingly, with an unmistakable twinkle.

Susan laughed and shook her finger at him, and Walter chuckled again. It was apparent to the others that they were sharing some private joke, so Len and Duffy picked up their conversation where they left off. Jason remained silent as he solemnly watched Susan refill Walter's cup.

As she returned the coffeepot to the element on the coffee maker, Walter pulled a dog-eared seed catalog out of his back pocket and carefully spread it on the table, an absorbed expression on his face. She came back to the table and slipped into the chair beside him, hunching over the catalog to study the colorful illustrations. "Do you have any poppies in the garden? You know, those big orange Oriental ones? A big clump of them would look fantastic behind the blue bachelor buttons."

He nodded. "There are some."

"Where are they?"

He gave her an impish smile. "Behind the blue bachelor buttons."

She gave him a menacing look then grinned as she punched him playfully on the shoulder. "I'm too big to have my leg pulled, Walter Chisholm."

Duffy brushed the crumbs off the front of his shirt and glanced at Walter. "Say, Walt, I was wonderin' if you'd have a look-see at that truck of mine. It's started missin' and poppin', and it's beginning to sound like it might hiccup itself to death."

"The older man nodded slowly. "This afternoon."

Susan looked at Clayton's cousin. "Sounds like you get all the fun jobs."

He shrugged, his expression bashful. "I like fixing things."

"Walter's probably the best mechanic in this here country," Duffy interjected with undisguised pride. "There ain't nothin' he can't fix. And he's a wizard with an engine."

Susan turned to the older Chisholm, her expression one of wry humor. "A wizard's just what I need. Maybe I can bribe you into saying a few incantations over my car. I've come to the conclusion that somebody's put a hex on it.''

He grinned. ''Apple pie should work pretty good.''

Susan stared at him blankly for a moment, then her eyes began to dance when she finally caught his drift. ''I think that could be arranged.''

Slapping at his thighs, Len pushed his chair back from the table and stood up. ''Well, I guess we'd better get back to work before I put down roots.'' He picked up his battered cowboy hat from the floor and settled it on his head, then nodded at Susan. ''That was a mighty fine snack, Susan. Appreciate it.''

Susan carried the dirty mugs to the counter, then dumped the remains of the coffee down the sink. She smiled at Len as she started loading the cups in the top rack of the dishwasher. ''I was just trying to put some fat on those scrawny bones of yours.''

The other men had left the table and were walking out of the kitchen when Jason paused and turned to face her. ''Why don't you leave this and take a walk down to the barn with me? There're a couple of horses you should be able to ride if you want, and I'll show you what tack to use.''

Her stomach did a weird little hop and a skip, and she nearly shoved the rack through the back of the dishwasher in her haste to comply with his unexpected invitation. He misread her reaction as one of desperation to get out of the house, and he cocked one eyebrow, amusement in his eyes. And for the first time in a long time, Susan felt a warm blush creep up her neck.

Shaking his head, Jason slipped on his Stetson and clapped her on the shoulder as she was about to pass in front of him. ''Well,'' he said softly, ''I'd say that just about finishes all hope for any blue-and-yellow pot holders, wouldn't you?''

The weight of his hand on her shoulder did incredible things to Susan's spine, and she felt as though her whole body were turning to warm porridge. She gave herself a quick mental lecture about reacting like a silly adolescent, then forced herself to take a deep breath before she glanced up at him. Her laugh had an odd throaty timbre to it, and her voice was slightly unsteady as she retorted, "The hopes were pretty slim to begin with, Jase."

He grinned back at her, and for one electric moment their eyes held. In that instant, Susan had the overpowering sensation that some incomplete part of her had just connected with something in him, and she felt a kind of closeness, a kind of harmony she'd never experienced with anybody else. The effect was staggering.

Jason drew in a ragged breath and his gaze slid to her mouth, his touch on her shoulder almost a caress as she said unevenly, "Then maybe we'd better make a trade—the rocking chair for a saddle." His voice was even more husky as he put pressure on her shoulder, prompting her to move. "And it could be a hell of a lot more interesting."

Susan really had to fight to gather the strength and willpower to move, and as she regretfully severed the physical contact, she felt suddenly dispossessed of the warm sense of oneness that had enveloped her. Struggling to regain at least some semblance of calm, she smoothed her hands down the front of her jeans and turned toward the door.

The screen door slammed loudly behind them, and Dudley came bounding around the corner of the house, a branch the size of a small tree hanging out of his mouth. He romped along in front of them, begging for someone to play with him.

Jason bent over and took the branch, then sent it flying in a long arch in the direction of a coppice of spruce. The dog went tearing after it and Jason hooked his thumbs on his belt buckle, an air of introspection about him.

They walked on in silence for a short distance, then he glanced at Susan. "Do you mind if I ask how come you went along with Clayton's idea?"

A light breeze caught her hair, feathering it across her

face, and Susan absently tucked the strand behind her ear as she lowered her head, her expression thoughtful. There was a pensive quality to her voice as she finally spoke. "I'm not sure I really know why. I've always had a fascination for the west…but there was more to it than that." She hesitated, trying to sort out her thoughts before she went on. "When he first mentioned it to me I had no intention of coming, then something changed and I found myself really caught up in the idea." Sliding her hands into the back pockets of her jeans, she frowned slightly as she kicked a small stone off the path. "Clayton's talked about it so much, it's almost as if he's given me a sense of—I don't know how to explain it—a sense of *rightness* about this country. It was almost as though I was compelled to come and see for myself."

"And now that you have?"

Susan looked up at him, her expression serious. "I love it," she said quietly.

He held her gaze for a second, then looked away, his voice suddenly gruff. "Yeah, so do I."

Jason followed a trail that led into the windbreak, and Susan ducked a low-hanging branch. "I don't know how Clayton can stay away when this country means so much to him."

Jason's manner was somewhat brusque when he responded, "He has his reasons."

"I know he does."

Jason shot her a sharp look, and Susan shrugged and gave him a sheepish grin. "Well, I don't know *exactly*, but I have my suspicions."

He tipped his hat forward, the shadow from the brim obscuring his eyes. "Close, but no cigar," he said, his voice touched with amusement.

"Thanks," she said dryly. They walked on in silence for a moment, then Susan spoke again. "What did happen, Jase?"

He glanced at her. "Have you ever asked him?"

"No."

"Why didn't you?"

She shrugged as she idly trailed her hand through some long grass beside the trail. "I guess I felt I'd be intruding on his privacy—that maybe he doesn't like to talk about it."

"He doesn't."

"Did it have anything to do with his never marrying?"

Jason caught a small branch and stripped the leaves off it. "He was married."

Susan shot him a surprised look. "When?"

"Years ago, to a Métis girl. It caused quite a storm in the district—marrying a Métis wasn't exactly socially acceptable then—and my grandfather nearly disowned him over it. She died of tuberculosis four or five years later, and from what I can remember it was months before Clayton came out of the back country."

A hollow feeling settled in Susan's stomach. "Do you remember her?"

"Yeah, I sure do. White Dove was the most gentle, tranquil person I've ever known. When she died, Clayton told Mattie that there would never be another woman to take her place."

Susan blinked back the sudden sting of tears. "How sad."

Jason looked at her, his eyes solemn. "No, it isn't, Susan," he said quietly. "He's had something that very few people ever find, and for the most part, he's grateful he had the time he did with her. Occasionally he gets down about it, but not very damned often."

"Memories are a poor substitute," she countered softly.

"Maybe, but I think Clayton would tell you that the memories he has are a lot better than the day-to-day existence most people live."

Susan frowned thoughtfully as she considered Jason's comment. Knowing Clayton the way she did, she knew his nephew was right. But one thing was clear: the Chisholm family had suffered its share of tragedy.

They passed through the wide belt of trees, and the rest of the ranch buildings came into view. The arena was at the most eastward end of the complex, with a series of corrals between it and a huge red barn, and on a knoll off to the west, a modern wind generator had been erected, its blades spinning soundlessly in the light breeze. Jason glanced at her, a tormenting glint in his eyes. "Too bad Clayton hadn't sent you out last year. All the buildings had to be painted, and it got to the point where I practically had to use a cattle prod on everybody to get it done. You would've had a great time."

She gave him a warning glance. "You're pushing your luck, Jason Chisholm," she said softly.

He just grinned and tipped his hat a little lower. As they walked past one of the larger outbuildings, Susan spotted several horses grazing in the field, and she slowed her pace. She had gone through a phase in her teens when she nearly drove her parents crazy begging for a horse, but she could never quite convince them that she would simply die if she didn't get one. Her delirium of enthusiasm had finally passed, but the fascination had remained, and she watched them now with genuine interest.

There was a soft whinny and she turned. A sorrel gelding was in the corral right beside the barn and he came over to the fence, his head held high and his ears pricked in interest. She started toward him, but he threw is head and shied away, then trotted off to the back corner.

She hooked her elbows on the top rail, her chin resting on her forearms as she watched him prance around. Jason leaned against the fence. "That's old Riley. Mattie broke him over twenty years ago and he's still going strong."

Susan's expression was one of amazement. "You don't still ride him, do you?"

Jason rested his foot on the bottom rail as he braced his shoulder against the post. "Sometimes. We use him at roundup, and every once in a while Clayton saddles him up, but he's usually turned loose in the big pasture. The only reason he's in here now is because he needs his hooves trimmed.''

He gave a low whistle and the horse threw his head, then trotted over to the rail and nuzzled Jason's shoulder. Jason smiled and rubbed the animal's nose. ''Mattie and he used to have some rare old go-arounds. He shies at anything that moves, and he used to pile her regularly. I think it eventually developed into a simple battle of wills.''

Susan slowly stroked the gelding's neck as she listened to Jason, her eyes sparkling. When he finished, she shook her head and laughed, a look of pure mischief on her face. ''It sounds as if the Chisholm contrariness is a common characteristic around here, doesn't it?''

Jason turned his head and looked at her, a warning tone in his voice. ''Don't push *your* luck, lady, or you'll be back in the kitchen.''

She shook her head, her hands raised in a gesture of refusal. ''Not a chance.''

With a hint of a smile, he straightened and motioned toward the barn. ''Come on. I'll show you around.''

Inside, a fragrance of horses and dried hay rose up to meet her, and Susan squinted, waiting for her eyes to adjust to the dim interior. There was a tack room inside the door, and with one quick glance at the large box stalls lining the structure, Susan followed Jason into the small room. A number of specially built brackets mounted on the wall held all the saddles, each with a saddle blanket draped over it. On the end wall two rows of wooden knobs held a variety of halters, bridles and martingales, and along the bottom of a row of shelves stood several pairs of boots.

Dust motes hung suspended on the shaft of light that slanted in through the grimy window, and a large white cat lay in the splash of brightness that fell across an old sheepskin saddle pad.

Jason flipped a halter off a hook, then indicated the boots. ''You should be able to find a pair that'll fit you. And do wear them, Susan,'' he cautioned. ''Wearing shoes without heels is asking for trouble.''

She nodded, and he turned away. Draping the halter over his shoulder, Jason stuck his hand into a large bag then handed her the huge pellets he'd picked up. ''I'll give you Breezy to ride, and she'll come in with a whistle if you use the right bait.''

Susan followed him out of the tack room, and as Jason headed for the other end of the barn, she fell into step with him. ''How many horses do you have?''

''I have about fifty head right now, but ten of those have been sold to an oilman from the States. He wants to try them out as polo ponies. They'll be shipped out in another couple of weeks, as soon as they've shed out.'' He slid open the big door at the end of the barn and they stepped out into the sunlight. ''Can you whistle?''

She nodded and gave him a dubious look.

He let out two shrill whistles and the horses in the field raised their heads, but one started loping toward the barn. Jason turned and smiled, an almost sheepish look on his face. ''Well, it beats walking out there to get them.''

Susan suppressed a smile. ''Sure it does.'' She extended her hand as the horse trotted up, and Breezy eagerly nuzzled the pellets out of her palm.

Speaking quietly, Jason slipped the halter, which was made of a sturdy red twill, over the horse's head. ''Do you want to take her for a ride now?''

She glanced at her watch and shook her head. ''I won't have time. I still have to make lunch for you to take with you.''

Patting the mare on the shoulder, Jason unsnapped the shank from the halter, then turned the horse loose. ''I'll leave the halter on so it'll be easier to catch her.''

Susan watched the horse gallop off, her eyes glowing with pleasure. She turned to say something to Jason, and her heart flip-flopped when she found him watching her with solemn eyes, an unfathomable expression on his face. The wind feathered her hair across her cheek and as if drawn against his will, Jason reached out to smooth it back. Before he actually touched her, he hauled in a deep breath and turned away, his voice uneven. "I'd better get going. Len and Duff will be waiting for me."

And an aching emptiness overcame Susan as she watched him walk away.

CHAPTER FOUR

THE REST OF THE AFTERNOON passed in a daze. Susan was actually relieved when the kids finally got home from school, bringing with them enough commotion to distract anybody. She'd spent most of the day trying not to think about their father, which was a lost cause. She tried to rationalize her way out of it, block it out, then finally tried to sweat it out by scrubbing down both bathrooms in the main house. But that didn't work, either. At least at the rate things were going, two more encounters with Jase Chisholm and she'd have the whole house cleaned from top to bottom.

The only thing that snapped her back to reality was when Michael came racing in the back door, wound up like a top because Todd had a snake—a green snake with dots on its back that wriggled when you squeezed it. And Todd, being a normal, red-blooded boy, was threatening to stuff it down his brother's neck. By the time Susan caught Todd as he tore by, hauled him up short and discovered the snake was a rubber one, she had so much adrenaline racing through her system that *nothing* affected her.

She confiscated the snake, made the boys set the table and listened to Lucy try to list all the words that rhymed with "stink." It wasn't until she had the potatoes peeled and on the stove that it dawned on her she hadn't seen Patricia. Drying her hands on her jeans, she went into the main house and finally found the girl huddled in a big chair in the living room, sobbing her heart out.

A look of concern crossed Susan's face as she crouched beside her and smoothed back her hair. "What's the matter,

Trish? Did something happen on the way home from school?''

Patricia vehemently shook her head, sobs racking her whole body, and Susan made a sympathetic sound as she slipped her arms around the teenager and cuddled her to her. "Come on, honey. Stop crying and tell me what's wrong. Maybe I can help.''

The girl buried her head against Susan's shoulder, her flood of tears soaking through her blouse. Susan's expression was very solemn as she gently rocked her, remembering how much things hurt at that age. She pressed her face into the child's hair, her tone gentle as she murmured, "Did somebody say something or did something happen?''

Patricia dragged in a ragged breath, her voice muffled and distorted by weeping as she ground out vehemently, "I hate being fat! I hate it! I'm tired of everybody poking fun at me, and I'm tired of pretending it doesn't matter.'' She burst into a fresh flood of tears. "Because it does matter. It does!''

Susan cuddled her closer and kissed her on the forehead. "I know it matters, Trish. I was really overweight when I was your age, and I hated it, too. And everybody thinks because you're fat, you're supposed to be a good sport about it.''

Wiping her face with the back of her hand, Patricia pulled out of Susan's embrace, her weeping suddenly checked. She wiped her nose on a balled-up tissue then raised her head. Her face was splotchy and swollen and her mouth was puffy, and she looked utterly miserable. But there was the tiniest glimmer of hope in her eyes as she looked at Susan. "Were you really, Susan? Fat, I mean? You're so tall and slim now.''

Susan suppressed a smile as she brushed back wispy strands of hair that were clinging to the girl's face. "Yes, I was, Trish. And I hated it, too.''

Patricia wiped her nose again then looked down as she agitatedly twisted the Kleenex into a rope. "One of the neighbors up the road—I baby-sit for them all the time—

she joined Weight Watchers last year and she said I could go with her. But Grandma didn't want me to go. She said wanting to be thin was silly and that it was a waste of money and that I'd slim down in my own good time. I said I would pay for it with my baby-sitting money, but she said no.''

"Did you talk to your dad about it?"

Patricia lifted her head and met Susan's gaze. "I tried, and I think he would have let me go if it hadn't been for Grandma. But he didn't want to upset her."

Susan frowned and chewed absently on her bottom lip. "I see," she said thoughtfully.

"Mrs. Donaldson gave me the books so I could go on the diet by myself, but every time Grandma caught me measuring my servings, she'd get all worried. She was afraid I was going to turn anorexic or something." Sighing tremulously, Patricia lowered her head. "I really love Grandma, and I didn't want to do anything that was going to upset her so I quit trying."

There was a look of speculation on Susan's face as she stared at the child. "Do you still have the books?"

"Yes."

"Will you get them for me?"

Patricia stared at the woman's face. "Why?"

"Well, I don't want to do anything to upset your grandmother either, Patricia, but I think we can work this without anyone ever knowing. We won't be able to say anything to anybody, and we'll have to be careful, but I think we can do it."

For a moment, Patricia continued to stare at her, then her eyes filed with tears again, only this time they were tears of happiness, and she flung her arms around Susan's neck and hugged her fiercely. "Oh, Susan, I'll do anything—*any-thing*—if you'll just help me."

There was an odd tightness in Susan's throat, and she tried to overcome it before she answered, "Well, the first thing you can do is go get the books."

Patricia gave her another hug, then scrambled off the

chair and went flying up the stairs, her eyes bright. Susan
sighed and slapped her thighs as she stood up. "Wonderful," she muttered to herself. "Now I'm conspiring with a
child behind her grandmother's back." She felt a sharp
twinge of conscience as she walked out of the living room,
but she was still going to help the kid, conscience or not.

By the time supper was ready, Susan had read the pam-
phlets, fixed a scribbler for a daily record book, noted Patricia's weight and had a week's worth of school lunches
planned. And Patricia was floating on air.

Todd looked at his sister, who was happily humming to
herself as she made the salad for supper, his expression suspicious. "What's the matter with her? Why's she so happy,
anyway?"

Susan patted him on the head and answered him airily,
"Why, Toddy! She's all happy because she gets to go to
your baseball game tonight."

He rolled his eyes heavenward and muttered, "Gimme a
break."

"Would that be one leg or two?"

Todd screwed up his face in total incomprehension. Then
the lights went on in his eyes and he let out a hoot of laughter. "Gimme a break—one leg or two! One leg or two!"
He flopped on a chair and tipped his head back, convulsing
with a fit of giggles. "I'm gonna remember that. I am."

Susan watched him with a wry smile, or at least she did
until it hit her how much he looked like his father, then she
gave herself a stern mental shake and went to mash the
potatoes. She was whipping them with a mixer when Mattie
came, the traces of sleep still on her face. She shook her
head in disbelief, her tone apologetic. "I don't know what's
come over me, Susan. I truly don't. I've done nothing but
sleep since you've arrived."

Susan smiled at her as she switched off the appliance.
"There's no need to apologize, Mattie. I'm having a great
time bossing everyone around."

The older woman attempted a facsimile of a stern expression as she surveyed her grandchildren. "Well, they certainly could do with a little bossing."

Michael grinned at her as he carried the buns to the table. "You're so mean, Grandma." He set the basket down then looked back at his grandmother. "Are you going to come to our baseball game tonight? We're playing High River and I'm going to pitch."

Weariness flashed across the older woman's face, and Susan was about to intercede, but Todd beat her to it. "It's okay if you don't come, Grandma. Honest. Susan and Uncle Walter are coming, and Dad said he would really try to make it later."

Mattie sat down at the table, a conscience-stricken look on her face. Michael went over and put his arms around her shoulders and gave her a little hug. "Maybe it'd be better if you didn't come, then I won't feel so dumb if I mess up."

Mattie smiled at him and gave his hand an affectionate pat. "You'll do just fine, Michael. But maybe I will stay home if you really don't mind. I'm so very tired."

He smiled reassuringly. "It's okay, really. Maybe Todd and I will mess up so bad, we'll spend the whole game sitting on the bench."

Mattie shook her head in amused affection as she sighed wearily. "That would be worth watching, Mikey. I don't think I've ever seen you just *sit*."

THE CHISHOLM FAMILY VEHICLE was a big nine-passenger Suburban, and Susan felt as if she were behind the wheel of a tank after her Volkswagen Beetle. She had not expected to drive, but Walter had handed her the keys and shook his head when she tried to hand them back.

He gave her directions, and by the time they arrived at the ball diamond, several other vehicles were already parked along the road. Susan felt a little hesitant as they approached a group of parents who had gathered behind the team bench.

But Michael would have no part of that. He caught her hand and dragged her into the group, a big grin on his face.

"Hey, guys, this is Pete Lynton's sister and she works for my Uncle Clayton."

Several people turned to look, and Susan felt as if he'd just put her on sale. An extremely attractive woman in her mid-thirties approached her, smiling at Susan as if they were old friends. "Well, hi there. You must be Susan. I'm Carol Redding. We live just up the road from the Double Diamond."

Susan took her outstretched hand and smiled back. The three Redding boys spent considerable time with the Chisholms, and they had the same open smile as their mother. Carol introduced her to everyone, and in less than ten minutes she felt as comfortable as she would at a community gathering at home.

There was a swarm of boys milling around in blue-and-gray striped uniforms with the Dodgers crests on them, and the coach, a big man with a booming voice, clapped Susan on the shoulder. "I'm short some help tonight. How would you feel about warming this crew up, Pete Lynton's sister? And if you're as good as Todd says you are, we'll hire you," he added with a hearty laugh.

She laughed, and still feeling somewhat conspicuous, pulled a bat out of the equipment bag and picked up three balls, then went to stand at home plate. Signaling for the stocky redheaded catcher to catch for her, she started batting infield flies. If anyone had any doubts about her qualifications, they were soon dispelled as she expertly peppered the field with a mixture of grounders and line drives.

"Hey Wilson," somebody yelled at the coach. "Give us a break and play your new assistant."

Susan glanced over to the first-base line. A tall blond man was watching her, his arms folded across his chest, an unholy grin splitting his face. He was one of those lean wiry men who had a certain athletic grace about them—tough and with endless stamina, and who stood out in a crowd. Only this one *really* stood out with his Robert Redford good looks and an utterly engaging grin.

She was so busy watching him, she missed an incoming ball, and he shook his head, his expression schooled into one of woe. "Geez, I don't know about these imports, Wilson."

The agonized look on his face made her laugh, and Susan missed another incoming ball. The catcher rolled his eyes heavenward and muttered something about dopey women.

By then, the opposing team had arrived, and with a signal from Mr. Wilson, the Dodgers trotted in from the field. Susan caught a ball with one already in her hand, then tossing the bat to Todd started walking toward the bench.

The blonde was watching her, a truly wicked sparkle in his eyes. When she got close enough, he stuck out his hand and introduced himself. "I'm Tyler Redding. All those Redding boys who hand around the Double Diamond are my nephews."

Susan had already suspected he was the much talked about Tyler Redding, and she had certainly heard enough about him. He was a championship chuck-wagon driver and had, for two years in a row, taken top money at the Calgary Stampede, his fame making him an idol for both his nephews and the Chisholm boys.

She smiled and took his hand. "I'm Susan Lynton.'

He nodded, his lips pursed. "So I've heard." He grinned at her suddenly, flashing a set of perfect teeth. "You're some ball player."

She grinned back. "You're some heckler."

He watched her intently, his grin turning into a thoughtful half smile. "So," he said softly, as though he were thinking out loud, "this is the reason ol' Jase is in a sweat."

Feeling as though he had suddenly poured ice water over her, she stared at him, her expression frozen. She felt at an utter loss for words, and she turned away, trying to cover up her discomfort. Needing something to do, she knelt by the equipment and started arranging bats on the ground.

Tyler squatted beside her, his voice suddenly quiet and

serious. "I apologize for that crack. Sometimes I put my mouth in gear while my brain's still in neutral."

Before she thought about what he was saying, she answered sharply, "Yes, you do."

That made him laugh and she glanced up at him as he shook his head, his voice still heavy with laughter. "Man, you're a flinty one, aren't you?"

"I try," she answered wryly.

He laughed again. Then his expression grew serious as he studied her and added thoughtfully, "I think something worthwhile has finally turned up in Jase Chisholm's life."

There was nothing flip about his observation, and it took Susan a second before it registered that he meant every word. She didn't know quite how to respond or what to say, and she fingered one of the bats before she looked up at him. "I think I'll take that as a compliment," she said, trying to smile.

He nodded. "You do that," he said quietly. "It was sure in hell meant as one." He continued to watch for a moment, then clapped her lightly on the shoulder and stood up. "See you around, Susan Lynton." And she watched him walk away, a funny sensation settling inside her.

It was the top of the third inning when Susan's internal antennae started tingling, and she glanced around. Jason had just arrived and was standing with Tyler and Walter behind the team bench. Lucy distracted her as she came running up behind her and looped her arms around her neck, then leaned against Susan's back. Right then, the boy who was batting for the Dodgers hit a pop fly to center field, making the third out for the inning. Lucy continued to hang off Susan's neck, bobbing her head in time to the music as she made up words to a song she was singing under her breath.

The Dodgers took the field, and Susan's expression changed as she watched Michael pitch. Unfortunately the first two batters got on base because of outfield errors, but even so, Michael was doing a very credible job. The third batter came up, and Susan could tell by the way he settled himself at the plate that this kid was fully capable of bringing those two runs home. Michael's expression became more intense, then with his face twisted in concentration he made his pitch. One strike. He wound up again, and as soon as he let the ball go, Susan knew it was a hit.

The batter connected with sizzling line drive to the left of the shortstop, but somehow Todd, who was well behind the baseline, managed to stretch out and trap it in his glove, the velocity of the ball yanking him off his feet and rolling him over. He came up with the ball still clutched in his glove, a dazed look on his face as the runner who was headed for third whirled to return to second. Susan yelled for a triple play, and Todd reacted, firing the ball to second base. The second base man made the tag and fired the ball to first, catching the other runner.

But there was no elation on Susan's face as she disconnected Lucy's arms and got to her feet. She knew by the way Todd had caught the ball and by the look on his face that he had really hurt his hand. He was fighting to hold back tears as he came to the bench, his face white.

Susan knelt down in front of him as she carefully slipped off his glove. "Did you catch it on the edge of the fingers or did they get bent back?"

"Bent back," he whispered as he inhaled sharply.

Susan winced when she saw that the fingers were already starting to turn purplish. "I wish we had some ice. If we could stop that swelling, we could tape them so you could finish the game."

Jason crouched beside her and inspected his son's hand. "Bring him over to Redding's car. Carol has a cooler of pop for the kids in the trunk, and she said there was plenty of ice in it."

Susan glanced at Todd. "Okay, Todd? How about we do that?"

He nodded, his face even more ashen than before. She picked up his glove and stood up, then put her arm around his shoulders, gently guiding him toward the parked cars.

By the time they reached the vehicle, Jason had the cooler lifted out and the lid open.

Taking Todd's arm by the wrist, she carefully submerged his hand in the chipped ice and gently packed it around his fingers. The boy looked up at her, his eyes dark against his waxen face. "I won't be able to finish the game, will I? I'm one of the best batters on our team, and we're ahead by one, and I won't be able to play. Maybe we could beat them this time."

Crouching beside his son, Jason draped an arm around the boy's hips. "You've sprained your fingers pretty bad, son. Your hand's going to be really sore, and if they swell much more, you aren't going to be able to hold the bat."

With an age-old maternal gesture, Susan lightly brushed his damp hair off his forehead and then let her hand rest on his shoulder. "That was a great play you made, Todd," she said as she gave him a reassuring shake. "If you hadn't hung on to that ball, they'd have scored two runs—and just think, you put three out in one play."

Todd shrugged with embarrassment then grinned at her. "I heard you yell 'go for the triple' and I figured I'd better make it or else."

She ruffled his hair and stood up. "Or else is right." She lifted his hand and looked at it, then she grinned down at him. "Well, at least you didn't sprain all four fingers. By the looks of it, there are only two that are really bad."

He looked up at her, his expression hopeful. "I can still play, Susan. Honest I can. They don't hurt that bad."

There was a doubtful look in her eyes as she smoothed her hand down his arm. Uncertain about what to say, she glanced at Jason and found him watching her, his head tipped to one side, a strange contemplative expression on his face. His eyes remained unreadable for a moment, then he smiled and said, "Seeing you're the expert on sprained fingers, what do you think?"

She grimaced then crouched and rechecked Todd's hand. "Well, if we can get our hands on some of the stretchy adhesive tape, I can strap his fingers so he'll be able to play." She looked at Todd, her tone warning as she said, "I can tape them so they won't get sprained any worse, but it's going to really hurt if they get hit again."

He thought about it for a minute then grinned. "I can stand it."

His father smiled and stood up. "Okay, kid. Then let's go."

Jason put the cooler back in the trunk, and they walked toward the bench. There was a large first-aid kit by the equipment bag, and Susan sank to her knees and opened it.

Todd crouched behind her, a conspiratorial tone in his voice as he whispered, "I thought I'd dropped the ball when I fell. It wasn't until you yelled I realized I still had it in my glove. Boy, was I surprised."

Jason overheard him, and handing Susan the roll of tape, he gave his son an amused glance. "You weren't the only one."

Tipping his head back, the boy squinted up at his dad, a pleased look on his face. "It *was* a pretty good catch, wasn't it, Dad? Just like a real shortstop."

Susan bit back a smile. "Then why were you standing there if you weren't the real shortstop?"

He gave her a playful punch on the shoulder. "You know what I mean."

Jason glanced down at her and shook his head, a glint of laughter in his eyes. "Maybe he ought to stick to saving baseball cards."

Michael came tearing over and dropped down by his father, his face flushed and slightly grimy as he crowded in next to Todd. "Are you still gonna be able to play? You gotta play." Then his face lit up with an enraptured grin. "That was some catch! And a real triple play! Wow! Just like a real shortstop."

Susan's gaze connected with Jason's, and somehow she managed not to laugh as he raised his eyes to the heavens in a beseeching gesture, then cleared his throat and turned away. "I'll go tell the coach you're still in the game."

Susan forced her face into a deadpan expression as she deliberately lowered her head over Todd's hand.

Michael crowded closer to scrutinize his brother's hand. "That's gonna hurt, isn't it?"

"Nah," Todd said nonchalantly, trying to seem totally disinterested.

There was a flash of amusement in Susan's eyes. One thing she'd learned over the years was that small boys would rather die than admit to pain. Very carefully, she shaped his swollen fingers into a slight curve, and Todd sucked in his breath sharply. She glanced up at him and gave him a reassuring look. "If I tape them with the right curve on them, you'll be able to hang on to the bat and still be able to get your glove on." She dried off his hand on the tail of her blouse, adjusted the position of his fingers and started wrapping. "I'm going to tape all your fingers together. That way, the two good ones will act as a splint, so if you do get hit again, you won't sprain them any more."

Todd let his breath go as he watched with interest. "Did you used to tape your brother's hands when he got a sprain?"

She could tell by the tingle down her spine that Jason was back and was standing very close to her. His presence unnerved her, and she fumbled clumsily with the strip of tape, accidentally twisting it so that it adhered to itself. Crouching beside her, he reached over and straightened the tape, his hands making contact with hers. A frantic fluttering in her chest paralyzed her lungs, and she had to fight to draw a breath.

"Well, did you?"

It took a second for her to collect her wits enough to answer him. "Not often. It was usually me who got all the sprains. He just stood out there firing fast balls at me."

"Wow," Todd said in awed tones. "Just think, you used to catch for Pete Lynton."

Susan cast him a slightly caustic look. "I used to do his dirty laundry, too, but I don't suppose you view that with quite the same reverence."

Jason grinned as he held the tape where Susan indicated. "Hardly. As far as Todd's concerned, clean clothes are something that just miraculously happen. It doesn't have the same glamour at all."

Todd grimaced. "Aw, come on, Dad. I'm not that bad."

"Nearly." Jason turned over his son's hand and smoothed down the tape. "You must've sprained a lot of fingers to develop this technique."

"I did. My mother was convinced I was a confirmed tomboy and that my feminity would never amount to a hill of beans."

His voice had a sudden husky texture to it and he said softly, "Didn't your mother ever tell you there's something very appealing about a tomboy?"

She was transfixed by his amused gaze, and Susan felt as if everything were going into a long slow spin, leaving her light-headed. "My mother was too busy wallowing in despair over my lack of social graces."

Todd broke the spell. "Michael's up to bat. Can I go watch?"

Tearing her eyes away and collecting her wits, Susan cut free the roll of tape, her voice unusually low. "Sure. But Todd, I want you to watch the pitcher. He has a favorite slot for right-handed batters. About every third pitch, he throws one that just catches the corner of the plate low and inside. If you widen your stance and wait for that one pitch, you should be able to put it over the fence. And with that angle of swing, you won't put too much strain on your hand."

He grinned at her and scrambled to his feet. "Right, Coach!"

Brushing the dried grass off her slacks, she stood up and

watched him go, keenly aware of his father standing beside her. She expected Jason to rejoin Walter and Tyler, but he remained beside her, his hands rammed in the back pockets of his jeans, his legs locked, his attention focused on his younger son. She studied his profile for a second, then turned her attention to Michael.

Michael got on base with a clean grounder to third and flashed Susan and Jason a delighted smile from first, then bent over, his hands on his knees, trying his best to look like a "real" ball player.

When Todd came up to bat, there were two out and two on base, and Susan's expression became intent. Jason grinned down at her. "You'll hear about this for the rest of your natural life if you're wrong, you know."

She grimaced. "I know."

The first pitch was a perfect strike across the middle of the plate, but Todd let it go by, then glanced at Susan, his expression questioning. She reassured him with a nod and he turned back to face the pitcher. The second pitch was a ball, and the third, true to Susan's scouting, was low and inside, and Todd connected. As soon as he made contact, he winced and yanked his hand away, an expression of pain flitting across his face as he headed for first. The ball sailed away over the left field fence as she had predicted.

Jason raised his eyebrows in surprise, then looked at Susan. "Have you ever considered the fact that maybe you're in the wrong business?"

She laughed and shrugged. "I'm always in the wrong business." Just then Walter came over to Jason, a strange glazed look in his eyes. Jason spoke to him quietly, then handed him the keys to his truck, his expression one of concern as he watched the older man walk away.

Susan looked up at him. "Is something wrong?"

He sighed and shook his head. "Not really. He just wants to go home. He has spells occasionally when he develops very severe headaches, and when that happens he just wants to go off by himself."

Susan was going to question him further about Walter's condition, but she changed her mind when she saw the taut look around Jase's mouth. She suspected that there weren't many days when Jason wasn't reminded, in one way or another, of the enormous family responsibilities he shouldered.

By the time they returned to the Double Diamond, it was very late. Lucy had fallen asleep on Susan's lap during the long drive home, and even the boys had finally wound down from their much sought-after win.

As they pulled into the driveway, Susan gently shifted Lucy's weight as she slipped the girl's arms around her shoulders, then glanced at Jason. "If you want to check on Walter, I'll get the kids to bed."

He parked beside the caragana hedge and switched off the lights and ignition before he answered her. "I think I'd better. He sometimes forgets his medicine when he's like that." He opened the door and turned to get out. "I'll carry Lucy in first."

"No, that's okay. I can manage. You go ahead."

He stared at her for a moment, the interior light in the vehicle casting his face in dark shadows, then he nodded and climbed out, closing the door behind him.

Subdued by sleepiness, the two boys trailed into the house behind Susan as Patricia held the door open for her. With Lucy draped over her shoulder and still dead to the world, Susan entered the darkened porch, then addressed Patricia in a whisper. "There's a bunch of carrot and celery sticks in a plastic bag in the fridge, and there's some salad left from supper in a little white container. You can have those if you want, Trish, and you can have one more glass of milk."

Patricia opened the door leading into the main house and turned on the kitchen light. "Thanks, Susan," she whispered gratefully. "I was getting so hungry."

"You go have your snack, then you better come right up to bed, okay?"

"Okay."

Lucy stirred and twisted her head on Susan's shoulder, and the woman cuddled her closer as she turned toward the living room and the stairs. "Shh, honey. We'll have you in bed in just a minute."

The boys were dragging themselves toward their room as Susan came upstairs. "You guys make sure you brush your teeth before you go to bed, okay?"

"Aw, Susan."

"Teeth first," she whispered firmly as she turned down the hallway toward Lucy's room. She heard them grumbling as they entered the bathroom.

Patricia had already come upstairs by the time Susan had Lucy ready for bed, and she heard the older girl speak to someone before her bedroom door closed. Susan listened for a minute then bent over the sleeping child and gently brushed back the dark tumble of curls. She tucked the comforter around her and shut off the small night-light.

When Susan turned around, Jason was standing in the doorway, his hand resting on the knob, his body silhouetted against the light from the hallway. Silently she slipped out of the darkened room, inadvertently brushing against him as she passed in front of him. The physical contact set off a flurry of electric sensations within her, and she felt him tense, as though he had just received a shock. Without looking at him, Susan went quietly downstairs, trying not to let her suddenly wanton thoughts get the best of her.

Jason followed her down and paused by the living room bookshelves, a pronounced set to his jaw. Sensing he had something to say, Susan hesitated, a strange anticipation unfolding in her.

There was a certain edginess about him, as though he were dealing with a very awkward situation, and his hands weren't quite steady as he rolled back the cuffs of his shirt. "I want to thank you for going out of your way for the boys tonight," he said quietly, an odd huskiness to his voice. There was a strained hesitation, then he finally raised his gaze and looked at her, his eyes dark and very solemn. "It meant a lot to them having you there. I think they sometimes feel a little left out because they're the only kids on the team who don't have a mother there rooting for them."

His frankness touched a disturbingly responsive cord in her, and suddenly needing something to keep her hands occupied, Susan picked up Lucy's sweater from the arm of the sofa and began folding it. "It wasn't any big sacrifice on my part," she responded, her own voice uneven. "It was a good game and I really enjoyed it." She finally raised her eyes to meet his, the intensity radiating between them sapping her of strength. She could feel her pulse accelerate as she took a slow breath, then murmured, "You've got a good bunch of kids, Jase. You can really be proud of them."

He looked down and refolded one sleeve, his voice so strained she could barely hear him. "I am."

There was something in his voice that made her long to go to him, as if some force were drawing them together.

Nor was she the only one affected. She sensed he was fighting to hold his distance, but knowing that only intensified her overwhelming feelings. It was though they were separated by some chasm that was impossible to span.

It seemed that they stood there forever, neither of them speaking, the silence compounding the tension between them. Unable to endure it any longer, Susan finally screwed up her courage. "I think we need to talk, Jason," she whispered.

He had moved away and stood staring out the window, his arm braced against the frame, an unyielding set to his profile. There was a strained silence, then he answered raggedly, "I think it's better if we don't."

It didn't take much insight to realize he was experiencing feelings he was having trouble dealing with, and Susan gazed at him, a nearly suffocating ache unfolding inside her. She wanted so badly to go to him, but she also knew she didn't dare. She realized it was going to be up to her to lighten the tension between them, so she said softly, "If we can't talk, how about a coffee and a piece of pie?"

He made no response for several moments, then finally he turned and looked at her, a halfhearted grin creasing his face. "How about a riding lesson instead?"

Her eyes lit up. "Are you serious? It's not too late?"

There was a touch of wry humor in his eyes as he said gruffly, "It might be too late if we stay in this house."

For some reason, his reply uncorked an incredible effervescence inside her, and she laughed, a heady sensation bubbling through her. "I think you're a coward, Jason Chisholm."

The tense look left his face and he grinned back at her. "Under the circumstances, I'd rather think of myself as prudent." They were standing close enough for the fragrance of him to fill her senses, but what she was feeling toward him went far beyond simple physical attraction. It was much deeper than that, and she was finally forced to face the real reason that she had this unholy need to be close to him, to touch him. Susan knew right then and there that she was utterly lost. She had already fallen in love with him; it was that plain and simple.

CHAPTER FIVE

"CAN I, SUSAN? Can I? Grandma said I could if it was all right with you."

Susan gave her head a shake and stared vacantly down at Lucy, who was hopping around, anxiously waiting for the verdict. Not having heard one word the child had said, she exhaled sharply as she leaned against the sink and focused on the little girl. "Can you what?

Lucy gave a sigh of exasperation and repeated her question. "Can I bring the box of old curtains down from the attic? I want to play dress-up with them, and Grandma said I could if it was all right with you."

"I don't see why not, as long as you promise to clean up your room first."

Lucy skipped off, her curls bobbing in agreement. "I promise."

Susan turned back to the counter and stared down bewilderedly at the bowl of ingredients sitting there. For the life of her, she could not remember what she'd already added to the batter, and she knew if she didn't get it finished soon, she wouldn't even be able to guarantee what it was supposed to be.

With an absent look in her eyes, she started mixing in two eggs, her thoughts drifting back to the night before. The few hours she'd spent with Jason had been, quite simply, the best few hours she'd ever spent in her life. Once he relaxed his guard a little, she'd found out what the real Jason Chisholm was all about. Not only did he possess a keen sense of humor and an inquiring mind, but she discovered he had a down-to-earth philosophy that she fully appreciated.

But there had been more than that. When they'd left the arena after the lesson, Susan had been overwhelmed by the brilliant canopy of stars that hung overhead, and she'd gazed up, transfixed by the wonder of it. Unwilling to go in on such a perfect night, she had poked along, fascinated by the heavens and how close they'd seemed. Jason had started pointing out various constellations and somehow or another, they ended up watching the heavenly display from a stack of bales, the fragrance of hay and the silence of darkness enveloping them. In the privacy of night, each had the chance to quietly discover the fiber of the other, and in that short space of time, Susan felt closer to him than she'd ever felt to another human being. And not in one of her past relationships had she experienced the kind of easy compatibility she'd felt with him.

It hadn't been until she climbed into bed that her euphoria betrayed her, allowing intimate and provocative fantasies to infiltrate her mind. She lay there in the dark, acutely aware that he was lying just on the other side of the wall, less than an arm's length away. But it wasn't the physical act of loving him that she longed for; rather the simple, almost unbearable need to have him hold her.

"How come the batter's all lumped over on one side? Is it supposed to be like that?"

Susan snapped out of her reverie with a jerk and stared down at Michael, who was standing by the counter, his head propped in his hand, watching what she was doing with considerable interest. "What's it going to be?"

Susan smiled lopsidedly as she had a good look at the concoction in the bowl. "Who knows?" she answered dryly.

"Can I lick the beaters when you're done?"

"Have you finished cleaning up your room?"

He pulled a rueful face. "Are you gonna make us clean our rooms *every* Saturday?"

"Do you want me to help you with your pitching?"

He gave her a grin that was intended to melt her heart. "I could do it one Saturday and Todd could do it the next," he offered hopefully.

She stared down at him. "Wrong. You can clean up your own messes, Michael Matthew, and quit hauling out the Chisholm charm." She removed the beaters from the mixer and held them in her hand. "Now, is your room done?"

"Yes."

"Vacuumed and dusted?"

He licked his lips in anticipation. "Yes."

"The bed's made and your laundry's gathered up?"

"Yes."

"Okay, then. Here you go. One for you and one for your brother."

"What about Lucy and Patricia?"

"Lucy gets the bowl when she'd done her chores, and Patricia doesn't want any."

"Can I have her share?"

Susan glanced down at him, biting back a smile as she poured the batter into a cake tin. "What a little pig."

Michael grinned and shrugged. "Dontcha know I'm a growing boy?"

"Yes, Grandma," Susan responded solemnly, and Michael giggled.

"What do I get?"

The now familiar fizzle shot through Susan, and she steeled herself as she turned to face Jason, who was leaning against the fridge, his thumbs hooked in his belt, an amused yet somehow intimate look lighting his eyes. Susan's heart skipped a couple of beats and a host of butterflies unfurled in her midriff as her gaze connected with his. It took considerable effort to keep her voice steady. "You can have a cup of coffee—" she hesitated and glanced at the clock "—and some muffins."

Michael glanced up at her, a glint of mischief in his eyes.

"How come you aren't going to ask him if he cleaned up his room and picked up his dirty laundry?"

"Because he's too old to train."

Jason cast her a quick glance, his own eyes glinting, then helped himself to a cup of coffee. Susan put the cake in the oven, then stacked the baking utensils in the sink. Jason half sat on the counter, his legs stretched out in front of him, and every nerve in Susan's body responded to his closeness.

Todd came in and saw Michael painstakingly licking the beater. "Hey, do I get one?"

Susan handed it to him and he went to sit by his brother. He glanced up at his dad, a touch of disgust in his voice. "Susan made us clean our rooms."

Jason tipped his head slightly. "Good for Susan."

"She's going to make us do it every Saturday."

There was a quirk at one corner of the senior Chisholm's mouth. "That's nice."

Realizing he was fighting a lost cause, Todd sighed dramatically and gave his father a woeful look. "She beats us, Dad, and makes us do awful things."

"Fine," his father answered.

Todd grinned and licked a smear of batter off his wrist. "And she took my rubber snake."

Lucy came bouncing into the kitchen, looking sweet and adorable. "My room's done. Can I lick the bowl now?"

Dropping a spoon in it, Susan handed her the bowl. "You be sure to put it in the dishwasher when you're through, okay?" Lucy nodded as she climbed up on a chair.

Patricia had followed Lucy into the kitchen, and Jason indicated her with a nod of his head. "Don't you think you'd better share that with your sister, Lucy?"

Patricia looked at Susan, her expression almost guilty. "No, thanks, Dad. I don't want any."

Jason's eyes narrowed slightly as he studied his elder daughter. Susan interpreted the look as she interjected hurriedly, "There's a dish of fruit left over from breakfast, if you'd rather have that, Trish. It's on the second shelf in the fridge."

He fixed his gaze on her, a contemplative look in his eyes as he took a sip of coffee and watched over the rim of the cup. Susan turned away and started filling the sink with hot water, suspecting he could read her like a book.

As if he decided to let it drop, he shifted his position and looked at his kids, who were all gathered around the table. "So, what have you guys got planned for today?"

Patricia shrugged, then looked at her father. "The boys are going to Reddings', and Susan's going to teach me how to sew." She glanced at Susan, then quickly looked away. "And we're going for a long walk."

"I see," he said softly, as though he really did see. He studied Susan for a moment longer, then looked at Lucy. "And what about you, Luce?"

"Susan's going to make me a new outfit for my Cabbage Patch doll." She pursed her lips and shook her head emphatically. "And we aren't going to bug Grandma or be noisy in the house, because Grandma's really tired." She glanced up at Susan, looking for confirmation. "That's right, isn't it, Susan?"

Susan nodded.

Lucy went on, her face animated with enthusiasm. "And Grandma said I could play with the old curtains in the attic, so I'm going to make a playhouse out in the trees. And have a tea party, maybe."

Jason's eyes were alight with both humor and affection as he watched his small daughter. "The main course being mud pies, no doubt."

Lucy screwed up her face in a guilty expression. "But I won't use Grandma's rolling pin this time, Daddy. I promise. I'll just use the things in the plastic tea set Mikey gave me for Christmas."

Jason's mouth twitched. "That sounds like a good idea."

Lucy gave him another sheepish grimace, then danced out of the room, her curls bobbing. Michael pushed back his chair and stood up. "Hurry up, Todd," he urged. "Dad said we have to pick up the loose papers that blew out of the burning barrel before we can go."

Susan wiped the mixer and put it away, then filled a basket with bran muffins. "Will Len and Duffy be in?"

Jason shook his head. "Not until dinnertime I don't imagine."

Todd put his dirty beater in the dishwasher, helped himself to a muffin and headed for the door. Michael followed him. "We'll be out behind the house if Davy calls, okay?"

Susan acknowledged him with a nod and grimaced slightly as the boys let the back door slam loudly behind them. She poured herself a cup of coffee and carried it and the basket of muffins to the table. Jason followed her and sat down across from her, his expression suddenly sober.

Susan stirred her coffee. "How's Walter?"

Jason sighed and leaned back in his chair. "About the same. It usually takes a while for spells like this to pass."

"Isn't there anything that can be done medically?"

Jason reached for the covered butter dish in the middle of the table. "Yeah, there is. He could have surgery that would relieve the headaches, but he has such a deep-seated fear of both hospitals and doctors, he won't even consider it."

Patricia put her spoon in her empty dish and looked at Susan as she stood up. "I'm going outside, but if you need me for anything, just call me."

"Why don't you give Lucy a hand with her playhouse? That way she won't drive the boys crazy."

She nodded and flashed the Chisholm smile. "She drives everybody crazy." She patted her father on the back as she walked past him to put her dish in the sink. "See you later, Daddy."

He watched Patricia leave the kitchen, then with his expression grave, he looked down and absently toyed with his coffee mug. After a moment, he raised his eyes and looked at her. "I know what you're trying to do for her, Susan.

She's a good kid, and she deserves a lot more than she gets.'' He looked away, the muscles in his jaw working, as though he were struggling to maintain a veneer of control. His voice was even more ragged when he continued. ''I know her self-image has really suffered this past couple of years, and whether you realize it or not, you've given her the kind of support she needs right now.''

Susan's expression became solemn as she gazed at him, her own voice slightly uneven as she tried to lighten his mood. ''I was a porker when I was her age so I know how she feels.'' She smiled halfheartedly as she quietly chastised him. ''Peeling carrots and chopping celery is no big deal, Jason. She's the one who has to make the sacrifices.''

There was a hint of a smile around his mouth as he raised his head and looked at her. ''Is anything a big deal with you?''

She grinned. ''Yes. The World Series and mud on a clean kitchen floor.''

The laugh lines around his mouth finally creased. ''I'll remember that.'' He sighed and dragged his hand across his face in a weary gesture. ''Has Mattie made an appearance since breakfast?''

Susan studied him briefly, then decided to try her hand at a little common-sense counseling. ''I know you're worried about her, but I honestly think most of her problem is plain old exhaustion. The rest she's getting is going to make such a difference.''

''That's what her doctor says.''

Without thinking about it, she reached out and covered his hand in an imploring gesture. ''Then listen to him, Jason. And quiet feeling guilty about it. Mattie wouldn't be here if she didn't want to be.''

His eyes darkened, and for an instant she thought he was going to turn his hand over and lace his fingers through hers, but he swallowed hard and eased his hand away. His face had a rigid set to it as he said gruffly, ''I guess I'd better get moving. I have to go into town for veterinary supplies.''

Susan watched him go, aching to know what was going on in his mind.

But she never got a chance to find out. From then on, and over the next few days, it was almost as though he were deliberately avoiding her. If he was ignoring her, it would have been different, but he wasn't—he was plainly avoiding her, and that nearly drove her crazy. He'd still get into verbal sparing matches with her at meals, and he had given her another riding lesson, but he always made sure someone was with them, that they didn't spend so much as a minute alone. She'd been raised in a home where everybody's feelings were always out in the open, where people talked about what was bothering them. Jason Chisholm, however, was not like that. He wasn't about to talk about anything.

Susan tried to convince herself that he wasn't *really* avoiding her, that he was just preoccupied because there was so much work to be done, but she didn't believe that for a minute. And maybe she would have never scraped up the nerve to confront him if it hadn't been for an incident one morning at the breakfast table. It had all started out so innocently.

She was refilling mugs with fresh coffee when Duffy raised his cup and took a sip and tipped his head in approval. "If you ever get hard up you could always auction her off, Jase. Any woman who can make coffee like that should fetch a good price on the open market." He looked utterly pleased with himself, and the others had a chuckle over Duffy's droll little aside.

Susan put her hand on her hip and glared at him, warning him he was treading on dangerous ground.

Jason glanced up at her then solemnly shook his head. "I don't know, Duffy. I don't think she'd train worth a damn."

Susan gave him a slicing look. "Maybe you need a little training yourself."

He grinned at her and gave her a noncommittal shrug. "Maybe."

"Maybe," she said in the same tone of voice, "all of you would like to make your own lunches from now on."

His grin broadened. "I don't think so."

"Then you'd better start treating the cook with a little more respect, or you'll find yourself standing directly behind an apron with a potato peeler in your hand."

The laughter in his eyes held her transfixed as he leaned back in his chair and deliberately baited her. "That's woman's work."

"If you don't quit while you're ahead, Jason Chisholm, you're going to find yourself in very deep trouble," she warned.

The sparkle died and Susan was sure something that closely related to pain flitted across his face. He managed to hold his smile in place as he tore his gaze away. "Yes," he said quietly, "I know."

Susan stared at him, her thoughts tossed into a complete muddle by his response to a seemingly offhand remark. There was a deeper meaning that she didn't comprehend, but she knew it had something to do with her.

Somehow she managed to get through the next half hour with an outward appearance of normalcy, but mentally she was functioning in a strange disjointed state, almost as though she were caught in a very unsettling dream. She made lunches for the kids, but by the time she hustled them out the door to catch the school bus, she could not even vaguely remember what she'd packed for them.

She'd had to chase after Todd because he'd left his homework lying on the counter, and by the time she returned, the men were leaving the table. Jason was already standing by the door, his hat in his hand, giving the men a list of duties for the day.

With his jaw set in stern lines, he brushed some dried grass off the brim as he spoke to her without making eye contact. "We've got a few chores to do around here, then we'll be pulling out for most of the day. Don't expect us back until around suppertime."

Susan felt oddly inept. "Then you'll want lunches packed."

He finally raised his eyes and looked at her, a soberness there she'd never seen before. "Yeah. If you would. We're trailering the horses over to our leased land, so you can pack everything in the cooler."

She nodded and he put his hat on, then he turned and left the room. The other three followed him out, the screen door slamming loudly behind them.

The silence that remained was cheerless, and Susan set about cleaning up the breakfast dishes and making the mens' lunches, her mood glumly introspective. She wasn't stupid. She could read people with the best of them, and she was almost certain that Jason Chisholm was battling with himself, and that a good portion of that battle had something to do with one Susan Lynton. And she didn't like the obvious explanations as to why. She was just finishing wiping off the counters when the door slammed again, and Jason came into the kitchen. Without speaking, he went to the fridge where he kept the veterinary supplies.

He took out a tube of something and stuck it in his pocket, then turned to go. Trying to ignore the fact that the butterflies in her stomach were the size of ostriches, she acted on a wild impulse and confronted him. "Why are you avoiding me, Jase?"

He turned and looked at her, his expression closed. "What makes you think I'm avoiding you?"

Susan gave him the same look she used on the kids when they were trying to pull something over on her. "Because you are."

"I don't know what you're talking about."

"Yes you do. If I get within five feet of you, you bolt like old Riley, and this is the first time in days we've been alone for more than twenty seconds. Is it the perfume I use? Do I have bad breath? Am I contagious or something?"

There was a hint of a smile in his eyes as he said, "Infectious would be a better choice of words."

She was in no mood to be humored by anything cute, and she put her hand on her hip as she glared at him. "I'm not asking you to reveal your bank balance, Jason. All I want to know is why you treat me like a leper."

He spread his legs in a wide stance and hooked his thumbs in his belt. "Maybe," he said in a low, pointed tone, "I avoid you because every time we say more than two words to each other, we end up arguing."

"We aren't arguing," she said hotly. "We're discussing a situation."

"Sounds like arguing."

"God, you're exasperating!"

He grinned and pulled his Stetson low over his eyes. "See you at supper."

He started toward the door and she jumped in front of him, spreading her arms across the open portal. "You aren't getting out of here until you talk to me, Jason Chisholm," she warned. "Damn it, all I want is a simple answer."

"Well, you aren't going to get it."

She could tell by the stubborn set of his jaw and the look in his eyes that she was beating her head against a brick wall. With a sigh of resignation she stuck her hands in her back pockets and looked away. He was about to brush by her when she laid her hand on his arm and he jerked away, almost as though she'd scalded him.

It was an unexpected reaction and she took a long shot. "Jason," she said quietly, "is it because of what happened before…with the kids' mother? Has that turned you off all relationships?"

Suddenly feeling that she had gone too far, she looked down, unable to hold his penetrating gaze. Lord, but she had got in over her head *this* time, she thought wildly as she felt unexpected tears burn her eyes. What a stupid thing to say.

She heard him draw in a deep breath, then with infinite gentleness, Jase hooked his knuckles under her chin and forced her head up. There was a different kind of solemn-

ness in his eyes as he met her gaze with heart-stopping
directness. "It has nothing to do with Eileen, Susan," he
said very quietly. "Whatever wounds were inflicted then
have healed long ago."

There was so much emotion unfolding inside her that Susan could barely breathe as she whispered, "Then what is
it, Jase? I need to know."

For the longest time he simply looked at her, his eyes
giving nothing away. But she sensed a deep discontentment
about him, as if he were enduring some inner struggle. And
she couldn't stand that. Reaching up she touched his face,
her voice breaking as she said, "Something's happening
between us, and I'm getting in so far over my head, I don't
know what to do. Without even trying, you landed this on
me and I can't even fight back."

He shut his eyes in a grimace as he pulled her hand away.
"Sue," he whispered raggedly. "God, Sue...don't."

"Talk to me, Jase," she pleaded. "I'm not asking for
much. I just want you to talk to me."

He opened his eyes, eyes that were dark and smoky, and
as if drawn against his will, he cupped her face in his cal-
lused hands and softly stroked her cheeks with his thumbs.
"Just because you're attracted doesn't mean it's anything
more, Susan. It doesn't mean those feelings are real."

Who's he trying to kid? she thought, her senses thrown
into a mindless muddle by the feeling of his hands on her
face. *This is as real as anything is ever going to get.* But
for once, she didn't argue. Not now, not while he was looking at her the way he was. She had a nearly uncontrollable
urge to step into his arms, but even in the daze she was in,
she knew that Jason Chisholm would withdraw the minute
she did. As much as she loathed to do it, she knew she had
to put some distance between them. And somehow she had
to get him talking.

"Then it's not just me, is it? It's happening to you, too."
There was a flash of something in his eyes that resembled

anguish, and it aroused such a fierce protectiveness in her she had to fight to keep from responding.

There was a quiet, almost desperate seriousness about him as he slowly stroked her lips with his thumb. "Yes, it's happening to me, too."

"Then why—"

He pressed his thumb firmly against her mouth to silence her. "I'm old enough to be your father, Susan."

"You aren't."

She could see the faintest glimmer of amusement in his eyes as he said firmly, "Yes, I am."

That small exchange helped to break the tension, and Susan pressed the issue, knowing that by doing so they were steering away from dangerous ground. "You are not."

The glimmer intensified and he said warningly, "Susan—"

"Well, then, you must have been a very precocious teenager."

He grinned and let his hand slip to her shoulder. "My teenage years have nothing to do with it. I'm forty-four years old. I was *seventeen* when you were born, for Pete's sake. I'm telling you, I'm old enough to be your father."

She lifted her chin in a gesture that was unmitigated defiance as she said slowly and very distinctly, "But you *aren't* my father."

His grin deepened. "Thank God."

She narrowed her eyes, but before she could respond, he patted her on the cheek as if she were Lucy's age, then eased past her. "I'll see you at supper," he repeated as he brushed by.

The screen door slammed behind him, and she could hear the sound of his footsteps fading as he headed toward the barn. Her knees refused to support her one moment longer and she numbly sank to the floor, her back graced against the doorjamb. She was hot and cold, and she felt as though she had just stepped off some hair-raising ride at a fair.

Closing her eyes, she tipped her head back and weakly

rested it against the wall, waiting for her pulse to return to normal. But the recollection of the galvanizing sensation of his hands on her face did incredible things to her heart rate, and she clenched her fists against the warmth that pumped through her. If he could turn her into such a wreck with a single touch, she wondered what kind of state she'd be in if things ever really got out of hand between them. It would be so unbelievable....

There was a feather-light touch against her temple, and with a massive effort she opened her eyes. Jason was crouched beside her, his hazel eyes glinting green, his expression softened by a heart-stopping tenderness. With infinite gentleness he rested his knuckles against her jaw and slowly smoothed his thumb across her cheek, an irresistible half smile pulling at his mouth. "Don't tell me I finally won a round," he said, his voice low and husky.

Feeling as though her whole body were paralyzed by the magic of his touch, Susan gazed up at him, her expression soft and misty. "You fight dirty, Jason Chisholm," she whispered unevenly.

Very lightly he drew his thumb across her bottom lip. "So do you."

"I don't."

The dimple appeared. "I knew you were trouble the minute I laid eyes on you."

Susan drew a shaky breath, then spoke, her voice still unsteady. "You were only guessing."

He slowly shook his head, his eyes darkening as his expression sobered. "No, I knew."

Susan felt drugged by the intensity that enveloped them, almost afraid to breathe for fear she would shatter the spell that bound them. He continued to caress her face and she closed her eyes, losing all sense of space and time beneath the mesmerizing effect of his touch. Finally opening her eyes, she moistened her lips and was about to speak.

Once again Jason touched his thumb to her mouth, his hand curving against her jaw, his fingers caressing the soft skin of her neck. "Don't, Susan," he whispered, his voice ragged. "It's so damned hard to keep things in perspective right now, and I have to."

She pressed her face against his hand, her eyes as readable as a book. "Why?"

He inhaled sharply, his eyes sliding to her mouth. He clenched his jaw then swallowed. "Because I'm a generation older than you. It's as simple as that."

Susan was experiencing so much right then that she could barely speak, but somehow she managed an unsteady smile. "That's your opinion. Maybe you're just too cagey to be caught."

The lopsided grin appeared. "There's an old saying about fools rushing in where wise men fear to tread. And under the circumstances, I think I'd better rely on wisdom."

She smiled at him softly, her eyes luminous. An unspoken harmony seemed to radiate between them, and that feeling of intimate companionship was so powerful it was almost as if they were physically bound together.

Jason sighed as he molded his hand against her jaw, and she covered it with her own. "I don't suppose you'd hold me right now, would you?" she whispered unsteadily.

She caught a flash of laughter in his eyes before his voice dropped warningly. "No."

"Could we discuss it?"

He finally laughed aloud, his hands slipping threateningly to her neck. "Lord, but you're impossible."

"I'm a determined woman," she said, half laughing, half serious.

"So I've discovered."

Her expression changed, her gaze becoming intent. "Jason—"

He firmly shook his head. "No, Susan. We are not going to talk about it."

She stared at him a moment, then decided on a different tack. "Why did you come back?"

"I saw Breezy hanging around the corral and I thought

she was looking a little bored. So I thought the two of you might like to come with us.''

She stared at him a split second longer, then her eyes lit up. ''Are you serious?''

Smiling, he gently smoothed back a loose curl as he nodded. ''Yes.''

Her face grew sober. ''Do you want me to come, or are you asking me out of some warped sense of duty?''

His voice was very husky. ''I want you to come.''

For some insane reason Susan found herself fighting tears and she blinked rapidly, trying to hold back the intense feelings that were growing in her.

Turning his hand beneath hers, he laced his fingers through hers and stood up. ''Come on,'' he said quietly as he pulled her to her feet. ''Let's get moving before this gets out of hand.''

He didn't release his hold on her immediately, and there was something deeply reassuring about that physical link. He gazed at her a moment longer then let her go, a gleam in his eyes. ''Well, woman, you'd better jump to it.''

With her feeling of well-being soaring, she grinned at him. ''And you know where and how high you can jump.''

He grinned back at her as he pulled his hat low over his eyes. ''That's what I like about you, Susan. You're so servile and obedient.''

She made a face at him and he tapped her firmly under the chin, then turned to go. Susan suddenly remembered Mattie and Walter, and her high spirits took a nosedive. Exhaling sharply, she suppressed a sharp pang of regret. ''I can't go. What about lunch for Mattie and Walter?''

He shrugged off her concern. ''Walter can manage. I'll go tell Mattie you're coming with me, and I'll catch Walter on the way to the barn.'' He checked the pocket of his jean jacket for the tube he'd taken out of the fridge, then started toward the door. ''How much time do you need to get ready?''

"Ten minutes. Your lunches are ready to go. I just have to pack the cooler."

He looked at her from beneath his hat brim, a smile tugging at his mouth. "Don't you think you'd better pack something for yourself? It's going to be a long day."

She laughed and gave him a wave of dismissal. "I'll eat grass."

He was still grinning as he went out the door. "You'll have to fight off a herd of cows to get to it."

Susan flew into action the minute the screen door slammed. By the time the men pulled up by the back door, she'd taken a pot of tea and some toast up to Mattie, packed the lunch in the cooler, filled a huge thermos and changed into a long-sleeve shirt.

She was carrying the large Styrofoam cooler into the porch when Jason came in with a pair of cowboy boots and a hat. "Here, you'd better put these on."

Susan set the cooler on the floor and took the gear Jason handed her. "Did you find Walter?"

"Yeah. He said he'd come in and check on Mattie." Jason picked up the cooler and turned toward the door. "What have you got in here—bricks?"

Laughing, she twisted her hair on top of her head and covered it with the straw Stetson. "That and some grass."

He gave her a sharp look as he hit the latch on the door with his elbow. "Not funny, Susan."

She kicked off her runners and pulled on the boots, then picking up the huge thermos and a light jacket, she dashed out the door behind him. The truck was parked by the hedge, the sounds of horses and creaking saddles coming from the blue-and-silver six-horse trailer hitched on behind.

Jason placed the cooler in the back of the vehicle, and Susan set the thermos beside it. Len was stretched out in the back on a pile of hay, his hat tipped over his eyes, his hands laced behind his head, idly chewing on a piece of straw. She laughed and caught the toe of his boot and gave it a shake. "What's the matter, Len? Won't they let you ride in the front with the big boys?"

He peeked out from beneath his hat and woefully shook is head. "I had a rough night last night, Susan. A rough night."

Duffy's drawl came from the cab. "You should quit your tomcatting around if you can't handle it." He chuckled and stretched his legs out in front of him in a satisfied pose. "Don't go in the kitchen, boy, if you can't handle the heat."

"Someday I'm gonna punch your lights out, Duff," Len responded mildly. "Sure as hell, I am."

Shaking his head in amusement, Jason opened the door on the driver's side and Susan stepped in and slid past the wheel. Duffy moved over to make room for her, then draped his arm across the back of the seat and grinned. "I hope you brought a sticky saddle for her, Jase. Remember the last time ol' Clayton brought one of them eastern dudes out here? We jest about had to tie him on a horse. Every time that old cow pony'd make a turn, he'd slide out of the saddle neater'n a whistle."

Susan gave him a sardonic look. "Who did you give him to ride, old Riley?"

Duffy chuckled and stuck a toothpick in his mouth. "Hell, no. We put him on Breezy. She got so fed up with him that she finally laid down on him. It was funnier 'n hell."

Jason was grinning when Susan glanced at him for confirmation. Putting the truck in gear, he slowly pulled away, verifying Duffy's tale with a nod. "It was pretty bad, all right. I'd wanted Len to take him out in the truck, but Clayton was sure he could manage. And the guy insisted that the only way he could form any realistic concepts about ranching was to ride." He laughed and shook his head as he glanced at Duffy. "You don't need to worry this time, Duff. Susan has a better defined anchorage than he had."

Duffy chuckled. "Yep, with them long legs of hers, she'll stick on that horse jest like one of them old clothes pegs."

"Look, Duffy," Susan said firmly, "if you're nice to me today, I won't give you the piece of cherry pie with all the pits in it at lunch."

Folding his hands across his chest, he slouched in the seat and chuckled again. "Sounds fair."

As it turned out, Susan was the one who got the piece with all the cherry stones in it, much to the delight of the three men. But by then she was flying so high, she could have eaten a whole gravel pit, and done it with a smile on her face. It had been a wonderful morning, and she reveled in every second of it.

They had decided to eat the noontime meal overlooking a shallow stream on a grassy slope purple with crocuses. Off in the distance, cattle dotted the rolling hills. Len had taken the horses down to water them as Susan watched, silently wishing she had brought her camera.

Jason was stretched out on a horse blanket he'd taken from the trailer, his hands laced behind his head as he watched the clouds. Susan was sitting cross-legged beside him, relishing the wind, the sun on her back, and the rich smell of spring. Duffy was seated on the ground with his back propped against a rocky outcrop, rolling a cigarette, a cup of steaming coffee propped between his knees.

Susan reached out and raked her fingers through the dry grass. The ground was dust dry and there were very few spikes of green amid the brown. She glanced at Jason. "How bad is it?"

He rolled onto his side, then put on his hat and reached for the thermos. "Bad enough. It takes more than one season for this land to recover and even longer if it's overgrazed, and this is the third year in a row we've had practically no rain. We may have to reduce the size of herd this year, but with careful range management, we'll be okay. His expression grew sober. "There'll be a few who won't be so lucky, though."

Duffy chuckled. "If it don't rain soon, we're going to spend the whole damned summer shuffling cattle from one pasture to another. We'll put in more miles than a traveling salesman.''

Susan grinned and looked back at Jason. ''Clayton said the Double Diamond covers a little more than thirty thousand acres. With that much land, why would you have to cut your herd?''

''We normally run about a thousand head of cattle, but if you want to manage the range effectively, you need about twenty-two acres per cow-half unit. And when it gets bad like this, you need considerably more—maybe even double that. And the condition of our range is always our primary concern.''

''Clayton says you lease land.''

''About a quarter of the acreage is crown land leased from the government. The rest is deeded—most of it's been in the Chisholm family for years.''

Len came up the hill leading the four horses, and pushing his hat to the back of his head, he dropped the reins and came toward them. ''I seen that old blue cow down by the willow thicket with two calves in tow. That must be the fifth year in a row she's had twins. If she keeps that up, she could make you a rich man, Jase.''

Susan's expression was one of amazement. ''A thousand head of cows, and you know the performance of *one*?''

Jason laughed and stood up. ''Some are more memorable than others.''

Duffy sighed wistfully. ''Sort of applies to females in general, don't it?''

Len slapped his thigh and let out a loud guffaw and Susan, realizing she was faced with an incurable situation, shook her head. ''You guys are really hopeless, do you know that?''

Still grinning, Len challenged her. ''Now that ain't so, Susan. We've always got hope.''

That brought a snort of amusement from Duffy, and Jason warned, ''You'd better quit while you're ahead.''

She gave him a rueful look. ''I think you're right.''

Len had looped the reins over his horse's neck and, without using a stirrup, caught the horn and swung effortlessly into the saddle. Susan watched, awestruck. "I'd give my right arm to learn how to do that."

"Aw, hell. That's easy," Duffy offered as he picked up his reins. "There's a little trick to it. Here. Watch."

He repeated the process for her, and Susan watched intently, then shook her head as he settled himself in the saddle. "Never, never in a thousand years could I manage that. You have to be part gymnast to do that."

"Get ol' Jase to show you how. He can get on from both sides, and hell, there was one time we made a few bucks on him. Remember, Jase? It was roundup at the Flying U and ol' Tyler said you couldn't do it at a gallop, and you said you could. So we ran that mean-mouthed half-broke gelding past you, and you caught that horn and was in that saddle before Tyler could blink. Ol' Tyler jest stood there dumb like, not believin' what he was seein'. Hell, we had a good laugh over that."

Susan looked at Jason. He was busily prodding a clump of grass with his toe, and she could swear his neck was turning red as he tried to shrug it off. "It was nothing more than a stupid stung." He finally glanced up and gave her a sheepish lopsided grin. "And I damned near ripped my arm off doing it."

Susan laughed, delighted that there still was some boy left in the man. "Sounds like the kind of thing that legends are made of."

Len stroked his chin and chuckled. "It's a good thing ol' Tyler's a few years younger 'n you, Jase. I figure you two would have done some serious hell-raising if you'd been twenty at the same time."

Jason had held Susan's horse while she mounted, and laughed as he handed her the reins. "Tyler did just fine all by himself."

By the unmitigated Chisholm charm and the glint of devilry in his eyes, Susan strongly suspected the same could be said for Jason Chisholm.

CHAPTER SIX

THE PHONE RANG, and Susan closed the dishwasher door, set the switch, then turned to answer it. The muscles in her thighs protested with every movement, and she groaned, thinking that she was certainly paying the price for the day she'd spent riding with Jase. Drying her hands on the towel she had draped over her shoulder, she cradled the receiver against her shoulder. "Double Diamond Ranch."

A man answered. "Hello. Could I speak to Mr. Chisholm, please?"

Susan glanced at the clock on the stove. "He won't be home for another hour or so. Could I take a message?"

"Is Mrs. Chisholm available?"

"I'm afraid Mrs. Chisholm can't come to the phone. She's resting right now."

There was a pause, and Susan sensed a thread of urgency in his voice when he finally spoke. "Is there any way you could get word to Mr. Chisholm?"

"Yes, if necessary." Something—a certain timbre in the man's voice—got to her and she caught herself frowning. "Is something wrong?"

"Yes, I'm afraid there is. This is Mr. Carter. I'm the principal of the school Michael and Todd attend. We've had a—a freak accident."

Alarm shot through her. "What happened?"

She could sense him considering how much to tell her. "The classes were dismissed for recess when a thunderstorm hit." There was a frightening pause before he explained. "Lightning struck in the playground."

Her alarm escalated to fear, and Susan could barely breathe. "Who?" It was all she could say.

As if realizing what grim thoughts she was thinking, Mr. Carter hastened to explain. "No one was actually...was critically injured." The way he said it sent a cold shiver down her spine. She forced herself to stay calm as he continued. "Seven students and one teacher were close to the spot where it struck, and they were all badly shaken up. Michael was one." The principal was obviously skirting the seriousness of the situation, but at least Michael was still... She couldn't even think about what *could* have happened to him.

She forced herself to concentrate on what Mr. Carter was saying. "It would take too long to get ambulances out, so we've arranged for private transportation to take them to the hospital in High River. The district nurse will be with them."

With her fear neutralized by the need to act, Susan's mind finally clicked into gear. Walter had taken her car apart that morning, Len had taken the Suburban to town for parts, and there wasn't another vehicle on the place. She wasn't even sure where Jase was. And she didn't have a clue how long it would take her to track him down. And someone had to be at that hospital for Michael. How? Who? A new thought cut into her frantic thoughts. Wherever Michael was, Davy wouldn't be far away. "By any chance, is David Redding another one who was hurt?"

"Yes, but I haven't been able to reach his parents—there's no answer." For the first time, the professional cool of the principal gave way and he sounded extremely agitated.

But Susan didn't allow herself to think about that. They were wasting time. "I'll contact the Reddings." She knew Carol was home; she'd stopped in less than an hour ago for coffee. Susan's mind raced. They'd never be able to get to the school before the makeshift ambulance left, it would make more sense if she and Carol headed right for the hospital. If they drove like hell, they might even be able to beat them there. "Tell Michael and Davy we'll meet them at the hospital."

"I'll tell them. And you're going to contact David's parents," he said, making certain the directions were clear.

"Yes."

"Fine then. We'll see you at the hospital."

Susan hung up the phone and pressed her shaking hands tightly against her thighs as she groped for the right words to tell Carol what had happened. Taking a deep breath to steady the awful churning in her stomach, she dialed the number. One ring. Two. Three. Susan whispered urgently, "Come on, Carol. Answer the damned phone." Seven. Eight. Nine.

"Hello!" an irritated voice answered.

"Hi, Carol. It's Susan."

There was a groan, then a laugh. "Your ears must be burning. I called you every name in the book for dragging me in from the garden."

Susan's voice was surprisingly steady as she said quietly, "There's been an accident at school, Carol." Then, calmly, she told Davy's mother what had happened.

Carol's voice showed signs of stress when she said, "Is everyone okay?"

"Mr. Carter said no one was critically injured, but you could tell he was pretty worried."

"I'll leave right now."

Susan glanced at the clock and wiped her hand on her jeans. "Carol, could you pick me up? I don't have a clue where Jase is, and I don't know how to track him down. And somebody has to be there with Mike."

"Just a minute." Susan could hear muffled conversation, and she paced back and forth as far as the cord would allow, chewing worriedly on her lip.

"Derek just came in. He's going after Jase, and I'll pick you up in five minutes—no, ten. I have to put some slacks on."

"I'm going to tell Walter what happened so he can keep

an eye on Mattie, then I'll go out to the road and meet you there.''

"What are you going to tell Mattie?"

"Not the truth, that's for certain. At least not until I find out how he is.''

"I think that's wisest.'' There was a pause, then Carol continued, her voice sounding oddly hollow. "I'll be there as soon as I can.''

Susan hung up the phone and raced out the door into the porch, letting the screen door crash shut behind her as she flew down the stairs. She found Walter puttering in the garage. Once again she related the story. "I need you to stay in the house, Walter, in case Mattie needs anything.'' She rested her hand on his arm, her face marked by anxiety. "But you mustn't tell her what's happened. I'm not going to wake her, so when she does get up, you just tell her that I went to town with Carol to pick up some things, okay?"

Walter nodded and methodically wiped his greasy hands on a rag. "I'll watch her,'' he said with painstaking slowness. "You go to Mikey.'' He picked up a small tool kit and started toward the house. "I'll fix the basement door. Then she won't wonder why I'm inside.''

Susan didn't have the time to waste, but nevertheless, she put her arms around him and hugged him. "God bless you, Walter. I'd have never thought of that.''

He patted her awkwardly and smiled in encouragement. "You go to Mikey.''

And Susan went. She dashed into the porch, through the kitchen and into her room, stripping off her blouse on her way. She grabbed a clean shirt from the closet, thrust her arms into it, snatched her shoulder bag and raced out the door, buttoning up the front of her blouse as she went. She hit the driveway at a dead run, and for the first time since she got the phone call, she couldn't block out thoughts of what she might be facing at the hospital. *Please, God,* she prayed silently, *let him be all right. Let them all be okay.* Thunder rolled overhead, rumbling down the valley and fading off in the distance. She was breathing hard and her body was damp with perspiration by the time she reached the main road, and she found it hard to catch her breath in the clammy, still heat. She had started down the road toward the Reddings' when she finally saw the plume of dust approaching. The vehicle hadn't rolled to a stop before Susan had the passenger door open. Carol braked sharply then rested her head on the steering wheel. "You're going to have to drive, Sue," she said unevenly. "I'm shaking so bad, I can't."

Susan didn't argue. She went around the car and slid behind the wheel, slammed the door and put it in gear. It was a big old Buick that responded with a throaty reverberation of power and a hail of gravel as she tramped the accelerator. There were enough horses under the hood to make this thing move, she thought grimly, and she was going to use every one of them.

She glanced at Carol. "Does speed bother you?"

"No."

"I don't know the road that well so you're going to have to tell me where the rough breaks and the curves are."

"Okay." There was a brief silence, the Carol said with a quiet kind of dread, "I've got this awful feeling in my stomach."

Susan's worried frown deepened and she gripped the wheel tighter. "I know. So have I."

Susan pushed the big car to its limit, and the miles flashed by. The only time either of them spoke was when Carol voiced a caution and Susan acknowledged it. By the time they pulled into the parking lot at the hospital, they were both tight-lipped and pale.

And then they had to wait.

The hospital had been notified about the incoming injuries and as edgy as she was, Susan was aware of the state of readiness, and it didn't help to know that two additional doctors had been called in from their offices. Knowing that made it all the more frightening; it was as if they were preparing for the worst.

When word came that the casualties were being unloaded, Carol and Susan exchanged one long anxious look then followed the nurse. The first stretcher they brought in was totally shrouded, and through the tunnel vision of her own fear, Susan saw Carol go deathly white as she mouthed something, then her knees started to buckle beneath her. But Susan moved quickly, managing to catch the woman before she went down. Susan felt a horrible chill slithering through her; she, too, recognized the battered running shoes that showed beneath the blanket. They were David's.

A man in a crumpled shirt pushed through the medical staff and hurried over to them. "Mrs. Redding, it's not what you think," he said frantically. "He's not—his face was burned and we're concerned about his eyes. The nurse didn't want them exposed to light until the doctor has a chance to examine him."

Carol closed her eyes and hauled in a deep breath. "Oh, God, I thought he was—"

"Mom, is that you?" came a scared little voice from beneath the sheet.

Carol drew in another shaky breath, then visibly steeling herself, she went over to the stretcher and grasped the small, grubby hand that had wormed its way out. Her voice was calm and reassuring as she took it in both of hers. "Yes, honey. I'm right here."

"My eyes hurt."

Her steadiness wavered slightly as she said, "I know, sweetheart." Just then an attendant grasped the gurney to wheel it into another room. Still holding the boy's hand, Carol followed, speaking quietly to her son.

Susan turned away, her heart in her throat. Finally she spotted Michael. He was chalk white with a definite redness down one side of his face. There were streaks of blood under his nose and down his T-shirt, and his pupils were so dilated his eyes appeared to be black. He looked so scared. She didn't really give a damn about "procedure," and she didn't really give a damn about the vexed look the nurse gave her. All she cared about was giving that child some measure of comfort. Overpowered by an overwhelming relief that made her feel shaky, she pushed her way through some empty stretchers to get to him. She didn't dare speak as she slipped her arms around him and held him close against her.

He wound his arms around her neck in a strangling hold and managed to choke out her name. "Susan..."

"Shh, love. It's okay. Everything's going to be okay."

"I thought Davy was dead after."

Susan had to wait a moment before she dared answer him. "But he's not, Michael. His mom's with him right now, and the doctor's checking him."

She felt him tremble, as though he was trying hard not to cry. "He can't see. Is he going to be blind?"

Gently bracketing his face in her hands, she tried to think of an honest comparison, to give him something familiar to relate to. "You know how your dad always makes you kids stay away when he's welding because it can hurt your eyes?"

Dragging his hand across his face, Michael nodded.

"A flash of lightning that close would be the same. If he wasn't looking right at it, maybe David will just have really sore eyes for a while." She gently smoothed his hair as she smiled at him with reassurance. "They'll take good care of him here, love, so try not to worry."

He slipped his hand into hers and hung on for dear life. "Where's Dad?"

"Mr. Redding has gone to get him. They should be here soon."

He looked away, and she could see tears along his lashes as his grip became almost painfully tight. "I'm glad you're here, Susan. I was so scared."

It was a tough battle to keep her smile in place, but somehow she managed it. "I'm glad I'm here, too." Her expression was filled with compassion as she studied his profile. "Do you want to tell me about it, Michael?"

He turned his head and looked at her, his pale face very solemn. "It was so freaky. We were out playing soccer at recess and a big thunderstorm came in really fast. Miss McDougal came to get us in, then wham. There was this awful crash and the next thing I knew, we were all down on the ground."

He was beginning to warm to the retelling of the drama, and an amused, knowing look kindled in Susan's eyes. Once he got over the shock and the fear, Mike would revel in this. He wiped his nose then continued. "Everybody started to get up, and they were all acting really dopey like, but Davy didn't move. Then Miss McDougal crawled over to him. You know, we couldn't find her shoes, then Mark found them by the backstop. That lightning must have blew them right off her feet. And my nose was bleeding and—" He swallowed as he became even paler. "I'm going to be sick, Susan."

There was a stainless-steel basin on one of the stretchers and Susan grabbed it, and grasping Michael around the shoulders, she raised him up as he started retching. His nose started to bleed again, and suddenly there was a crowd of medical people around him. One doctor started snapping out orders. Susan held the boy securely against her and kept talking to him in a soothing tone of voice. "It's okay, love. It's okay." The bout of sickness passed and she glanced at the doctor, knowing what he was bound to be thinking. She quietly explained, "He's prone to bad nose bleeds, Doctor."

The doctor acknowledged the information with a nod, then smiled down at Michael. "Okay, son. Let's get you into an examining room and have a look."

Susan was just about to enter the room when Carol came half running down the corridor toward her, her face drawn. "They're sending Davy to Calgary, Susan. The doctor here wants to have a specialist look at his eyes."

For a moment, Susan thought *she* was going to be sick,

but seeing the stricken look on her face, Carol quickly explained. "They don't think there's any permanent damage—more of a temporary trauma—but they want to be on the safe side." She managed a weak grin. "It isn't every day they get a kid in who sees lightning strike."

"You aren't driving, are you?"

"No, I'm going in the ambulance with David. When Derek comes, tell him they're sending him to the Calgary General."

"Sure. Are you leaving right now?"

"As soon as they finish bandaging his eyes." She took a deep breath. "How's Mikey?"

Susan absently wiped blood from her hands as she gave a worried shrug. "He's been sick to his stomach and his damned nose keeps bleeding—and he's shaken up, but I think he's all right. The doctor's checking him over now."

"They're ready to go, Mrs. Redding," called a nurse.

Carol squeezed Susan's arm as she turned away. "I'll give you a call as soon as I can, Sue." She stopped and dug the car keys out of her purse and shoved them into Susan's hand. "Here. I'll leave these with you. You might need the car."

Susan nodded, then gave her a quick hug and whispered shakily, "I don't care if it's four in the morning—just let us know."

"I will."

It was well over an hour later when Derek and Jase finally arrived. Susan had called the Double Diamond and was pacing up and down the hallway outside of X ray, her arms folded rigidly across her breasts as she nervously chewed her lip. The doctor's examination had turned up a nasty swelling on the back of Michael's head, and they were now x-raying his skull. She looked up to see the two men striding down the corridor toward her, both of them with anxious looks on their faces.

Somehow she managed to glue a smile on her face as she went to meet them. She never gave them a chance to speak.

"They're both fine." She took one look at Jase's face and she wanted to cry, but she made the smile stick and tried to keep her voice steady. "They were both shaken up, but there's nothing seriously—"

"Where's Davy and Carol?" Derek interrupted, his concern making him agitated and abrupt.

Susan took a deep breath. How could she tell him without scaring him half to death? But she told him. And he listened with far more composure than she expected. But the whole time she was explaining about the freak accident and what had happened, she was acutely aware of Jase standing beside her, his whole body stiff as he stared blindly down the corridor. If it wasn't for the way he had his jaw clenched and the haggard look on his face, she would have wondered if he was even listening to her. *Like a rock,* she thought, as an intolerable ache started to unfold in her chest.

She could cope with almost anything, but she couldn't stand to see him endure one crisis after another with such rigid stoicism.

Derek jerked her back from her solemn thoughts. "When did the ambulance leave?"

"A little more than an hour ago."

"I'm heading off now. I'll make up some time on the road."

Susan dug the keys from the back pocket of her jeans. "Carol left me the keys to your car. Will you need it?"

He took the keys from her. "Yeah. We came in Jase's truck."

"You need gas, Derek. There's less than a quarter of a tank."

"Right." He caught Jason by the shoulder. "We'll talk to you later, Jase. Tell Michael we're thinking about him."

Jason only nodded and raised his hand in a silent farewell as Derek turned to leave. He stonily watched his neighbor walk down the corridor, and it wasn't until Derek disappeared from view that he finally spoke. "How long has Michael been in X ray?"

His voice was devoid of emotion, and Susan avoided looking at him as she answered, "They took him in just before you came." She motioned toward a small sitting area a short distance down the corridor. "Why don't we sit in there. I imagine he'll be a while yet."

Wordlessly Jason followed her and sat down beside her on the small settee. Resting his arms across his thighs, he hunched forward, his hands clasped between his knees as he stared at the floor. The lines around his mouth were deeply defined by anxiety and he looked so tired and so worried that Susan couldn't stand it any longer. She forced her hand between both of his.

He didn't look at her, but she heard him draw in a ragged breath as he finally relaxed a little, and pressing palm against palm, carefully laced his fingers through hers. He tried to speak, then stopped and swallowed heavily before he finally whispered, "Thank God you were here, Susan. Knowing you were here...that he wasn't alone—" His voice broke, and he abruptly looked away. Fighting her own battle, Susan simply tightened her hold on his hand.

Several minutes passed before he leaned back, and resting his head against the wall, he finally looked at her. "Is he really okay?"

"He has an awful lump on his head and I think he has a bit of a flash burn on his face, but other than that, he seems to be fine." She smiled at him and gave his hand a little shake. "You know Michael. This is going to be the highlight of the school year for him—something that broke up the tedium. It'll be one of his adventures, and you know damned well he'll milk it for all it's worth."

Jason's eyes finally lost that bleak look as he gave her a warped smile. "Do you mean I'm going to hear about it a few hundred times?"

"Mr. and Mrs. Chisholm?" A nurse had appeared. Jase gave Susan an intent look, but she only grinned and shrugged. Her grin deepened even more when he acknowledged the nurse without bothering to correct her mistake, then continued to hold Susan's hand as they stood up.

"They've taken Michael to a room. You can wait with him until the doctor has a chance to talk to you." She started down the corridor. "If you'll come with me, I'll take you to him."

"How is he?" Jason asked, unconsciously tightening his grip on Susan's hand.

The nurse smoothly sidestepped the question with an ease born from experience. "The doctor will be with you shortly and he'll be able to answer all your questions."

They found Michael sitting up in bed, a disgruntled look on his face. "They made me pee in a bottle," he said with disgust.

Susan managed not to laugh. "That's one of life's little curve balls, Mike."

"That's not funny, Susan."

"I'm not laughing."

He gave her an accusing look. "Inside you are." Then he looked at his dad and said brightly, "Hi, Dad. Did Susan tell you it blew Miss McDougal's shoes off? And the doctor says Davy's going to be okay, it just scorched him a little. And did Susan tell you I barfed out there?" he said, waving vaguely at the door.

Susan could see the anxiety literally drain out of Jase, and he sat down rather suddenly on the edge of the bed, his hand still gripping hers. "How are you feeling?"

"Fine," Michael answered airily. "I've got a headache, but the doctor says that's because it looks like somebody hit me on the back of the head with a baseball bat. But I don't know how because I was flat out on my stomach when I woke up. How could I have a lump on the back of my head, Dad?"

"Maybe," his dad offered with a hint of a grin, "it was one of Miss McDougal's shoes."

"Do you 'spose?" Mike asked wide-eyed. "Hey, that's right on." He gingerly touched the back of his head. "The doctor says I have to stay in the hospital tonight so they can keep me under obser...obsurd..."

"Observation," Susan supplied with an amused smile.

"What does that mean?"

"It means they're going to watch you."

"Watch me do what?" he asked, suddenly suspicious.

"We're going to watch you sleep, young man," said the doctor as he came into the room. He directed his attention to Jason and Susan. "He has a slight concussion, so I'd like to keep him overnight. The principal was very definite about us not taking any chances." The physician turned to face Michael, a kindly smile on his face. "We have some supper here for you. So why don't you let your mom and dad head home to theirs, and they can come get you first thing in the morning."

Michael didn't move a muscle. It was as though he were digesting the entire concept of what the doctor's comment suggested. Susan could feel a flush creeping up her face and she opened her mouth to explain, but with a wicked grin, Michael smoothly intercepted her clarification. "That works for me," he said, mimicking one of the catch phrases of a favorite TV star. With perfectly contrived innocence, he turned to Susan and his father. "Why don't you guys go home and I'll see you in the morning."

Susan could have strangled him. She knew that look; he was up to something. But he never gave his game away until she bent over to kiss him goodbye. He gave her a big hug, then in a voice loud enough for his father, the doctor and half of the hospital to hear, he said, "Good night, Mom." She saw Jase's mouth twitch and she thought she detected a hint of humor in his eyes, but he acted as though he hadn't heard.

The minute they stepped out of the room, Susan could feel Jason withdraw into himself, and they walked in total silence to the truck. Susan was dumbfounded to see how low the sun was on the horizon. It didn't seem as if she had been at the hospital that long, but when she glanced at her watch, she realized it was well after seven o'clock.

As they approached the vehicle, Jason fished the keys out of his shirt pocket. Without looking at her, he said, "Do you mind driving?"

She cast a troubled glance at him as she reached out her hand. "No, I don't mind." She couldn't see his face that clearly, but she sensed he was suddenly exhausted beyond words.

How does he manage all this on his own, she thought soberly as she climbed behind the wheel. *He's faced with a severe drought, he has a mother who is definitely not well, he's trying to raise four kids without their mother, and he has at least eight people dependent on him for their welfare. And today he came within a hairbreadth of losing a son.*

As she started the vehicle, she glanced across the cab at him. He was slouched in the seat with his head back and his eyes closed. He wouldn't sleep; he was simply shutting himself off. This way he wouldn't leave himself open, he wouldn't have to talk. And Susan was torn between wanting to shake him and wanting to stop the truck and simply hold him. But she did neither. She drove home, the mugginess pressing down on her like a wet blanket. Ahead of her, against the jagged outline of the mountains, the water-laden thunderclouds rolled up against the peaks in dark banks, trapped against the rocky barrier, unable to move east to the dry land. And to the north, she could hear thunder rolling across the heavens. There would be no rain tonight.

Once they reached the Double Diamond, Jason went directly upstairs to see Mattie. Susan dealt with the kids, assuring them that Michael was really find, and that he would be home tomorrow. Walter had remained in the house and between him and Tricia, they had made supper. Susan opened the cupboard to get the filters for the coffeepot, then checked the other cupboard doors. Every hinge had been oiled and tightened, and the loose handles had all been fixed. She'd bet the farm that there wasn't a loose screw, a squeaky hinge, a burned out light bulb or a dripping faucet in the whole place. When she experimentally opened and closed the cupboard drawer that used to stick, she realized that Walter was quietly watching her inspection. She grinned at him. ''Apple pies for you tomorrow, Walter.''

He gave her a sly smile. ''Tomorrow I fix your car.''

Susan caught his drift and holding up her hands in surrender, she laughed. ''Okay, okay—you made your point. Apple pie *and* Yorkshire pudding.'' Chuckling to himself and nodding in approval, Walter picked up his tool kit and shuffled out.

She was still smiling to herself when she turned around, and her stomach did a funny little lurch. Jase was standing at the dining room archway with his hands stuck in the back pockets of his jeans, his shoulder braced against the framework. He was watching her with a steady, unnerving look.

She felt oddly uncomfortable, as though he'd caught her doing something he disapproved of, and it was all she could do to keep from fidgeting. ''How's Mattie?'' she asked, her voice suddenly faltering.

''She's fine. Tricia had her settled for the night.''

There was an awkward silence, and suddenly the championship they had shared the day before seemed like a distant memory. For one heart-stopping instant they stared at each other, invisibly linked by an acute awareness, then Jase's expression altered dramatically. Looking suddenly very gaunt, he turned away. ''I have some paperwork I'd better catch up on,'' he said gruffly. Susan felt as though he were severing a vital link as she watched him walk away. He had barricaded his feelings behind an unyielding belief, and both of them, unfortunately, were going to have to live with his decision.

Trying to block out the ache that had settled in her chest, she went into the main kitchen and started making apple pies with a vengeance, her mood swings bouncing from righteous anger to absolute misery. But mostly she felt as though all the lightness had been drained from her, leaving behind a leaden heaviness.

It was after ten when she finished cleaning up the kitchen and put the last four pies in the oven, then went for a quick bath. Instead of putting on her regular clothes, she slipped into a brightly colored cotton wrap that her brother had sent her from the Bahamas. It was really a beach cover-up, but it was cool and comfortable, and the kitchen was so unbearably hot after having the oven on for so long.

The phone rang just as she was taking the pies out of the oven, and she itched to answer it, but she knew Jason would. She was sure it was Carol with news about Davy, and she simply could not wait to find out what the specialist had said. She started for the door, then turned back to the cupboard and cut Jason a large wedge of hot pie, topping it with a scoop of ice cream. Pouring a single cup of coffee, she picked up a fork and once again started down the corridor that led past Jason's room.

She found him in the living room, stretched out on the sofa with one arm draped across his eyes, a grim set to his mouth. A single lamp cast the room in heavy shadows and a cool breeze wafted in from the screen door that led onto the veranda.

Her eyes solemn, she quietly set the coffee and dessert down on the coffee table.

He lifted his arm and looked at the large wedge of apple pie then glanced up at her, a touch of humor in his eyes. "What happened to good old chicken soup?"

She smiled and sat down on the corner of the table. "Don't you know anything? You get chicken soup when you have the flu, and you get apple pie and ice cream when you feel like holding your head in the watering trough."

That made him smile, and he hauled himself up and leaned back against the wide arm, then reached for the plate. "Walter will kill me if he finds out I was into his apple pie."

"Who are you kidding? Walter has trouble killing flies."

She watched him for a moment, then asked quietly, "What did Carol have to say about Davy?"

He didn't look up, but she sensed that same tight control she'd witnessed at the hospital. "He's okay. The specialist wants him to stay out of the sun for a couple of days and not expose is eyes to any irritants, but there's no damage."

She let out a sigh of relief. "Thank God."

His voice had little strength to it. "Those kids were so damned lucky."

Susan didn't know what to say to ease his mood so she said nothing and watched him eat his pie in silence. When he finished, he slid the empty plate back on the table and, still without looking at her, he finally spoke. "I don't know how to thank you for being there for him today. It could have been such a frightening experience for him if he hadn't had someone with him."

"Don't thank me," she admonished gently. "I went because I wanted to."

He finally looked up at her. "I know that." He gazed at her for a moment then leaned his head back and stared at the ceiling. "You never think about what a big space a kid fills in your life until something threatens him. Then it hits home how very fragile life really is." He rested his arm across his eyes again, and she saw him swallow hard before he continued, his voice strained. "I don't know what I would have done if something had happened to that kid. I really don't know."

Susan slipped over to the sofa and sat down beside him, and with the ache in her throat nearly suffocating her, she gently took his hand in hers and drew his arm down. There was a wealth of understanding and compassion in her eyes as she stroked his taut face. "Don't do that to yourself, Jase. Don't. That kind of thinking is usually motivated by guilt, and you have nothing to feel guilty about."

His hand tightened around hers. "But I do," he said hoarsely. "I came within an inch of rejecting that kid in the

most destructive way possible, and it's going to haunt me
for the rest of my life.''

Frowning slightly, she stared at him. ''I don't believe
you're capable of that.''

As if he was shutting out a grim recollection, he closed
his eyes, his grasp on her hand becoming almost painful.
When he finally spoke, his voice was so ragged it was barely
audible. ''When Michael was five, I discovered he wasn't
my son.''

Susan felt as if she'd just been dropped into ice water.
''You *what*?'' she whispered, her voice rasping with disbelief.

Heaving a heavy sigh, he looked up at her, a desolate
look in his eyes. His voice was quiet, almost devoid of emotion when he started to speak. ''It was just before Eileen
pulled out for the last time, and Michael had to have his
tonsils out. Things were pretty rocky here at home, and the
kids were beginning to feel it.'' He exhaled sharply and
began to absently caress the back of her hand with his
thumb, his face looking more haggard with each passing
moment. He sighed again, then continued. ''I was at the
hospital when he came out of surgery and had planned on
spending most of the day with him. His chart was lying on
the table by his bed, and without really thinking about it, I
started reading it. I got as far as his blood type, and then
the whole damned world caved in on me. I knew my blood
type and Eileen's were both O. Michael's was B. There was
no way he could have been mine.''

Susan laced her fingers through his. ''What happened
then?''

''Not much. I spent most of the night driving around half
out of my mind. She had taken off a couple of times after
he was born, but I didn't have a clue she'd been sleeping
around before that. After she'd come back the second time,
I convinced myself we could put everything back together,
and Lucy was the result. But when I found out about Mi-

chael, I couldn't stand to look at her." He hesitated, then added stiffly, "Or him."

Susan smoothed her hand up his arm in a comforting caress, a quiet urgency in her voice. "But that was understandable, Jason. You saw that as the ultimate betrayal, and there isn't a man walking this earth who wouldn't have felt exactly the same way."

His self-condemnation made his tone harsh. "But that doesn't excuse the way I acted."

"What happened when you confronted her with it?"

He stared at her rigidly for a moment then looked away, the muscles in his jaw rigid. "I never did confront her with it."

Susan frowned, her expression thoughtful. "Why not?"

There was a tone of bone-tired weariness in his voice when he answered. "Because I was so riled, I didn't trust myself to go near her."

"Didn't she wonder what was going on?"

Jason gave her a bleak smile then looked away, haunted by the pain of recollection. "One of her old boyfriends showed up here a day or two after Michael came home, and I accidentally caught them together in the bunkhouse. I told her to get the hell out, and she packed her bags and left."

"And Mikey?" she asked softly.

"It was a couple of nights after she'd gone, and I was sitting in the kitchen getting quietly drunk. He came creeping in and climbed up on my knee and put his arms around my neck." His voice broke and he clenched his jaw and looked away, plainly struggling to maintain a veneer of composure.

Susan was having a struggle of her own, but she sensed that Jason desperately needed to say it all. She swallowed against the awful tightness in her throat, then whispered huskily, "And?"

His voice was low and unsteady. "He looked so worried, and I could tell he'd been crying, but his concern was for me. He told me not to feel sad, that everything would be all right. He said that he would look after me when I got old, and he'd never leave me alone.''

Trying to ease a breath past the awful constriction in her chest, Susan reached out and took his face between her hands. "Look at me, Jase," she whispered jaggedly, her eyes glimmering with unshed tears. Slowly he responded to the pressure and turned, his face carved by the kind of anguish that scars men's souls. With infinite tenderness, she smoothed her hand along his jaw, her touch firm and comforting. "You don't have to hide your feelings from me, Jason. I really do understand."

"I know you do," he whispered roughly as he caught one of her hands and pressed it tightly against his chest. "I know you do." He hauled in a deep shaky breath then met her gaze, a tormented look in his eyes as he continued. "Something happened when he said that, Sue. It was as if something snapped inside me and I realized that he was my son—maybe not mine biologically, but mine in the ways that matter." He closed his eyes and twisted his head in a gesture of pain. "I go cold every time I think how damned close I came to packing him off with his mother and totally destroying his whole world."

"But you didn't," she said with quiet conviction. "And I don't believe you ever could. Never in a million years. You've dragged all that guilt around with you for something you're utterly incapable of doing."

He wearily tipped his head back, a grim retrospective expression in his eyes. "I never felt so helpless in my life as I did on the way to the hospital today. And so guilty. I couldn't remember the last time I spent fifteen minutes alone with that kid."

There was a trace of a smile in her expression as she gave his hand a reassuring squeeze. "Let me tell you a few things about kids, Jason Chisholm," she said with an air of surety. "I came from a big family, and I can tell you from experience that having time alone with a parent isn't that important. What *is* important is letting your kids know you're there for them, and whether you realize it or not, you do that in a hundred different ways. I'll bet there isn't a night goes by that you don't go upstairs and check on each one of them before you go to bed. And one of the most reassuring things in the world is being covered up when you're half asleep and cold. That's the kind of thing that really matters.''

The rigid set of his face relaxed a little as he watched her with thoughtful intensity, unaware that he absently stroked the back of her hand. ''How can someone so young have accumulated so much common sense?''

She gave him a rueful smile. ''I got it from my grandmother. She's heavy into common sense and minding your own business.''

That brought a gleam of humor into his eyes and his mouth quirked in a hint of a smile. ''Well, I guess one out of two isn't bad.''

She gave him a narrow look, and his smile became more genuine. There was a short silence, then her expression sobered as she asked quietly, ''How many people know?''

He stared at her a minute, then looked down and smoothed his thumb across her knuckles. ''Just you.''

Susan experienced the strangest sensation, almost as though she were falling through a long tunnel, and it seemed to take forever before she could collect herself enough to speak. ''His mother must know.''

He shook his head. ''No, I'm positive she doesn't. If she'd known, she would have used it to her best advantage when she left. And she would have enjoyed doing it.''

''Could anyone stumble on it accidentally?''

''The only way that could've ever happened was if someone started checking out her medical records, so I made damned sure all of them were forwarded on to her.''

Susan hesitated to ask the next question, but it was one she was going to have to ask sooner or later. ''Do you know who the father is?''

His tone had a brittle edge to it. "No, and I don't give a damn. As far as I'm concerned, Mikey's mine now."

She tightened her grip on his hand. "Of course he's yours. In a lot of ways, he's even more like you than the others—the way he walks, the way he holds his head, how he talks. He wants to be just like you, Jase, and no father can ask for more than that."

Jason closed his eyes and swallowed hard and Susan knew that he was so torn up inside, he couldn't respond. With her own vision blurred with tears, she loosened her hand and slipped her arms around him, trying to give him some measure of physical comfort.

His voice hoarse from the unbearable strain, he whispered her name as he enfolded her in a crushing embrace, his arms like vises around her as he pressed his face into the curve of her neck. Hauling in a ragged breath, he turned on his side and drew her down onto the sofa beside him, their bodies welded together by the intensity of his embrace. Susan closed her eyes, her body trembling from the explosion of emotion that slammed through her, unconscious of everything except him.

His hold on her eventually slackened, and sighing softly he slowly combed his fingers through her hair, his touch gentle and oddly soothing. Her heart raced wildly as she savored the galvanizing feelings that coursed through her. It was like no other sensation she'd ever experienced, lying clasped in his arms this way. And if she'd had any doubts about her feelings for him, they would have been swept away the moment he touched her.

Cupping his hand against the back of her head, Jason nestled her more closely against him, his breath warm against her skin as his lips lightly brushed her temple. "I think I just made a very big mistake, Susan Lynton," he murmured.

She smiled and slipped her arm around his chest. "That's a matter of opinion."

He tightened his hold on her. "You sure in hell don't fight fair, do you?"

"Not if I can help it."

He laughed softly, his amusement fading on a sigh of capitulation. "I should never admit this, but you're exactly what I need right now."

"What you really need is to quit feeling guilty about Michael," she counseled softly.

His expression softened as he slowly rubbed his knuckles along her jaw. "Do you know that you have an unlimited talent for putting things in their proper perspective?"

She smiled, an impish gleam appearing in her eyes. "I'm glad you feel that way. There's one other matter I'd like to put in it's proper perspective, if you don't mind."

He gave her a long, level look, reproach in his eyes. "As a matter of face, I do mind."

The gleam faded and she sighed heavily. "Why can't we just talk about it?"

His chin took on a stubborn set. "Because talking won't change a thing."

"It might."

Jason smiled lopsidedly as he let his hand rest against her neck. "You never give up, do you?"

"No."

He stared at her a minute, his eyes suddenly dark and intent, then as he exhaled sharply, a shudder coursed through him and he pressed her even more fiercely against him. His movements unleashed a storm in Susan that robbed her of all rational thought, and she lay against him, unable to think, immobilized by an unbelievable excitement that overrode all else. She tried to twist her head, desperately wanting the moist, hungry contact of his mouth, but Jason caught her head, holding her motionless against him.

His breath was driven from him on a nearly inaudible groan, and his voice was hoarse and touched with desperation as he ground out raggedly, "God help me, Susan, but this is wrong. All wrong. But holding you like this feels so damned good I don't think I can ever let you go.''

Touched beyond belief by the agony in his voice, Susan fought down a sob of raw emotion, her chest banded by an overwhelming ache. She responded by tightening her hold on him, her body beginning to tremble from the upheaval he had aroused in her. Jason's mouth was warm on her forehead as he nestled her head against his shoulder, then reached back and switched off the table lamp behind him. He shifted his position slightly then pulled her on top of him. The darkness enveloped them in a safe cocoon, and Susan closed her eyes, taking immeasurable comfort from the sensuous and physical intimacy. For now, this was enough, knowing that he desperately wanted her, knowing that he couldn't let her go. And she also knew, that for her, there would be no turning back, that she had passed her point of no return, that Jason Chisholm had claimed a part of her that she could never take back. And off across the ridge of mountains, like some ominous forewarning, she could once again hear the sound of distant thunder.

CHAPTER SEVEN

EARLY MORNING TWILIGHT was infiltrating the room when Susan awoke, the chilling mountain breeze from the open door touching her back with a skin-shrinking crispness. She shivered as she carefully eased away from Jason's warmth and pulled the afghan, which was draped across the back of the sofa, over them, then nestled back in his slack embrace. Stirring in his sleep, he shifted his position, then gathered her firmly against him, his cheek resting on the top of her head, the rough stubble of his beard catching in her hair. She slipped her knee between his and snuggled down, savoring the quiet pleasure of waking up in his arms.

As she stared into space, absently aware of the soft rise and fall of his chest, her thoughts drifted back to the staggering revelation he had made the night before.

It took a special kind of person to accept a child under the circumstances Jason Chisholm had, and it could have been such a tragedy for Michael if his father hadn't been the man he was. But maybe there was a supreme justice after all, she thought solemnly, when one considered how that small boy had turned away from his natural mother out of the love for the man who had chosen to keep him.

"What are you thinking about?"

Attuned as she was to his every breath, Susan had no inkling of his awakening, and she tipped her head back and gazed up at him in surprise. "What do you do, just open your eyes and you're awake?"

He gave her a slow lazy smile as he smoothed his hand across her back. "Don't you?"

"I don't know. Do I?"

The laugh lines around his eyes creased, then Susan felt the pressure of his lips against her hair as he murmured softly, "Beats me, but I do know you're a hell of a lot nicer to wake up to than four kids and a dog."

For some reason, his words stirred a profoundly poignant feeling in Susan, and she gazed up at him, loving him so much it hurt.

His expression softened, and his warm gaze seduced her as he said huskily, "What *were* you thinking about?"

She gently caressed his mouth with her fingertips, her voice even more husky than his. "I was thinking how very much I love you, Jason Chisholm." Susan felt him tense and his expression became suddenly guarded as a muscle twitched in his jaw.

She pressed her fingers against his mouth before he had a chance to speak. "I know you didn't want to hear that," she whispered unevenly, "but I had to say it, and no matter how hard I try, I can't change how I feel."

He stared at her for a moment, then hauling in a ragged breath he closed his eyes and thrust his hand deep into her tousled hair, roughly nestling her head against his shoulder. His voice was gruff when he finally spoke. "God, if I had any sense I'd send you packing right now."

But in spite of what he'd said, his hold on her remained fierce and unrelenting, and Susan closed her eyes, trying not to give way to the suffocating tightness of suppressed tears. Long moments passed before Jason smoothed his hand across her hips then whispered unsteadily into her hair, "Why weren't you around ten years ago?"

That brought a spark of humor to Susan's eyes, and she lifted her head and looked up at him, her laugh husky. "Great. Then I would have been only seventeen, and you would have really thrown a fit."

Some of the seriousness left his face, and he gave her a wry grin. "That's not exactly what I had in mind."

She shifted position, propping her arm on his broad chest

and resting her head on her hand. "I know exactly what you had in mind, Jason Chisholm," she said as she slanted an amused look down at him. "And I think it's a rotten trick—taking ten years off yourself and hanging them on me. Especially when I come from a long line of women who consistently lie about their age once they're past thirty."

Laughing softly, Jason looped his arms across her back. "By the sounds of it, all you Lynton women like to make it tough on your men."

Her teasing expression altered, and her gaze became almost wistful as she slowly stroked his bottom lip. "Does that mean I can consider you my man, Jason?" she murmured. His expression darkened with a troubled frown, and Susan pressed her fingertips against his mouth and gave him a crooked smile. "Forget I said that," she said quietly. "Neither patience nor subtlety has ever been among my virtues."

He reached up and brushed back her tousled hair, his touch light and lingering. There was something in his eyes that revealed a depth of disquiet that was almost haunting, and Susan responded to his somber mood. With immeasurable gentleness she caressed his taut face, trying to smooth away the worry lines from around his eyes. "I don't expect anything back from you," she whispered. "But I do love you, Jase, and nothing you say or do is ever going to change that."

He finally met her gaze, his own bleak. "There's more than our age difference to be considered, Sue. I could never load you down with the responsibility of raising my kids or coping with the pressures around here. I couldn't do that that to you."

"Why?"

"Because it's too much to ask of anyone. Look what it's done to Mattie. Right now all this is a new challenge for you, but what happens when the novelty wears off and the never-ending work and responsibility turns into a never-ending grind? What then?''

Her gaze was unwavering and her voice was steady as she answered softly, ''I would never pack up and leave, Jason. I'm not made that way.''

The muscle in his jaw twitched and he abruptly looked away, his expression guarded. And it hit Susan that the collapse of his marriage had most certainly left some scars. Maybe the wounds had healed as he said, but he had been badly hurt once, and though he didn't realize it, he was unconsciously wary. She watched him, compassion stirring in her as she gently took his face between her hands and asked the question she'd dreaded asking. ''Do I look like her—does having me around remind you of her?''

He met her worried look with a level gaze. ''Because of how much Michael looks like you, you mean?''

Susan nodded and Jason tightened his hold on her as he shrugged off her question. ''At first maybe a little, but your personalities are so different that the physical similarities don't really register. What really threw me was how much Michael looks like you.''

''Does it bother you?''

He hesitated as he considered her question, then shook his head, his eyes connecting frankly with hers. ''No, it doesn't bother me.'' A hint of smile appeared around his eyes as he answered huskily, ''In fact, I think I like it.''

The grandfather clock standing at the base of the stairs chimed out the half hour, and Jason slipped his hand into her hair, again cradling her head against his shoulder. Enfolding her in a close embrace, he nestled his cheek against her hair. ''We haven't much time left,'' he whispered, his voice low and uneven. ''And I don't want to waste it talking about something that's buried in the past.''

Susan turned her head, pressing her face into the curve of his neck, and Jason's hold tightened as he said, ''God, but it does feel good to hold you.''

The huskiness in his voice infused her with a sudden

weakness and Susan's breath caught as her body responded to the closeness of his. But as much as she wanted to give way to the deep pulsating need that was swelling in her, she knew that now was not the time.

Somehow she found the strength to resist the nearly over-powering attraction of his mouth, wondering how she was ever going to endure it when she finally had to separate herself from his enveloping warmth. If she could be granted one wish right then, it would be that this moment could last forever. Jason sighed and shifted his hold, his voice tinged with reluctance. "I hear somebody moving upstairs. We'd better get up."

He made no move to release his hold on her, and Susan raised her head, amusement lighting her eyes as she looked down at him. "Maybe it's only Todd's mice breaking out."

Jason gave her a sharp look. "What mice?"

She grinned as she idly raked a nail across the silver stubble on his chin. "The mice he has stored under his bed. He has five of them penned up in the old fish aquarium, and by the size of them, I'd say he's had them for quite a while."

Jason stared at her for a second, then let his breath go in a rush of exasperation. "I'll kill that kid, so help me. The last time it was a garter snake, only it got out, and Lucy refused to come into the house until we found it. You'd think he'd learn, damn it."

Susan laughed and gave his ear a gentle twist. "Boys never learn, Jason. Having been one, you should know that." The gleam in Susan's eyes intensified. "Besides, you can't convince me you never had things stored under your bed that Mattie didn't know about."

He gave her a wry look. "Whose side are you on, any-way?"

She shrugged. "I'm on the side of truth and justice."

His expression was shrewd. "In a pig's eye. I have a sneaking suspicion you're aiding and abetting."

She kept a straight face as she shook her head. "On my honor, I'm not. I found them when I was vacuuming."

"And why were you vacuuming Todd's room? I thought he was supposed to clean his own room."

He'd caught her fair and square with that once, and Susan grimaced sheepishly. "It was just a quick once over."

"I thought we made a deal."

She slowly traced the shape of his ear as she said in a throaty tone of voice, "Do you want to fight about it?"

He laughed. "Not right now. Although it might make good ammunition for later."

There was another sound of movement from Mattie's quarters. Susan's expression became serious and her voice had a strange catch in it as she murmured, "The last thing I want to do is move."

The laughter went out of his eyes as he gazed up at her, the pulse in his neck suddenly noticeable. He spanned her jaw with his hand as he answered softly, "I know." Then he started to draw her head down.

Susan read his intent and a shudder ran through her as she hesitated, her eyes darkening. She knew if he kissed her now, her resistance to him was so low that she would be lost. And in spite of how much she wanted it to happen, she didn't relish the thought of a bunch of kids and an aged mother hanging over the banister when it did. She felt as though she were suffocating as she gazed down at him, longing to relent but knowing she didn't dare. Her voice was fragmented when she whispered, "Don't Jase. I don't know what'll happen if you do."

His eyes mesmerized her and his touch was infinitely gentle as he dragged his hand through her hair and caught her by the back of the head, forcing her head down. His lips were warm as he brushed a corner of her mouth with a whisper of a kiss, then roughly pressed her against him, his breathing labored. "Lord, Susan, don't say things like that. It only makes it that much harder to let you go."

Susan stroked his head and smiled softly. "I'll remember that."

Jason laughed and raised himself on one elbow, then looked down at her. "I knew you were trouble," he said softly. "You have that too-innocent look."

"You were only guessing," she teased as she looped her arms around his neck.

"Like hell," he said, his eyes gleaming. Rolling her beneath him, he grasped her around the waist and stood up, lifting her easily to her feet. He barely gave her enough time to catch her balance before he propelled her forward. "I think it's time we moved to safer ground," he said succinctly, and Susan wondered a little dazedly what he had in mind.

They reached the hallway leading to the main kitchen and Susan shivered, partly from the early morning coolness that had seeped into the house and partly from the absence of Jason's physical warmth. He paused by his bedroom door and looked at her, his dark eyes smoldering with need. He didn't say anything as he tightened his grip on her, then pulled her into his room.

He kicked the door shut and gathered her against him in the same movement, then exhaled a long sigh. It was the first time Susan had stood near him when he had his boots off, and she realized he was only an inch or two taller than she. Their closeness in height became even more evident as he widened his stance and locked her lips against his, fusing their bodies together from shoulder to thigh in a perfect, intimate match. She sensed he was fighting his own battle, and struggling for some thin thread of composure, she turned her head and whispered against his ear, "Just hold me for a while, Jase, until everything stops spinning."

With his arm angled across her back, he slid his hand up the back of her neck, his hold oddly protective. Finally he spoke, his tone mildly censuring. "You aren't making this any damned easier, you know."

There was something about the way he said it that made

her smile. "Good," she answered a little shakily. "You deserve it."

He laughed softly and hugged her closer. "You're impossible."

"I'm not, either."

"You are, Susan," he said firmly, his voice still tinged with laughter. "Bloody impossible."

"You're just too damned set in your ways."

"It's my age."

Susan eased back in his embrace and gave him a terse look. "Jason Chisholm, it has *nothing* to do with age. It's that rotten streak of Chisholm bullheadedness."

He grinned at her. "How come when you're talking about Clayton it's tenacity and with me it's bullheadedness?"

"It boils down to the same thing."

His expression softened and he gazed at her with a hypnotizing warmth, then whispering her name, he nestled her against him.

There was something infinitely calming about the way he held her, and the initial flash of desire slowly eased, her unfulfilled longing eventually replaced by contentment. She sensed that he, too, was finding a kind of tranquility after a very turbulent struggle.

Beautiful, silent moments slipped by as they stood locked in each other's arms, until the first rays of daybreak broke above the horizon and filtered into the room. With the golden shafts of light came the stark reality of another day, and sighing heavily Jason eased his hold on her. He slowly brushed his knuckles along her jaw, his mood solemn as he said softly, "I wish we could've had made it last forever, Sue."

Susan wasn't quite sure what he meant, but she had a nagging feeling he was referring to their entire relationship rather than their night together. Even if that was the case, she didn't want to mar the closeness they were sharing with another argument. Instead, she gazed at him, her eyes misty. "Right now, I'd settle for ten more minutes."

He grinned as he smoothed his hand across her shoulder and up her neck. "How long does it take," he asked with suggestive huskiness, "for you to make breakfast for this crew?"

She tipped her head to one side, an impish look in her eyes. "As long as it takes to open two boxes of Corn Flakes and get the milk out of the fridge."

He laughed and hugged her against him, pressing his face against the soft curve of her neck. "Susan, Susan, what in hell am I going to do without you?"

Susan tightened her arms around him and closed her eyes, trying not to think about a few things she'd like to suggest. She deliberately steered away from that very tempting but dangerous ground, and instead endeavored to keep the mood light as she said pointedly, "You could quit giving me a hard time."

He gave her another quick hug then lifted his head and looked at her, his eyes dancing. "You haven't even begun to know a hard time, lady."

"I already suspected that."

Not about to be caught in another verbal sparring match, Jason only grinned and sidestepped the trap. "What would I have to do to get a cup of coffee out of you?"

She gave him a steady stare. "You could try saying something nice."

"That could be a very risky move."

"Chance it."

His grin broadened as he said softly, "Not right now."

"When?"

"Later."

The conversation was entirely nonsense, and Susan realized it. But their bantering had effectively defused what could have been a very explosive situation, and for that she was grateful. At least now she could leave the warmth of his embrace and walk out of that room without feeling as though she were being torn in two.

Patting him firmly on the cheek, she eased out of his arms

and managed a disinterested expression. "Well, let me know. I'd hate to miss it."

He let his hand trail across her hip with deliberate slowness. "I'll think about it."

She gave him a pithy look then turned to go. She had just opened the door when he said softly, "Has anyone ever told you you have a great set of legs?"

There was something about the way he said it that made her insides go into dizzying loops, but she managed to keep her voice light. "Not really. My eldest brother said with legs like mine, I should have been the front half of a giraffe."

Jason laughed, and for a split second it was as though time stood still, and Susan knew that would be one memory of him that would stay with her forever. He had his hands on his hips and was standing with his back to the window, his head tipped to one side so that part of his face was touched by the rising sun. His expression was animated with laughter, and there was an incredible vibrancy in his eyes that seemed to reach out and physically touch her. And she knew, in the clarity of that one single moment, that he really did love her. It took all the strength she had to step through the door, close it behind her and walk away.

By the time she had a quick shower and got dressed, Susan had more or less regained her equilibrium, and a vitalizing energy made her feel as if she were walking on air.

She was humming to herself as she entered the kitchen. Jason was leaning against the cupboard, a steaming cup of coffee in his hand, a grin on his face. "You look as if you're ready to move mountains."

She gave him an airy flip of her head. "I am."

"That's disgusting."

She laughed and made a face at him. "Why don't you give up and quit nagging?"

He turned and poured another cup of coffee and handed it to her. His eyes had a familiar glint in them as his gaze connected with hers. "I may as well. You totally ignore me anyway."

She took the mug from him, then leaned against the cupboard beside him, their arms lightly brushing. She took a sip then slanted an amused glance up at him. "And who says you can't teach an old dog new tricks."

That made him laugh, and he shook his head in amazement. "You must drive Clayton damned near nuts."

Susan gave him a pained look. "You should know Clayton Chisholm better than that." She glanced at the clock on the wall, then checked her watch. "I hope you realize you got me out here half an hour early."

He grinned at her. "I wanted to give you plenty of time to open the Corn Flakes boxes."

She caught him in the ribs with her elbow. "Don't bug me at five-thirty in the morning," she warned. "My sense of humor is a little thin before the cock crows."

"So I see," he responded, his eyes twinkling. He moved slightly and braced his arm behind her, the heel of his hand resting on the lip of the sink. There was something about the way he did it that revealed a very comfortable familiarity, and Susan experienced a warm rush. She would never have believed she could find so much pleasure from simply standing at a cupboard with someone, especially at this ungodly hour in the morning.

She leaned against his arm, liking the feel of his warmth against her. She took a sip of coffee, then glanced up at him. "What time are you going to call the hospital?"

He shot a quick look at her, the looked down, an almost sheepish tone in his voice. "I did already."

She bit back a smile. "And?"

He finally met her gaze. "He's fine. The doctor had been called in for another patient, so he checked on Mike, and left orders that he could be discharged."

"I can go get him if you want."

"No," he said quietly, "I'll go get him."

Susan left it at that and tried to lighten his suddenly heavy mood. "So what Zane Grey scenario do you have lined up for this week?"

His expression didn't change but a sparkle appeared in his eyes as he answered, "I don't know for sure. I was thinking about lynching the cook."

That made her laugh, and Susan retaliated with a threatening look. "Sure. And then what?"

Jason grinned, then shifted his weight and hooked one ankle over the other. "We always brand the first week in June, so that only gives us the rest of this week and all of next to get ready."

"And what does that entail?"

"The corrals need some repairs this year, and it'll take us a couple or three days to round up the cattle. We can usually separate the calves from the cows in a day if the weather cooperates, but from now on we'll be pretty busy."

Susan knew from the stories Clayton told that branding time was very much a cooperative venture in the ranching community, with ranchers from one spread helping out at another. Which meant, she suspected, that she was going to have extra people to feed. She looked at him with amused speculation. "Under the circumstances, it seems like it'd be a bad time to lynch the cook."

The laugh lines around his eyes crinkled. "Could be."

Jason emptied his cup and set it on the counter then glanced back at Susan. "Mattie said Clayton called yesterday while we were at the hospital, and he'll be flying in either Tuesday or Wednesday."

"Did he say how long he'd be staying?"

"She didn't say, but he usually stays for at least a week or two."

Susan glanced at the clock, sighed, and reluctantly straightened up. "Well, I'd better wrangle that damned stove into submission."

Jason's mouth twitched. "You have a problem with the stove?"

She gave him a rueful smile. "It hates me."

He laughed aloud, and straightening up he gave her a reassuring pat on the shoulder. "Everybody needs something to hate, Susan. It makes life interesting."

"Why don't you get lost, Jason."

He was still laughing as he walked away. "I haven't time."

By the time Susan made breakfast, fixed four lunches and rummaged through the laundry looking for two pair of matching socks, the few hours she'd spent alone with Jason seemed like a half-forgotten dream. But there was one instance, when she looked up and found him watching her in a way that made her breath catch, that she remembered every intoxicating detail of how it felt having his body molded against hers. The same feelings came rushing back, making her head swim, and she finally had to look away.

She had the kitchen cleaned and chicken fried for supper by the time Jason returned from the hospital. But when he entered the kitchen, he was alone.

She glanced at the door, then at him. "Where's Mike?"

Jason gave her a rueful grin. "You know Michael. He couldn't miss the chance to revel in the glory, so he insisted he wanted to go to school. The doctor said he couldn't see why he shouldn't go, so I dropped him off on the way home."

Susan laughed and shook her head. "He'll love every minute of it."

Jason draped a pair of leather chaps over his shoulder as he got a package out of the small fridge. "I probably won't be home until late. If something comes up, I'll be checking fence over in the pasture where we keep the bulls. Walt knows where it is."

She nodded and screwed the cap on the thermos she was filling for him. "There's just enough coffee left for a cup. Do you want to have it before you leave?"

He dropped his hat on the counter and combed his hand through his hair. "I guess I could. Duff has to load the fencing supplies before I can pull out."

Susan filled his mug and handed it to him, then set the empty coffeepot in the bottom rack of the dishwasher. "Do you want me to hold supper?"

He glanced at the clock. "No, never mind. Len and Duffy should be back, but I likely won't make it home until after dark."

Susan put soap in the dispenser, closed the dishwasher door, then put the box of detergent away under the sink. She was wiping the taps when Jason reached in front of her and set his empty mug in the sink, and she glanced up at him.

He hiked up the chaps on his shoulder, then put on his hat as he shot her a quick look. "I'd better hit the road."

There was something about the way his body moved that made her pulse erratic and her voice was oddly husky as she said, "See you later."

Jason stopped, and as though drawn against his will, he turned and looked at her. Susan was rooted to the spot, and she felt the blood drain from her body as he came across the room. He paused in front of her, then without saying a word he smoothed his hand along her jaw, and his fingers tunneled into her hair. A galvanizing charge seemed to sizzle between them as their gazes locked, then silently he lowered his head, covering her mouth with a soft lingering kiss. Susan's whole body went weak, and she felt as if she were floating as his mouth moved against hers with immeasurable gentleness.

He hauled in a ragged breath, then murmured against her lips, "See you later." And with that, he turned and left the kitchen. Dazed, Susan watched him go. The sound of the back door slamming jolted her out of her state of shock, and she closed her eyes and let her legs fold beneath her, her back braced against the cupboard as she slid to the floor. Never in a million years had she expected him to do that. And she had a sudden horrible feeling that there was a damned good chance he might never do it again.

IT TURNED OUT to be another stifling day; not even a whisper of a breeze stirred the leaves that hung limply in the shimmering heat. And there didn't seem to be any relief in sight. The rain-laden clouds were again piling up against the ridge of mountains as the sun beat down, scorching the already dry earth. By shutting the windows and closing all the drapes and blinds, Susan managed to keep the house reasonably cool, but in spite of that, Mattie literally wilted.

After persuading her to take a cool shower, Susan set up an oscillating fan with a bowl of ice cubes in front of it. By the time the older woman came downstairs, the living room was cool enough for her to actually fall asleep. Susan checked on her periodically, concerned about how spent she looked, but Mattie barely stirred, her breathing smooth and even.

The day dragged on, the heat becoming more oppressive, and Susan found time weighing very heavy on her hands. It was simply too hot to do anything. She folded the last load of towels from the dryer, then went into her room, flopped down on the bed and tried to read, but her thoughts drifted.

Her life, she realized wryly, was turning into a baseball game. She was suddenly getting curve balls thrown at her, and she didn't have a clue whether she was going to strike out or not. Jason Chisholm was, after all, a very unpredictable game player. She turned her head to look at the clock on her bedside table, wondered how he was holding up, trying to work outside in this ungodly heat.

She finally sighed and sat up, her light blouse clinging to her damp body. Thank heaven she'd had enough foresight to have everything ready for a cold meal. She really didn't think she could stand having to cook anything for supper.

By dusk, a breeze was beginning to rustle through the leaves, bringing with it a breath of coolness from the mountains, its crispness making the inside of the house seem even more airless. Susan had thrown open every window and door, but she knew it would be midnight before the rooms really cooled down, so she used that as an excuse to let all the kids sleep out on the veranda. But the real reason she'd gone along with their idea was because she'd sensed that the other three had had a scare over Michael's close call, and needed to renew the family security of being together.

Since her arrival, the days had been noticeably lengthening, and even by ten o'clock that night, it was still light enough to see. She made a large pitcher of iced tea for herself and Walter, and the two of them sat out on the back step, watching the vibrant sunset colors fade from the darkening sky.

Mattie came out to join them, and for the first time Susan could see some sparkle in the older woman's eyes. "I must be getting old," she said as she sat down between them. "I can't ever remember it being so hot at the end of May."

Susan moved over to give her more room. "I didn't think it ever got this hot out here. It was certainly nothing Clayton ever bragged about, anyway."

Mattie chuckled softly. "Clayton doesn't see the warts, Susan. He believes there's no place as wonderful as this anywhere in the whole world."

Walter shrugged and hung his head. "Clayton is a Chisholm," he said softly, almost self-consciously.

Mattie patted his arm in a kind, maternal gesture, her tone soft with understanding. "Yes, he is, Walter. To the core."

Susan pointed to the folding lawn chairs stacked at the corner of the house. "Can I get you one of those, Mattie? You'd be more comfortable."

The older woman gave her a wry smile. "Thank you, my dear, but no. I've sat on these steps for a good many years, and I think I have the wherewithal to sit on them for a few more, in spite of Jason's fussing."

With her arms resting across her thighs, Susan hunched over as she studied Jason's mother with affection. "I think Jason had good reason to fuss. You were not looking well."

"Frankly, I wasn't feeling well, either." Mattie smiled and patted Susan's hand. "But I'm much better now, thanks to you, my dear. Clayton certainly knew what he was doing when he sent you to us.''

Susan wondered if Clayton had *any* idea what he was doing when he'd suggested she come.

Walter clapped his hands on his knees in a gesture of finality, then stood up. ''My house should be cool now,'' he said haltingly, then glanced down at the two women. ''See you in the morning.''

Susan smiled up at him. ''Good night, Walter. If you stay out of trouble tonight, I'll make you blueberry pancakes for breakfast.''

He chuckled as he shuffled away. ''I'll try, Susan. I'll try.''

Mattie watched him go, her face suddenly lined with sadness as she said quietly, ''He is such a fine, decent man, and that senseless accident was such a tragedy. He deserved so much more out of life.''

''I know,'' Susan answered softly. ''He's such a pet. It just doesn't seem fair.'' She turned to look at the other woman, her voice catching a little as she added, ''But at least he's not alone. He has all of you, and his family means a lot to him.''

Mattie sighed and shook her head. ''But sometimes, my dear, that doesn't seem like enough.'' She heaved another deep sigh and slowly got to her feet. ''Well, it's after ten. I think it's time I called it a night, too.'' She paused, taking a deep breath of the clean night air. ''Walter always plants evening scented stalks in the flower garden, and I always look so forward to that first whiff of their fragrance. Reminds me of my youth, for some reason.'' She shook her head as if dismissing her pensive mood, and touched Susan on the shoulder. ''Good night,'' she said warmly. ''And don't ponder the universe too deeply tonight. It'll still be here in the morning.''

Susan smiled and tipped her head in acknowledgement. ''I won't, Mattie. Pondering can be so...'' She paused, searching for the right word.

A twinkle appeared as Mattie offered, ''Ponderous.''

Laughing, Susan nodded. ''Exactly. Ponderous.''

Mattie gave the younger woman's shoulder a squeeze. ''Good night. And sleep well.''

''You, too, Mattie. See you in the morning.''

But in spite of what Mattie had said, Susan found herself pondering a lot of things. She wondered about the tragedy of Clayton and White Dove, and if he would ever talk about his dead wife. She wondered about Jason's ex-wife, and why she'd done what she had. And she wondered about Jason and herself. And she was still sitting on the doorstep, ''pondering the universe'' when Jason came home.

He didn't see her sitting in the dark until he was almost at the step, but despite how exhausted he sounded, there was still a hint of amusement in his voice. ''What are you doing out here? Did the kids lock you out of the house?''

''No. I was wondering why life has to be so complicated.''

''That sounds grim.''

She laughed softly and stood up. ''It is grim. Would you like some supper?''

He opened the screen door and held it as she preceded him. ''No. Don't bother. I ate the last of the lunch on the way home.''

The porch was illuminated from the light from the kitchen, and she turned to look at him. ''You're sure you don't want any fried chicken or potato salad? Or fresh strawberries with whipped cream?''

He managed a tired grin as he hooked the heel of his boot in the bootjack. ''When you put it like that, maybe I'll reconsider.''

He looked so damned exhausted that Susan longed to slip her arms around him and simply hold him up, but she suspected he needed something to eat more than he needed support.

By the time he'd washed up, she had a place set for him and his plate filled. He slumped wearily into the chair, and tipping his head back and closing his eyes, he drank thirstily from the bottle of beer she had set by his plate.

Susan sat down in the chair across the corner of the table from him, her head propped on her head, a sympathetic look in her eyes. "You must have had a hell of a day," she said quietly.

Heaving a deep sigh, he set the bottle down and looked at her and smiled halfheartedly. "I've had better."

She gave him a wry look. "We've all had better. Mattie said she could never remember it being so hot this time of year."

Jason rested an arm on the table, then picked up his fork. "How did she weather the heat?"

"She slept most of the day. I really think she's beginning to feel better, Jase. There was some sparkle in her eyes tonight."

"I hope so. I should've never let her get so run down in the first place."

Susan's expression was thoughtful as she watched him, knowing it was pointless to try to ease his conscience. Instead, she changed the subject. "Carol Redding stopped by after she brought Davy home. She said he was doing just fine."

Jason glanced up at her. "What kind of day did Michael have?"

Susan grinned. "Michael is loving every minute of it. The teacher had the class write a composition about it, and she's going to put them all in a book and give each of the kids a copy. It'll be his claim to fame."

Jason's smile didn't quite reach his eyes, and there was a telltale gruffness in his voice as he said, "Some claim. I wonder if he has any idea what a close call he had."

"Kids never see things like that, Jase," Susan counseled softly. "They'd never take their first steps if they did."

He looked up at her, a spark of humor in his eyes. "Yes, Grandma," he said solemnly.

She made a face at him, then changed the subject again.

"Carol said she's coming over to give me a hand during branding. I think she's afraid I'll serve cucumber sandwiches and dainty hors d'oeuvres or something."

Jason laughed and shot her an amused look. "Who knows? You could start a whole new trend." He broke his dinner roll open and buttered it. "But just to put your mind at rest, the Double Diamond and the Flying U have always joined forces for brandings and roundups, and almost anything else that comes along. It's been going on for generations."

Susan propped her head in her hand, a wistful look in her eyes. "That must be nice, having those kinds of roots. Especially now when most city people don't even know their next-door neighbors."

"Yeah," he said softly. "It is."

Pushing his empty plate away, Jason leaned forward and rested his arms on the table, and Susan lightly caressed his arm. "Are you ready for some strawberries and whipped cream?"

"No, thanks. It was so damned hot, I'm surprised I ate what I did."

Susan stood up and cleared his place, tossing the place mat on the pile in the middle of the table, then carried his dirty dishes to the counter and put them in the dishwasher. She heard him push his chair away from the table, and she glanced up at him. "Just in case you go upstairs and find all the kids missing, I'd better let you know that I haven't stuffed them down the well. It was so hot I let them sleep out on the veranda."

He smiled back at her, exhaustion lining his face. "Well, at least I don't have to climb the stairs to check on them." His expression sobered and he absently rolled back his cuffs, his manner suddenly preoccupied. He hesitated, as though trying to find the right words, then looked up at her. "I don't know where in hell I'm at, Sue," he said huskily. "You've turned my life upside down, and I don't know whether I'm coming or going."

Sensing that he desperately needed some distance between them, she stuck her hands in her pockets and tried to ignore the awful flutter in her chest. "Just go with it, Jason," she said softly. "And don't imagine obstacles where there aren't any."

She saw him swallow hard, then he looked down and began rolling his sleeves with unsteady hands. "It's more than just the obstacles." He hesitated, then continued unevenly as he tried to explain. "I'd resigned myself to the fact that a part of my life was over, that there was nothing more ahead for me. Then you came along, and suddenly I'm experiencing the same basic drives and feelings of a man half my age." He looked up and met her gaze, his voice so strained it was barely audible. "I'm in such a damned tangle emotionally that I'm not sure if you're the best thing that ever happened to me...or the worst."

She smiled at him through a sudden blur of tears, her chest aching with an immeasurable surge of love. "I'll settle for that. At least you know I'm around."

He stared at her for the longest time, them came to her. Slowly he reached out and lifted a tendril of hair off her neck, molding his hand against her jaw. His face was cast in a very solemn expression as he stroked her cheek with his thumb, then finally he smiled, his eyes filling with an intoxicating warmth. "Oh, I know you're around, all right," he said softly. "I'm so damned aware of you it scares the hell out of me."

She covered his hand with hers, a silent entreaty in her eyes. "Just give us a chance, Jase. That's all I ask."

He gazed at her for a minute, then lowered his head and lightly brushed his mouth against hers. "After last night, I don't have a choice."

Realizing he needed some time and space, Susan let her mouth linger against his for a brief, electrifying moment, then whispered against his lips, "We're playing with fire, love, and I don't have much resistance where you're concerned."

He drew in a deep breath and crushed her against him. "God, I don't have any." He didn't say anything for several moments, then reluctantly eased his embrace and looked down at her, his eyes smoky. "I think you'd better go to bed, and I'd better go have a shower," he murmured as he caressed her back. "And I think we'd better give ourselves some time to deal with all this."

And Susan knew that to hold him, she was going to have to let him go.

CHAPTER EIGHT

SUSAN KNEW she was in for a hard time when Tyler Redding glanced at her, then turned to Jason, his face deadpan. "You ought to make a deal with Clayton when he gets here, Jase. See if he'll swap you his executive assistant for that mule-headed colt you're trying to break. You'd save a pile on oats, you know."

Mattie bit back a smile. "Are you trying to stir up dust again, Tyler?"

"Tyler's always trying to stir up something," Susan interjected dryly. And she spoke with some authority. Tyler had been at the Double Diamond for the past week helping with the spring roundup and branding. They had finished branding the day before, but he was back to cut out some of the Flying U cattle that had wintered with a small experimental herd of Jason's. And Susan had had plenty of time to discover he was an inveterate tease. Tyler grinned at her, and Susan gave him a withering look as she set a platter of sausages and pancakes on the table. "But one of these days," she warned, "Mr. Redding is going to bite off more than he can chew."

Jason grinned as he reached for the platter. "Don't count on it. Some women have grown old waiting for that."

Susan waved off his comment with a disdainful gesture. "Just wait. Sometime in the not-too-distant future, some little piece of fluff is going to walk all over him, and he's going to crumble like cake."

Tyler's grin broadened. "Now are we talking about a

genuine piece of fluff or just ordinary lint? I do have *some* principles, you know."

She raised her eyebrows. "Really? Who would have guessed it?"

Duffy chuckled and shook his head. "I'd back off if I was you, Tyler. She has a feisty streak, and she's apt to cut off your groceries if you get her dander up. And you gotta admit, she ain't a bad cook, even if she is one of them back-east dudes."

Before he'd even finished speaking, Susan whipped his plate from in front of him and was marching toward the door. "I'm sure Dudley will enjoy this *without* the cute wisecracks."

"But you know, Tyler," Duffy continued without taking a breath, his eyes glued hungrily on his disappearing break-fast, "she's gotta have the best caboose I've seen any-where." Amid a ripple of laughter, he raised his voice hope-fully as she disappeared into the porch. "And she looks fine in them blue jeans." Realizing he was getting nowhere, he sighed and hunched over the table in woeful dejection. "You may as well give it to the dog. I couldn't get a bite in no how. My foot's stuck so far in my mouth, there ain't room for nothing else."

Susan's eyes were gleaming with suppressed laughter as she came back into the kitchen and returned his plate. "Then let that be a lesson to you."

"Yes, ma'am," he answered contritely, then unable to resist, he gave her a sly grin. "But you do have a great caboose."

She let on she didn't hear him as she went to the counter, poured herself a cup of coffee, then returned to the table and sat down beside Mattie.

Len reached for the syrup, then looked at Jason. "What time is Clayton getting in today?"

Jason glanced at the hired hand. "He said he was hoping to catch an early flight." He turned his attention to his mother. "Did he let you know?"

She nodded. "He called last night and said he's due in around ten this morning. Walter said he'd drive me in to pick him up, so you don't have to take the time to go get him."

"He probably won't get here in time for dinner, so you can tell him we'll be out in the south pasture if he wants to ride out."

Susan barely heard what the conversation was about. Ever since the night of Michael's accident, Jason's attitude toward her had changed, but as the rapport between them grew, so did his deep misgivings. She knew he was still battling with himself, but there were times when his refusal to even talk about it left her feeling very alone. And she finally realized there was more than years and family obligations that separated them: there was also the fact that they came from two different generations, and because of that, they saw things differently.

To make matters worse, they'd had very little time together, and with him so busy, practically none alone. Needless to say, she'd spent a few very restless nights, and she knew from the sounds from his bedroom that so had he. But the strain was definitely beginning to get to her.

She heaved a sigh and looked up to find him watching her, his expression inscrutable, his gaze kindled by thoughts she could only guess at. After a moment he inhaled sharply and looked away, the muscles in his jaw suddenly tensed. Susan experienced a dull consuming ache, wanting to go to him so badly, knowing she couldn't, wishing they could spend at least a few minutes alone together. She looked away, too, trying to ease a breath past the awful constriction in her chest, then pushed her chair back from the table and stood up. She could not sit there doing nothing, feeling as though every nerve in her body was rubbed raw.

She cleaned off the counter and was at the sink scrubbing the skillet when the nerves down her back began to tingle. She knew he was right behind her before he even touched her. With his body shielding his movements from everyone at the table, he set his dirty dishes in the other sink then slowly smoothed his hand up her bare arm, his touch setting off a multitude of sensations. His voice was very quiet as he murmured, "You look tired this morning."

She tried to quell the wild flutter in her chest as she looked up at him. "I didn't sleep much last night."

His hand tightened around her upper arm, his voice becoming even more unsteady. "I know." He watched her, his eyes darkening as he murmured, "I'll try to arrange some time this afternoon. Maybe we can go for a ride."

The huskiness in his voice set off another flurry of excitement, and she longed to turn into his embrace and feel the weight of his arms around her. But she closed her eyes and swallowed hard, struggling for some semblance of composure. Finally she looked up at him and smiled. "How about fifteen minutes right now?"

He caressed her arm as he smiled back at her, flashing the Chisholm dimple. "What I have in mind makes a lousy spectator sport."

She laughed and Len interjected. "What are you two hashing up that's so damned funny?"

Susan shot Jason an amused look then turned to face the others. "We're discussing sports," she answered, straight-faced.

Tyler rocked back in his chair and chewed on a toothpick as he studied them with unnerving thoroughness. "Yeah, I'll bet," he said drolly. "Contact sports, no doubt."

Susan gave him a cutting look. "Aren't you supposed to be doing something constructive?"

He was grinning as he pushed himself away from the table and stood up. "Maybe you ought to reconsider a trade, Jase. She could be a handful to break. You'll have to keep her on a damn short rein."

Jason's eyes were gleaming as he settled his hat low on his forehead. "That's what I've always admired about you, Tyler. You like to live dangerously."

There was something oddly serious about the tall blond

man as he picked up his own hat, then looked at Jason. "You ought to try it sometime, Chisholm. It might be worth the risk."

SUSAN HAD A FEW SPARE MINUTES before everyone was due in for dinner, and she was at the sewing machine in the laundry room, altering a pair of Patricia's jeans. The teenager sat straddling a chair, her arms resting across the back, her chin on her hands as she watched. "Do you think I could get my hair cut, Susan? I'm so sick of it long."

Susan backstitched the seam, then lifted the pressure foot and removed the garment. She clipped the connecting threads, then looked at the girl. "I don't see why not. I think it would really suit you short." She smiled teasingly as she added, "For some reason, you're suddenly developing a very good jawline."

Jason's daughter grinned. "You mean uncovering. I didn't even know I had one."

Affection shone in Susan's eyes. "I'm so proud of you, Trish. Ten pounds is a lot to lose."

Patricia smiled ruefully. "And only ten more to go." She absently scratched at a mosquito bite on her arm, then looked up, her expression serious. "Will you ask Dad if I can?"

Susan turned the jeans right side out before she answered. "Why don't you ask him yourself?"

Patricia heaved a sigh. "Because he's so busy right now he won't have time to take me for an appointment—and Grandma will be so disappointed because she likes it long."

Swiveling to face the girl, Susan spread the pants on her lap and began clipping the remaining threads. "You have to learn to deal with things like that yourself, Patricia," she said quietly. "The appointment is no problem. I'll take you to town for that." She frowned slightly as she mulled over how to deal with the Grandma problem. "You can't give up the things that are important to you because someone makes you feel guilty, honey. I think your grandmother would feel terrible if she knew how much influence she had over your decisions. She wants you to grow up to be your own person, you know.''

With her head still resting on her hands, Patricia frowned and chewed her bottom lip. "Do you really think so?"

"Yes, I really think so. She's the type of person who'd try to see things from your point of view."

The girl considered what Susan had said, her frown changing to a contemplative expression. "You're right. I don't do a lot of things because I'm afraid I'll upset somebody." She finally looked up at Susan. "It's *my* hair. *I'll* talk to Dad and Grandma about it."

"That's the stuff." Susan tossed the pants to Patricia. "Try them on and see if I got the waistband small enough."

Patricia pushed herself off the chair and stood up. "Okey-dokey." She started for the door then turned. "Thank you, Susan," she said shyly.

Susan knew the teenager was thanking her for more than just the alterations, and she smiled back at her. "You're more than welcome, Patricia."

She shut off the machine and was just covering it when Todd came roaring into the room. "Hey, Susan! Tyler's here and he's got blood all over him."

To her horror, Susan discovered that Todd was not exaggerating about Tyler's condition. He did have blood all over him, and beneath his dark tan he was definitely pale.

Susan's voice was sharp with alarm. "My God. What happened?"

He gave her a weak grin as he lowered himself into the chair at one end of the kitchen table. "It really isn't as bad as it looks, but Jase thought for sure I was bleeding to death."

Susan frowned as she carefully checked him over. The source of the bleeding was a long jagged wound down the back of his head, and she gently parted his bloodied and dirt-caked hair to assess the damage. "What happened?" she asked again, her tone subdued.

Bracing his arms on the table, he lowered his head and leaned forward, trying to make it easier for Susan to see. His voice was slightly muffled when he answered, "One old cow went crazy and tried to go through the corral. She got hung up, but we managed to get her out without breaking her damned leg." Tyler swore softly as Susan pressed the large lump behind his ear, then he continued, "I had to twist her head to the side to pull her back, but I didn't let go fast enough and she went over with me."

Susan winced as she separated more of his matted hair. "How did you get cut like that?"

"Damned if I know. Must have been on one of the broken rails."

"It's a mess, but I don't see how it can be sutured. The skin's been scraped off and it's swelling so badly that I think stitches will simply pull out."

"Don't worry about it. I'm not going into the hospital for a couple of damned stitches anyway."

Susan stopped her probing and Tyler sat up. She frowned and shook her head. "Well, if you won't go to the hospital, we'd better clean you up."

"Yes, ma'am."

"Don't say that like I was your mother, Tyler."

He chuckled then winced again. "Damn, even that hurts."

She cast him an amused glance as she filled a basin with cold water and dropped a cloth in it. "You deserve it," she said, coming back to the table. She pressed his head down and started gently swabbing the long laceration, then stopped. "I'm never going to get it clean this way. Can you stand it if I wash it out under the tap?"

There was amusement in his voice. "Just don't drown me."

"If your mother managed to keep from drowning you, I'm sure I can."

He laughed and winced, and Susan managed to look a little sympathetic as she followed him to the sink. With a lump the size of that one, he had to have a blinding head-ache, but he never let on as he braced his arms along the edge of the sink and hung his head under the tap. There was more mischief than pain in his voice when he said, "Be gentle with me, woman."

"Don't 'woman' me, Tyler, or I *will* drown you."

She knew he was grinning when he answered contritely, "Yes, ma'am."

It took several minutes to clean the blood and dirt out of his hair, but finally the water ran clean. Turning off the tap, Susan gently pressed a towel against his head, then poured a liberal amount of disinfectant over the cut. She could tell he was light-headed as he straightened, and she watched with concern as he walked slowly back to the table and sat down.

She went to the freezer and got a pack of frozen peas to use as a makeshift ice pack, wrapped it in a clean cloth, then gently molded it to the back of his head. "I think the bleeding's pretty well stopped, but maybe this will help the swelling."

Holding the pack, he carefully turned his head and looked at her. "No wonder Clayton keeps you around."

"Clayton," she said pointedly, "keeps me around be-cause I mind my own business."

He grinned. "Don't kid a kidder, Sue." He turned so he could brace his elbow on the table, his expression growing sober as he watched her clean up the mess. Finally he spoke, his voice very quiet. "Sue?"

She turned to look at him. "What?"

"Has anyone ever told you anything about Eileen?"

Susan stared at him for a moment, then looked away. "No."

"Would you mind if I did?"

There was a stretch of silence before she answered him. "No."

Tyler frowned and stared across the room, then met her gaze with unnerving directness. "Jase is ten years older than

I am, so I never really had much to do with him until about twelve years ago. I started training horses with him about them, and it wasn't long after that I accidentally discovered Eileen was screwing around on him.''

''What did you do?''

''Nothing. I wasn't going to be the one to tell him. But everybody knew what was going on. I don't know if it was because she felt life was passing her by, or if she resented being tied down with the kids, or if she was just too damned young when she got married. I don't know what in hell happened, but she turned into a real tramp.''

Somewhere deep in her gut, Susan knew this was a question she was going to regret asking. ''What do you mean— too young?''

Tyler stared at her for the longest time, then sighed heavily. ''Didn't you know that she was eleven years younger than Jase?''

Susan didn't know, and she felt as though he'd just knocked the wind out of her. She glanced away, afraid he could read the stark look of comprehension in her eyes.

Tyler continued, ''She put him through a living hell.''

Her voice was carefully impassive. ''Why are you telling me all this?''

''I know Jase Chisholm pretty well, Sue, and I knew two days after you got here that something or somebody had really shaken him up. Then when I saw you at the ball game I knew, sure as hell, who it was.''

She finally looked at him. ''You're making suppositions, Tyler.''

''The hell I am. I've been watching the two of you while I've been here. I can tell that there's something pretty special developing, but I know that he's going to have some major reservations about getting involved again. He has to be gun-shy, after what happened with her.'' Tyler paused and looked down, his face thoughtful. ''For what it's worth, I think you're the best thing that's happened to him in a long, long time.''

Susan tried to smile. "Now all we have to do is convince Jason of that."

Tyler grinned suddenly. "I've been doing my damnedest."

Her voice had an undercurrent of laughter as she admonished him. "I hope I'm around when you get yours, Tyler Redding."

Tyler was still sitting at the kitchen table with the frozen bag of vegetables pressed against his head when Jason came in. There was a trace of a smile around Jase's mouth as he scrutinized his friend. "Didn't anyone ever tell you never to try waltzing with a cow?" He pulled Tyler's hand away and lifted the bag to check the wound, then grimaced and shook his head. "That's the closest you'll ever come to getting scalped." He carefully laid the pack back on Tyler's head, then cast an amused glance at Susan. "Is this your idea of improvising?"

Susan waved off his concern. "Don't worry about it. I'll make him eat 'em when he's done."

Jason turned to Tyler. "I'll get you a clean shirt."

Tyler removed the bag of vegetables and winced as he felt his head. "You do that, and I'll trade you a hell of a headache for it."

Jason grinned. "Thanks, but I think I'll pass." He slapped Tyler on the back, then looked at Susan. "I thought Carol was going to give you a hand again today?"

Susan lifted a bowl of salad out of the fridge and set it on the counter. "No. She had an appointment with the specialist for Davy this morning, so I told her I could manage on my own."

"Why," he said as if thinking aloud, "do I have this feeling you could manage damned near anything?"

Tyler couldn't let that pass. "Why don't you give us all a break and let her take a whack at managing you?"

Jason cast the injured man a piercing look, then turned and left the room.

And Tyler Redding leaned back in the chair, looking immensely pleased with himself.

By the time everyone finished eating and Susan had everything cleaned up, it was midafternoon and the stifling heat had penetrated the house. She collected a seam ripper and another pair of Patricia's slacks and went outside. The backyard was heavily shaded this time of day, and Susan moved one of the big wooden lawn chairs to catch what little breeze there was. The heady fragrance of silver willows, which grew in heavy clumps beyond the driveway, rose on the heat waves and drifted in on a breath of wind, and Susan inhaled deeply. She had never encountered any perfume that could equal it.

"Why the faraway look?"

Susan looked up to find Clayton Chisholm coming through the trees. She smiled and shrugged. "I was just wishing that I could bottle that fragrance and use it all winter."

"There's nothing on Earth like it," he said as he pulled another chair over by hers and wearily sank into it, then dropped his battered straw Stetson on the ground. He closed his eyes as he tipped his head back and heaved a heavy sigh. "I keep forgetting what damned hard work this place is. And this heat...
I don't know how Jason keeps on going."

"I suppose he's used to it."

Clayton opened his eyes and looked at her. "Used to it. Hell, nobody's used to weather like this. They've had record-breaking temperatures for more than two weeks now." He sighed and closed his eyes again. "I wish to hell it'd rain. We could have problems with grass fires if something doesn't change soon."

Susan didn't respond as she carefully picked out a seam, her mind on other things. She studied his profile for a moment, then turned back to Patricia's slacks and began ripping out another seam, her expression pensive. She didn't know whether to bring up White Dove or not; maybe it was best to leave it alone.

She glanced at him again and found him watching her, an intent expression on his face. His voice was gruff when he finally spoke. "So what's on your mind, Suzy Q?"

"Why didn't you ever tell me about White Dove?"

He didn't respond for the longest time, then leaned his head against the back of the wooden chair and stared at the sky. "I always knew you were too smart for your own good—uncovering my dark secret."

"You make it sound as though you committed a crime."

"In those days, a lot of people thought I had."

Sensing her query had unearthed some half-forgotten memories, she lowered her head over her work. After a moment, she said gently, "I know it doesn't help much, but at least your feelings weren't misplaced, Clayton. From what Jason said, she sounded like a very special person."

Clayton looked at her, then reached across the space and grasped her hand. "She was. And she's the only one of my youthful illusions that still remains intact."

Fighting back the sting of tears, Susan tightened her fingers around his, and he smiled a crooked little smile as he gave her hand a gentle shake. "Don't despair for me, Susan. I'm not unhappy. I had more in five years than most people have in a lifetime."

She wiped her eyes with the back of her hand and forced a wobbly smile. "I know. It just seems so damned unfair." And she wasn't just thinking about the Chisholm who was sitting beside her.

The conversation with Clayton had an unsettling effect on Susan, and she found herself in an introspective mood for the remainder of the afternoon. As she prepared supper, she discovered she was reluctantly comparing his life to her own. And for the first time, she realized that even though she understood Jason's reservations, she had never really faced the fact that things might not work out for them. She had never once considered what would happen if they didn't. And what then? What would she do? The thought scared her to death.

"What's the matter, Susan?"

Susan hauled her attention back from her sober thoughts to find Patricia slouched over the counter with her elbows braced on the top, her chin in her hands as she was watching her.

She dredged up a smile and went back to slicing onions for the salad. "Nothing, honey. My mind was wandering."

Patricia hungrily grabbed a stick of celery from the colander in the sink and took a bite. "You looked really sad, though."

"You shouldn't talk with your mouth full, Trish." As soon as she said it, amusement flickered in Susan's eyes. Her mother used to do that all the time—switch topics when she was trying to avoid something awkward, and Susan had sworn on everything sacred in a teenager's life that she would never, *never* do it.

"I asked Dad if I could get my hair done. He said I could, but he said that I should talk it over with you so I don't get stuck with something I hate."

Feeling as vulnerable as she did, Susan looked away, not wanting Patricia to see how she reacted to that innocent comment. Without realizing it, Jason had unconsciously placed her in a mother's role. Somehow she managed to keep her voice level when she responded, "Tell you what...why don't you look through some magazines and find the styles that you like, then we'll check them out together."

There was an impish twinkle in the girl's eye. "How far out can I go?"

Susan laughed and tapped her on the nose. "Stop at burgundy highlights with lime green streaks in it."

Patricia giggled. "Wouldn't Grandma have a fit?"

"She wouldn't be the only one," Susan responded dryly.

Patricia grinned, then turned to go. She stopped at the door into the porch, then faced the young woman, her manner a little uncertain. "I'm really glad you came, Susan. This is the best summer ever."

Susan's expression softened as she smiled at Jason's daughter. "I'm glad I came, too, Trish," she answered gently.

Len walked in just then and fondly ruffled Patricia's hair as he passed her. "Say, Susan, have you seen Jase?"

"No, not lately. I know he was planning on going out to check the herd to make sure the calves were doing all right, but I don't know if he did or not."

"Yeah, he did. But his truck's parked down by the arena so he's around somewhere."

Susan glanced at the wall clock and frowned slightly. "I don't imagine he'll be in for another hour. Do you want me to send the boys out to find him?"

"Maybe you better. The bay mare looks like she's goin' to foal pretty soon, and Jase wants to be around when she does. She went right rank last year and lost her colt, and she's too damned good a horse to have that happen again."

Susan rinsed her hands under the tap, then dried them on a towel. "I'll see if the boys are watching TV."

He nodded and turned to go. "I'm goin' to have to leave it with you. I have a bull we was doctorin' loaded in the trailer here. I gotta haul him over to the north lease, so I have to hit the trail pretty quick to make it back in time for supper."

Susan waved him off. "You go ahead. I'll take care of it."

It was Susan who finally tracked Jason down. He was stretched out under a tree behind Walter's little house, his legs crossed, his hands laced behind his head, and he was, quite uncharacteristically, doing nothing. Clayton and Walter were sitting on the back step, each nursing a bottle of beer, idly rehashing some past fishing trip.

She shook her head, her tone disdainful. "Well, honestly. And to think I've been in there slaving over a hot stove, while you guys are out here lazing around."

Clayton grinned at her. "Slaving over a hot stove is such an old saw, Susan. Next thing we'll be hearing about how you've worked your fingers to the bone."

She gave him a caustic look. "Well, I have."

Jason grinned. "Slaving and bony fingers—sounds pretty bad."

Susan's tone held a certain amount of spiteful satisfaction. "I'm glad you think so. Because now it's your turn."

"It's always my turn," he responded with a warped smile. "What is it this time?"

She passed on the information Len had given her. Jason put on his hat as he got to his feet, an undercurrent of resignation in his voice. "This could be the beginning of a long night."

And it was. It was well after midnight and Susan was still lying in her bed wide awake, listening for him to come in. Jason had gone to check on the mare when Clayton had retired to Walter's house, and he hadn't returned.

She checked the luminous hands on the clock, then sighed and pushed back the sheet. There was no use lying there, staring at the ceiling. Slipping into a light housecoat, she went out to the kitchen and put on a fresh pot of coffee. A cool breeze was wafting in from the open window, and she shivered as she leaned across the sink to close it. Through the black barrier of the windbreak, the lights in the barn winked through the shifting branches. She glanced at the clock again, then went back into her bedroom and pulled on a pair of blue jeans and a sweatshirt. At least she could take him some coffee and something to eat.

It was very dark, and the dim lights in the barn sent out murky halos that didn't quite reach into the heavy shadows. The structure was blanketed in a peculiar hush, and Susan felt almost compelled to tiptoe as she slipped through the half-open door.

She found Jason in a box stall halfway down the barn, crouched in one corner, washing his arm in a pail of soapy water. The mare was lying on her side on a pile of straw, and as inexperienced as she was about horses, Susan could sense the animal's fear.

Not wanting to panic her, she kept her voice very quiet when she spoke. "I thought you might like a coffee and a sandwich about now."

Startled, he glanced up, his surprise only partially disguising his pleasure. He managed a wry grin. "I take it you're still working your fingers to the bone."

She smiled. "No. I'm working on being nice for a change."

He dried his hands and arms on a towel, then came over to the gate and opened it. "That sounds interesting," he answered, his voice suddenly husky.

Her eyes softened as she reached out and caressed his face. "Hungry?"

He slipped his arm around her shoulders and drew her into the corner of the stall. "Later," he murmured as he took the thermos and sandwich contained away from her and set them on a stack of bales. His expression was suddenly sober, and his eyes darkened as he took her face between his hands and kissed her softly on the mouth. Maybe it was because of the heavy shadows that cocooned them in privacy, or maybe it was because they were away from everyone, but that soft searching kiss was like a torch to tinder, and Susan's breath caught on a ragged sob as he gathered her roughly against him. His mouth moved hungrily on hers, sucking the strength out of her, and she yielded, her world slipping into a long slow spin, drawing her into a whirlpool of sensation.

A low animal sound was wrung out of him as she moved against him, and catching her by the back of the head, he widened his stance, welding her hips to his. The contact was galvanizing, and a shudder coursed through him so forcefully that it made her tremble. Susan's whole body was paralyzed by the wild excitement that pumped through her, and she could barely breathe her heart was hammering so frantically.

Taking in a strained breath, Jason tore his mouth away, his embrace crushing as he pressed her head roughly against his shoulder. "I touch you, and I can't think."

She kissed the warm skin of his neck, uncertain who was trembling more violently. "Then don't," she answered unsteadily. His silent response was to hold her more closely, the hardness of his body slaking the hunger in hers, and her voice caught as she tightened her arms around him. "I do love you, Jason."

Knowing the personal apprehensions he had, Susan didn't expect him to openly declare his feelings, and she was unprepared when he inhaled sharply and buried his face in her hair. His voice was hoarse as he whispered, "God, but I didn't think it was possible for me to need anybody the way I need you."

The undercurrent of desperation in his voice created an aching tightness in Susan's chest, and she blinked back tears as she gently stroked his head. "Just don't start worrying about what's right and what's wrong tonight, Jase. I don't want anything except some time alone with you."

He kissed the hollow behind her ear then murmured gruffly, "That's good, because I don't think I could let you go."

With infinite tenderness she caught his jaw and raised his head. She smiled softly into his eyes, her own glowing with love. "I think I can handle that."

He held her gaze for a moment, then whispering her name, he roughly tightened his arms around her. "What in hell am I going to do with you?"

There was a teasing tone in her voice. "Whatever you want."

He laughed huskily and eased his hold on her. "That's not exactly what I need to hear, Susan."

She stared at him levelly, a hint of amused defiance in her eyes. "That's too bad, Jason."

He laughed again and hugged her hard, then pulled a horse blanket off the stall partition and tossed it on the pile of hay beside the bales. He bent over and straightened it out, then caught her hand and pulled her down onto the fragrant bed. "Come here. I need to hold you."

She slipped willingly into his arms. The blanket had shifted as she lay down and the hay poked and scratched through her clothing. She raised up and straightened the bunched-up fabric, then snuggled against him, her face turned into the curve of his neck. The masculine fragrance of him filled her senses, and she inhaled deeply, then smiled.

"What's so funny?" he murmured against her hair.

She grimaced and shifted again. "I've just discovered that hay is badly overrated. It smells great but it scratches and pokes every time you move."

She felt him smile against her temple. "Good. That'll keep your mind off other things."

She gave him a playful punch on the shoulder as she raised up to try to pull the blanket under her more. Her breasts pressed against his chest as she leaned into him, and Jason's face suddenly took on an intently solemn expression. The muscles in his jaw tensed as he drew in his breath, then he caught her hips and pulled her on top of him. Overcome with a throbbing need, Susan's eyes drifted shut as she fell victim to a rush of desire so strong that it immobilized her, sending a jolt of fire and ice racing through her veins.

His voice was strained and unsteady as he nestled her head in the curve of his shoulder. "I've been wanting to hold you like this all damned day."

Susan barely had the strength to speak. "Jason—"

"Shh, Sue. Don't say anything, for God's sake." He shifted slightly, settling her firmly between his thighs, then clasped her against him in an unbreakable hold. "Just let me hold you for a while," he whispered.

Susan didn't think the storm in her would ever subside, but in time it did, and she slipped into a dreamy state. Lying molded so tightly against him, aware of every movement, every breath, every contour of his body, it was almost as

hough she were both physically and mentally a part of him.
And little by little, she could feel his ardor abate until all
hat remained was an indefinable sense of oneness.

Finally she collected enough strength to move, and she
ifted her head and gazed down at him. She smiled softly
nto his eyes as she caressed his mouth. "I feel like I've
ust found my other half."

His expression softened as he slipped his hand slowly up
ier neck and into her hair, sending shivers down her spine.
"You fill a few holes yourself."

"You make me sound like a wad of putty."

He smiled up at her. "Right now, I feel like a wad of
outty."

She laughed and gave his head a little shake. "Good. It
erves you right." As she continued to gaze down at him,
m electric tension grew between them and finally she low-
red her head and covered his mouth in a soft, searching
ciss.

With his hand thrust deep into her hair, he held her head
still as he responded, his mouth moving thirstily against
iers. Susan's breathing became labored and it wasn't until
he moved her hips against his, tormenting them both, that
ie finally eased her away. He gave her one last fleeting kiss
hen whispered hoarsely against her mouth, "Don't start
omething we can't finish, Sue." He raked his fingers
hrough her hair, then spanned her jaw with his hand as he
gently raised her head, his eyes dark with regret. "With the
nare down, anybody's apt to walk in here to check on her.
And I don't want something special spoiled that way."

She sighed and touched his mouth, her voice wistful. "I
mow." She closed her eyes. "I don't want that to happen,
either."

Nestling his cheek against the top of her head, Jason
gently stroked her back. "I was hoping you'd come."

She smiled and smoothed her hand against his jaw.
"Why? Were you afraid of being out here alone in the
lark?"

Jason tightened his arms around her, his voice laced with amusement. "No. I just needed a warm body."

Susan couldn't resist. "You had the horse."

Jason laughed and looped an arm across her back. "Definitely not my style."

Savoring the feel of his arms around her, Susan snuggled closer. "And how's she doing?"

"I just finished checking her when you came in. It'll be a while yet."

"Good," she retorted with obvious satisfaction. "That's the best news I've had all day." She felt his mouth brush against her hair as he tightened his embrace, his hold strong and secure. Susan closed her eyes, determined to savor every second she had alone with him.

It was just a little more than two hours later when, with Jason's assistance, the mare finally foaled, safely delivering a gangling long-legged colt with a perfect star on his forehead. The whole experience filled Susan with a kind of awe and she was in a quiet mood as they walked back to the house.

Draping his arm around her shoulders, Jason adjusted his stride to hers and drew her firmly against his side as they silently passed through the overhead arch of trees, still bound by the quiet harmony they shared.

The fragrance of the first lilacs hung in the cool night air and from the small willow-ringed slough on the other side of the road, a chorus of frogs pervaded the stillness. Jason pressed her more firmly against him, then he stopped walking and pulled her into his arms. With immeasurable gentleness, he brushed his mouth against hers, and Susan's lips parted. He groaned softly, enfolding her in a crushing embrace as his kiss suddenly became hungry, more demanding. Potent sensations enclosed them in a world of their own, and neither of them saw the shadow disengage itself from the corner of the house.

They had no idea they weren't alone until a male voice spoke from the darkness. "This was sure in hell not the kind of fireworks I expected."

It was Clayton Chisholm, and he was not amused.

CHAPTER NINE

FRAMED IN THE LIGHT spilling from the kitchen window, Jason slowly straightened, drawing Susan even closer as he turned to face his uncle. Anger radiated from him and his voice was dangerously quiet when he said, "I didn't think lurking in the shadows was quite your style, Clayton."

"I wasn't lurking," Clayton answered flatly. "I saw the lights on in the kitchen, and I thought you'd finished in the barn."

It was apparent that both men were angry, and Susan felt as though she had been inadvertently thrust into a rather nasty scene. It didn't make one bit of sense why Clayton should be so annoyed because he'd seem them together, yet it was evident that he was. And it was also evident that Jason was just as annoyed because he had.

"I think you'd better go inside, Susan," Clayton suggested, sounding very much like an irate father. "I'd like to have a few words with my nephew."

Susan's chin came out, vexation flashing in her eyes. "Don't treat me as if I were fourteen years old, Clayton," she snapped.

"This doesn't concern you," he snapped back.

"It certainly does, and anything you have to say, you can say right now."

There was a taut silence, and Clayton took a deep breath, his tone more subdued and reasonable when he finally answered, "I'd like to talk to you, Jason."

Susan glanced at Jase, apprehension shooting through her when she saw the unyielding set to his jaw. He was furious.

"It might be wise," he responded softly, an edge of steel to his voice, "if you gave it some serious thought before you interfered in something that is none of your damned business." Jason tightened his arm around her shoulders as he turned toward the house. "Come on, Susan. I'll take you in."

Susan didn't want to go. There was something coldly hostile about the tension between Jason and Clayton, and she had an unnerving feeling that if left to ferment, it would turn into the kind of animosity that lasted a long time. But she didn't know what to do or say to defuse the situation, especially when it seemed as if she were the cause of it. Silently she let Jason propel her into the house, acutely aware of the crunch of gravel as Clayton strode away.

Once inside the door, Jason removed his arm, allowing her to precede him into the kitchen. She set the empty thermos and the sandwich container on the counter and turned to face him. "I think you should talk to him, Jason," she said softly. "He probably reacted without even thinking."

There was still a rigid set to his jaw, and his tone was harsh. "You should know him better than that. He *never* reacts without thinking."

She laid her hand on his arm as she tried to reason with him. "Please don't leave it like this, Jase. I don't want bad feelings between you because of me."

Some of the hardness left his face as he looked at her, his expression inscrutable. "I think it would be best," he said very quietly, "if Clayton and I stayed out of each other's way until we've had a chance to cool off."

Susan watched him, a worried look in her eyes, disturbed that something like this should have ever happened. Her shoulders sagged as she sighed with resignation. "I suppose you're right."

In a preoccupied gesture, he brushed some stray curls back from her face. "You'd better turn in. It's getting late."

She didn't want to let him leave in the frame of mind he was in, but she knew Jason Chisholm would have to deal with what had happened on his own. With an anxious look in her eyes, she watched him walk out of the room.

Susan awoke the next morning feeling oddly disoriented, and it took a while for her to figure out why. From the angle of the light streaming in her windows, it was obviously mid-morning.

She tried to clear the fog from her head as she sat up. The hands on her clock indicated it was just after ten, but it took a moment before she realized that the clock had been moved and the alarm shut off. With no visible indications that he'd been there, Susan knew it had been Jase who had moved it. It didn't do much for her dazed state to know that he'd been in her room while she slept. Raking her hair back from her face, she closed her eyes, trying to shut out the sensual images taking shape in her mind, images of them together. Lord, he had been right beside her, and she hadn't even wakened. Swearing softly, she forced herself to take a deep breath, then climbed out of bed and resolutely headed for the bathroom.

Her mood was contemplative when she finally went into the kitchen, and she was so intent on her own thoughts that she was totally oblivious to everything else. But when she rounded the corner and saw Clayton Chisholm sitting at the table, hunched over a cup of coffee, her pensiveness was replaced by a guarded alertness.

He gave her a crooked smile. "I was beginning to think you weren't in there."

She didn't respond as she dumped out the old coffee grounds, then set about making a fresh pot, but there was no mistaking the intractable set to her jaw.

Hooking his arm over the back of his chair, Clayton studied her for a moment, then said quietly, "I'd like to talk to you, Sue."

She finally turned to face him, her eyes flashing. "Talk to me, or give me a talking-to?"

"Come sit down," he said patiently.

"No."

There was a hint of amusement around his mouth as he continued to watch her. "How many times have we crossed swords in the past?"

She stared back at him. "Who counted?"

He sighed and slouched back in his chair. "Come on, Susan. We've had disagreements before, and we've always been able to work them out."

Some of the fire went out of her eyes. "But it was never personal before. Clayton, what you saw last night was between Jason and me. It was none of your affair."

Looking down at the table, Clayton hunched over his coffee, his brow furrowed. There was a brief silence, then he spoke, exasperation in his voice. "Will you quit being bullheaded and come sit down?"

Susan relented with a sigh and sat across the table from him, then propped her chin on her hand as she reluctantly gave him a smile. "This had better be good, Chisholm."

He looked up at and met her gaze, a glint of humor in his eyes. "It will be, if you don't go off half-cocked."

She didn't say anything as she held his gaze, then sighing heavily, she again relented. "Okay. You made your point."

He laced his hands around his mug, silently considering what he wanted to say. Finally he looked at her. "Maybe I ought to do some explaining."

There was amusement lurking in Susan's eyes as she responded, "Be my guest."

He gave her a crooked smile then lowered his head again. "I wanted you to take this job because I recognized your rather formidable ability for getting a grip on things, for managing the unmanageable. For my own peace of mind, I wanted you here with Mattie. But quite frankly, it never once crossed my mind that anything could ever develop between you and Jase."

"And if it had crossed your mind?"

He considered her question, then raised his eyes and met hers, his expression deadly serious. "I'm not sure, but I don't think I would have asked you to come."

"Why?"

He shook his head and frowned, and several moments passed before he answered her. "Mostly because of you. I don't think you fully realize what you'd be letting yourself in for—raising another woman's kids, coping with an entirely different life-style, the enormous age difference."

Susan quit picking at the crack in the table and looked at him. "I'm not an adolescent, Clayton, and I'm not another Eileen. And it's not as though this is the first relationship I've ever been involved in." Leaning forward, she folded her arms and rested them on the table, an unsteady catch in her voice. "Had I been asked, I would've thought you'd be pleased."

There was a dispirited slump to his shoulders as he reached out and covered one of her hands with his. "If this had happened fifteen years ago, before Eileen messed up his life, I would have been. But this isn't fifteen years ago, Sue. It's now. And there are four kids and a whole generation between you."

Susan pressed her hands together as she tried to control their sudden trembling. "So you want to inflict the same emptiness on me that you've had all your life."

"No, Susan, I don't," he answered, sounding suddenly weary. "That's the last thing I want for you." He sighed and leaned back in his chair, his face lined with concern. "But I don't want you trapped in something that's going to suck the life out of you, either."

The first tentacles of panic stirred in her, and Susan felt as though a tremendous weight were pressing the air out of her. She struggled to keep her voice level. "I suppose you still intend on talking to Jason."

"I did. We talked last night."

That struck her as the closest thing to a betrayal she'd ever known, and the hurt was so intense that she had to either give way to tears or unleash her temper. She shoved the chair back with such force that it went crashing over backward, but she was so angry that she didn't even notice it. She longed to pick up his cup and smash it on the table in front of him, but she stormed out of the kitchen instead, her vision suddenly blurred. Damn them. Damn them all.

As she turned down the hallway, she bumped into Jason, who was coming from the main house. He took one look at her face and caught her arms, his voice low and urgent. "What in hell happened?"

Susan shook her head, fighting to hold back the overwhelming pressure of tears.

His grip on her arms tightened and a flinty expression glinted in his eyes. "Did Clayton say something to you?"

Unable to answer him, she made a helpless gesture with her hands, and his expression turned to one of fury. Swearing hotly, Jason released her and was about to storm into the kitchen when she grabbed his arm and restrained him. He took a look at her tear-streaked face and relented, and exhaling sharply, he opened the door to her room and drew her inside. Catching the door with his elbow, he swung it shut, then leaned against it as he gathered her to him.

She sagged against him, struggling to control the flow of tears as he slowly stroked her head, his cheek brushing her hair. He drew in an uneven breath and held her even tighter, his voice unsteady. "Tell me what he said, Susan."

Susan shook her head, still unable to answer him.

He caught her under the chin and gently raised her head, forcing her to meet his gaze. "He told you that he already talked to me, didn't he?"

She responded with a nod and he brushed away her tears with his thumb, his voice gruff with emotion. "God, Sue, I hate what this is doing to you."

Finally able to ease a breath past the smothering constriction in her chest, Susan touched his mouth with trembling fingers. "It's all right, Jason," she whispered tremulously. "It just hit me wrong when he said he'd talked to you last night."

He sighed and shook his head. "I was afraid of that—that he'd talk to you before I had a chance. I came in this morning, but you were so sound asleep I hated to wake you.''

She got the same flurry of feelings she had when she first realized he'd been in her room, and her voice had a strange unevenness to it when she said, ''I wish you'd stayed.''

His own voice wasn't quite steady as he slowly stroked her cheek. ''I didn't dare.''

The dark, smoky look in his eyes was so mesmerizing that it was hard for her to go on, and her voice had little strength when she finally did. ''Don't let him color your judgment, Jase.''

Slipping his arm around her shoulders, he pressed her against him, his jaw resting on her temple. His tone was solemn. ''But there's a lot of truth in what he says.''

''It's none of his damned business.''

Jason sighed and eased his hold on her. ''Maybe it isn't, but I have to agree with him. If you were to stay, it would be one hell of a change. No matter how you look at it, you'd be the one making all the sacrifices. And let's face it, dealing with the situation here for—what has it been…six weeks?—is a far cry from dealing with it for the rest of your life.''

She was getting damned tired of hearing about how hard it would be for her to cope, and she stared back at him, her chin taking on a stubborn set. ''Why are the two of you so damned determined to convince yourselves that I can't handle it? Give me some credit, Jason. I'm not some fourteen-year-old bubble brain with her first crush.''

His expression changed, and there was annoyance flashing in his eyes. ''Then don't act like one, Susan,'' he said, his voice a little too quiet. ''It's a legitimate concern.''

Her eyes narrowed, then indignation took over and her temper flared. ''Why don't you do a little growing up yourself,'' she shot back. ''Quit acting like a damned martyr and get on with your life.''

He stared at her coldly, then brushed past her and yanked open the door. ''I can see this was a waste of time.''

"Yes, it certainly was."

"Fine."

"Fine."

He gave her one last icy stare and stomped off down the hallway. Susan didn't know whether to laugh or cry, so she slammed the door instead.

The rest of the day didn't get much better. After her burst of temper, Susan ended up with a splitting headache, and she spent most of the afternoon in her room. Everything seemed so hopeless, and the oppressive weight of the weather didn't help. Heavy clouds had rolled in, darkening the sky and smothering the countryside in a muggy heat, yet there seemed to be little chance of rain.

Neither Jason nor Clayton showed up for the noon meal, but they came in for supper, both of them grim-faced and silent. Susan was well aware of the questioning looks that shot around the table, but even though every person there was acutely aware of the tension between the two men, everyone tried to either ignore it or let on that nothing was wrong.

But even though they tried to pretend otherwise, the tension affected them all, and any attempts at conversation were strained and subdued. Susan saw Mattie glance from one man to the other, and the older woman absently toyed with her spoon as she frowned, her expression thoughtful.

Finally she addressed her son. "Tyler phoned just before you came in, Jason. He said something about his going to Wyoming with you on Monday."

Jason reached for a bun without meeting his mother's gaze. "We're going down to the quarter horse sale in Cheyenne."

Mattie's frown deepened. "I thought you'd decided not to go."

"I changed my mind."

Mattie glanced at Clayton, then turned her attention back to Jason. "I see," she said quietly.

Todd turned to his father. "How long are you going to be gone?"

"We'll be back the following Sunday."

Todd and Michael exchanged a worried look, then Todd spoke again. "Me and Mikey are supposed to go to that ball tournament that weekend. Are we still gonna be able to go?" The coach had entered their team in a weekend tournament in Lethbridge, and along with a few parents as supervisors, all the boys were going to camp out for the weekend. They were to leave by school bus Friday night, and Michael and Todd had been counting the days.

Jason stared at his son, his expression passive. "I don't have to be here to take you to the bus, Todd. Of course you can still go." He continued to watch the boy for a moment, as though he didn't quite understand why Todd should need confirmation now, then he looked down, his face still expressionless.

Michael made a grimace of bewilderment at his brother, then looked at Susan. It was as though he could read something in her face that no one else could see, and he reached out in the only way he knew now. "Would you like to come with us, Susan? You could share our tent, and Davy and Mark could sleep somewhere else."

That solemn, sincere expression on his little face touched her in a way few things ever had, and for one awful moment, she didn't think she was going to be able to hang on to her composure, but somehow she managed to dredge up a smile. "Thank you for the invitation, Michael, but I'd better stay here with Lucy and Patricia."

He smiled, too, then gave an embarrassed little shrug and turned back to his dinner. Susan looked away, struggling to swallow the awful ache in her throat, but somehow, her gaze connected with Jason's. He was staring at her, his expression suddenly haggard, his eyes bleak. For a split second, their eyes held, then without a word, he pushed back his chair and left the table.

And it was Michael, little Michael with the wide blue

eyes and high cheekbones, the boy without the Chisholm smile, who laid down his fork and went after him. Susan watched them go, the painful contraction in her chest intensifying.

As soon as she finished cleaning up after supper, she used her headache as an excuse to go to her room and shut out the world. She lay on her bed, staring unseeingly at the ceiling, trying to come to terms with the direction her life was taking. And for the first time, she acknowledged that she had very little control over it. And there wasn't a damned thing she could do about it.

Time passed, the heavy, oppressive sky began to darken, and nightfall slowly crept into her room, masking the corners in a dimensionless gloom. Deciding she couldn't stay in there forever, she sat up and was about to climb off the bed when there was a soft knock at her door. She sighed and slowly slipped off the bed, reluctant to open it. She strongly suspected it was Clayton, and she didn't feel up to another confrontation with him now.

Exhaling sharply, she mentally braced herself and opened the door. But it wasn't Clayton Chisholm standing there.

Her insides twisted as her eyes connected with Jason's, and the strange flutter made it impossible for her to speak.

His expression was earnest. ''Can I come in?''

Stepping back, she silently motioned him in. As he closed the door, Susan crossed to the lamp and turned it on, and feeling as though her legs wouldn't support her much longer, she sat down in one of the velour chairs. She knew Jason was watching her as he moved the other chair closer to hers, but for the life of her, she could not meet his gaze. It wasn't until he sat down that she finally managed to look at him.

He studied her for a moment, then sighed and leaned forward. Resting his forearms on his thighs, he clasped his hands between his knees and stared at the floor. Several seconds passed before he looked up. ''I want to apologize for losing my temper this morning. Some of the things I said were really uncalled for.''

She managed a lopsided smile. "Yes, they were."

His face relaxed briefly, then his expression sobered. "I want to do what's best for you, Susan," he said quietly.

She stared back at him, then sighed and looked down as she began rolling the hem of her skirt between her fingers. "I know you do."

He reached out and absently trailed his finger across the back of her hand, his mood introspective. "I realized this afternoon that I was playing a few games with myself."

"Like what?"

"Like not being completely honest. I didn't want to admit that, to some degree, I was concerned about what other people would think."

Susan's tone held no trace of censure. "And what would they think?"

He finally looked up at her and gave her a dispirited shrug. "Some would approve, others would disapprove, others wouldn't give a damn. But that's not the point." He took her hand in his and began absently tracing patterns down her fingers. "The point is, that's one thing I shouldn't have let influence me."

Susan stilled his restless movements and laced her fingers through his. "Jason, we're all motivated by what people think. Every kid in the world would eat with his feet and wear his underwear until it rotted off if parents didn't worry about what other people thought."

He smiled. "Very graphic, but your perspective is a little warped."

She smiled and touched his face with her hand. "So is yours, Jason," she said softly.

His expression altered, and he abruptly looked down at their clasped hands. "Maybe it is, but I think it's because my feelings for you scare the hell out of me."

"Why?"

Jason tightened his fingers through hers, his grasp almost

painful. When he spoke, his voice was very husky. "If I ever let go with you, I'd be lost. I came close to that point last night, and that's what scares me."

Her vision blurred as she reached out and gently caressed his haggard face. "Is that why you're going to Wyoming?"

He closed his eyes and caught her hand, his voice so tortured it was barely audible. "Yes, that's why I'm going."

THE FOLLOWING WEEK was the worst one Susan had ever spent in her entire life. The days dragged on and on in the never-ending heat, the kids were wound up because they were nearly finished school, and Clayton kept treating her as though she were an abused puppy. Her only consolation was that Mattie wasn't there. She suspected that Jason's mother saw far more than she let on, and Susan had been relieved when the older woman had decided to travel to Montana with Jason and Tyler to visit an old friend.

The days were bad, but the nights were even worse. Susan would lie awake with every nerve in her body on fire, wanting him so badly that she could barely stand it. And when she'd finally fall asleep, disturbing dreams would drift through her subconscious, leaving her oddly disquieted when she awoke.

When Friday morning arrived, and Clayton and Walter decided to head up to one of the Double Diamond line camps for a day or two of fishing, Susan could not believe her good luck. Len and Duffy were usually away weekends, the boys were leaving Friday night, so that left only Lucy and Patricia at home with her. And the prospect of some quiet time with just the girls was like an unexpected reprieve. By the time Susan got the boys off, she was more than ready to put her feet up and accept Lucy's offer of a peanut butter and jam sandwich for supper.

Susan had been watching the cloud banks collect on the western horizon as Lucy put the finishing touches on some elaborate peanut butter swirls, and she grinned as she glanced at the youngest Chisholm's handiwork. "That looks wonderful, Luce. Very artistic."

Lucy pulled a face and opened her eyes wide, as though she weren't quite sure if it was wonderful or not. "Do you want grape jelly or raspberry jelly?"

"I think I'll have grape, please."

Patricia rolled her eyes in revulsion as she watched Lucy glob on a horrendous amount of jelly and muck it together with the peanut butter. "That looks disgusting, Lucy. It looks like you've been finger painting in it."

Lucy gave her big sister a prim look. "You won't be able to see once I put the lid on it—like this," she explained as she dropped another slice of bread on top and pushed it down with the heel of her hand. "It's just nice and thick."

"And disgusting," Patricia added under her breath as Lucy handed the creation to Susan. Susan managed not to laugh as she eyed the sandwich. "I think I'd better eat this over the sink."

Patricia made a face. "I don't think you should eat it at all."

Susan had so much peanut better stuck to the roof of her mouth that she couldn't come to Lucy's defense, but Little Miss Chisholm skipped off, totally unconcerned by her sister's comments as she sang, "Yummy in your tummy."

"It's 'I'm rumbly in my tumbly,'" corrected Patricia. "And it's from *Winnie the Pooh*."

This time it was Lucy who rolled her eyes, but with exasperation. "I know that, Patricia. I'm not stupid, you know."

Susan grinned and winked at Patricia. "She certainly isn't."

Patricia grinned back. "But she certainly is a pain."

The phone rang, and with her mouth mortared shut with peanut butter, Susan motioned for Patricia to answer it. She was so busy scraping grape jelly off the front of her T-shirt that she didn't pay much attention to the conversation until Patricia said, "Just a minute and I'll check with Susan."

As Susan glanced up, the teenager covered the phone with her hand. "It's Mrs. Donaldson. She wants to know if I can baby-sit tonight."

"I don't see why not."

Patricia made an anxious little gesture that forewarned of more to come. "She was going to take the kids over to Drumheller tomorrow to see the new museum—you know, the one with all the dinosaur bones and stuff—and she wants to know if Lucy and I'd like to go with them. And if we can, she wants us to sleep over."

She could tell by the expression in Patricia's eyes that she was dying to go, but Susan also knew the girl felt badly about leaving her alone. Susan wasn't so sure she liked the idea, either. She had been looking forward to a break, not total solitude, but she also knew that Patricia had never been to the recently opened provincial museum and wanted to go in the worst way. Which meant Miss Susan Lynton would have to find something to do to keep her mind occupied. She smiled and waved off Patricia's unspoken concern. "I think that sounds like a great idea. Tell her you'd love to go."

Patricia could barely contain her excitement as she concluded the conversation then hung up the phone. "I can hardly wait," she said, hugging herself. "Dad took us to the Badlands once when I was little and I loved them." Her effervescence faded and she gazed at Susan. "I wish you could come, Susan. I feel awful leaving you all by yourself."

Susan's tone was dry. "Don't worry about it. I could've spent the weekend with Michael and Todd."

The young Chisholm was unconvinced. "Do you hate staying by yourself?"

"If you're asking if I'm afraid to be by myself, no I'm not. In fact there are lots of times I really enjoy it."

Patricia finally grinned and gave Susan a quick hug. "I can wear the new slacks and top you made me."

"What time are they picking you up?"

"At seven." Patricia glanced at the clock. "I'd better g
pack."

"I'll come with you and get Lucy's things ready." Sh
wiped the last of the grape jelly off the counter and drie
her hands. "I'll give you some money for meals."

"I can use my baby-sitting money," she offered self
consciously.

Susan smiled at her and ruffled her newly cropped hai
"You'd better save that for something really important, lik
loud records or hideous posters for your wall."

The teenager flashed her an impish smile. "The *reall*
major stuff."

The house was unbearably quiet after the girls left. Susa
tried to watch TV, but there was nothing on but reruns. Sh
found some photograph albums on the bottom shelf of th
bookcase, but that fascination palled and only made her fee
worse when she came across several old pictures of Eileen
She ended up wandering around, picking this up, straight
ening that until her own fussiness started to get on he
nerves. Feeling oddly unanchored with nothing to do an
nobody around, she decided to walk down to the barn an
check on the foal.

The sky had changed from a dull oppressive gray to sin
ister shades of blue, and the dark billowing thundercloud
were now streaked with white. The rustling of the leave
forewarned of a storm, and the lyric song of a lone robi
heralded its approach, its melody an omen of rain. Dudley
looking somewhat woeful, came from around the house an
beseeched her with a hangdog look. She rubbed his head
her fingers buried in his fur. "So you're lonely, too, ar
you?" She straightened and patted her thigh, inviting hi
along. "Come on, then. You can come along with me."

The foal and its mother were in one of the large corral
beside the barn, and Susan hung over the top rail an
watched them, fascinated that something so young could b
so steady on its feet. A gust of wind sent dried leaves flur
rying along the ground, and the mare nervously tossed he

head and moved to shelter the colt. The bay stood with her head high, her ears pricked, and Susan decided the horse knew something she didn't. Motivated by the adage that it's better to be safe than sorry, she led the mare, followed closely by the foal, into their box stall in the barn.

Breezy trotted over and nuzzled Susan's pockets as she pulled the huge barn door closed. Susan grinned and stroked the horse's nose. "You don't get handouts for looking cute, girl." A speculative look appeared in her eyes as she slowly ran her hand down the horse's neck. She hadn't been riding for days.

The inside of the huge arena was illuminated by an eerie luminescence from the skylights, but the high corners were left in murky shadows, providing concealment for a flock of wrens. They fluttered and chirped as Susan partially closed the door, and Breezy shied, startled by the sudden movement. Talking softly to the horse, Susan switched on the rows of overhead lights then led the mare to the center of the arena. Dudley thoroughly inspected the place, then sat by the door, his head cocked to one side as he watched her. She tightened the cinch, then gathered up the reins, put her foot in the stirrup and swung into the saddle.

Susan rode for more than an hour, practicing the reining techniques Jason had showed her, exhilarated by a sense of power as the horse responded to her signals. Her body was damp with perspiration, her face flushed, as she cued the horse into a canter and took her through a series of flying lead changes that were as smooth as silk. Elated by her success, Susan could barely contain her delight as she rounded the corner.

"Very nice," came a voice from the door.

If it hadn't been for her unconscious will to survive, Susan would have fallen off right there and then, but somehow she managed to stay in the saddle as she circled the horse and checked her to a stop.

Her pulse went crazy, and she felt as though she'd just been tossed into thin air. Jason Chisholm stood in the partially open doorway, his shoulder braced against the frame, his thumbs hooked in his belt loops, a grin creasing his face. "You're turning into a regular Annie Oakley."

"Don't get cute, or I'll run you over."

He straightened as she rode toward him, and he reached up and pulled the reins from around the horse's neck as Susan dismounted. "How come you're back early? I didn't think you were planning on coming home until Sunday."

"Once we got the brood mares we wanted, we couldn't see the point of staying on." He grinned and shook his head. "And even I can only look at so many horses." He patted Breezy on the neck and glanced at Susan with approval. "You had her working really well. She's inclined to be lazy if she can get away with it."

Susan gave him a rueful look. "Let's face it. I'm learning more from her than she is from me." She ran her hand down the mare's damp chest then looked up at him. "Maybe I should walk her out a bit, Jase. She's pretty hot."

"We can put her on the hot walker for a while." He opened the door wider and waited for the horse and Susan to go through, then closed and latched it. "Are the mare and foal in the pasture or are they in the barn?"

"In the barn. She was acting uneasy when I came down so I thought I'd better put her in." The breeze blew hair across Susan's face, and she brushed it back as she looked at him. "How did Mattie manage the trip?"

He shrugged and smiled. "Fine, I guess. She's having such a good time, she decided to stay for a few more days and fly back." Jason changed the reins to his other hand as they started walking across the yard. "Where is everybody?"

Susan went hot and cold as that innocent question hit home, and suddenly her knees didn't want to work. She drew in a slow, measured breath, and studiously avoiding his gaze, she answered him. "Walt and Clayton decided to go fishing, and Tricia and Lucy are over at the Donaldsons'. They're going to Drumheller with them tomorrow."

He didn't say anything for the longest time, and she could not bring herself to look at him. There was not another living soul on the place, all his kids were gone and she fully understood the significance of what that meant; his most crucial deterrents were no longer there. And, she realized with a sudden shock, neither were hers. Those times she had been able to walk away from the very real need he aroused in her were no accident. They had been because both of them possessed a strong sense of responsibility, not only for what might happen, but because of the kids. The last thing Susan wanted was for one of Jason's family, especially one of his children, to find them in bed together. Now that concern had been removed.

Jason's voice was terse. "You'd better go back to the house before that storm hits. I'll finish up here."

She finally looked at him, acutely disturbed by both her thoughts and him. "Jason, I—"

"Just go, Susan," he interjected gruffly.

She stared at him a moment, then turned away, her movements stiff and unnatural as she walked toward the path that led through the trees. But with every step, she was more tied to him than with the one before. And she could feel him watching her, as though he was mentally reaching out to her with a consuming hunger. Her body grew heavy with a heated languor, her strength sapped by her desperate need to feel him against her. There was more than a thunderstorm building...much more.

By the time Susan reached the house, her heart was hammering so frantically she felt as if she'd run five miles. Feeling strangely light-headed, she went into the kitchen and closed her eyes as she sagged against the fridge, trying to battle the wild anticipation that was pulsating through her. The only thing she could think of was that she and Jason were utterly alone with a sexual tension that was slowly overpowering them both. Just the thought of what it would feel like to have him moving against her, his mouth hot and demanding, paralyzed her with excitement.

She groaned softly and turned, pressing her flushed face against the cool appliance, wondering desperately how she was going to be able to endure the pressure that was growing thick and heavy in her groin.

It seemed like an eternity passed before she heard him enter the porch and she turned toward the counter, her body beginning to tremble as she grasped the rim of the sink. Somehow she found the strength to face him when he finally entered the room.

He glanced at her, then looked away, his face like granite, the muscles in his jaw rigid.

Her voice didn't sound like her own when she asked, "Would you like some supper?"

Without looking at her, he shook his head, his manner abrupt. "No thanks. We stopped on the way." There was a charged silence and the tension rose to a nearly intolerable level before he spoke again, his tone harsh. "I shouldn't even be in here."

Susan felt the color leave her face as she stared at him, wanting to turn away, but so shaken she was incapable of moving. She closed her eyes, trying to inhale past the sudden unbearable pain in her chest. When she opened them again, Jason was standing at the window, his arm braced against his frame, his back to her. As she watched him, his hand curled into a tight fist against the oak trim.

She longed to go to him, ached to run her hands over his body, to lose herself in his arms, but instead, she whispered brokenly, "I'm not going to pressure you, Jason. It has to be your decision."

He turned slowly, his face carved by strain, his eyes dark and haunted as he stared at her. The tension between them mounted, their common need so powerful, so desperate that their battle for restraint had created an invisible barrier between them.

Susan was aware of nothing but him and the hot, throbbing clamor he was arousing in her body. Her breathing was suddenly erratic, her legs so weak she could barely stand.

Clenching his jaw, Jason came toward her as though compelled by forces beyond his control, his eyes welded on her, immobilizing her. His hand was unsteady as he touched her face, then slowly so slowly, brushed back a strand of hair. "God," he said, his voice a tortured whisper, "do you think I could leave you now?" And for a moment longer he simply stared at her, then hauling in a ragged breath, he gathered her against him.

A low sob was driven from her, the galvanizing shock of pleasure so intense that it drove the air out of her and set her trembling even more violently. As their bodies fused together, a shudder coursed through him, and he whispered her name over and over. A hoarse sound was wrung from him as he moved against her, arousing her to a mindless frenzy, her body responding to the erotic, thrusting rhythm of his. One arm was around her hips, locking them together as the tempo became more urgent, and with a low groan, he roughly caught her head, covering her mouth with a kiss that annihilated what little conscious thought she had. Their mouths moved frantically, hot and searching, famished for the nourishment to satisfy their hunger.

Susan moaned a protest as he dragged his head away and forced her face against his neck, his chest heaving as he fought to hang on to some rationality. She twisted against him, her movement tormenting him, his hold on her tightening as he whispered gruffly into her ear. "Don't, Sue, I can't think....

"God, I want you...."

He roughly stroked her head, his hand tangling in her hair, his tone so filled with emotion that his voice broke under the strain. "Shh, love. It's happening too fast. Not like that—not here." He slowly smoothed his hand across her hips and up her back, trying to soothe her, trying to regain some control.

The frantic beat of her heart echoed in her head as she closed her eyes and hung on to him, sure she would crumple to the floor if he let her go. The movement of his hand stilled and he enfolded her in a tight embrace. Susan thought of nothing but the secure feeling of his arms around her, the hardness of his body against hers, the warmth of his breath on her neck, and eventually the delirium eased. Finally she was able to relax against him.

He stroked her back once more as he kissed her softly on the neck, then without looking at her, he released his hold and caught her hand. ''Come on,'' he said softly, and turned toward the door.

Feeling unbearably bereft without his strength and warmth, she leaned against him, and he put his arm around her shoulders, cradling her to him as they went down the dim hallway.

As they turned into the room and her bed came into view, a current of anticipation shot through her, making her breath catch, robbing her of the power to move. Sensing what she was feeling, Jason encircled her with his arms, supporting her as she swayed. Her breathing was labored as she whispered jaggedly, ''I can't stand this any longer, Jase. I need you now.''

He inhaled sharply, his heart beating frantically under her palm as he took her face between his hands, his own a study of rigidly controlled emotion. As if recognizing her barely coherent state, he tightened his hold on her, his tone so tormented it was hardly recognizable. ''Sue, I have no way of protecting you. You know we're taking chances.''

A wild excitement coursed through her and her eyes drifted shut, her lips parting as heated sensations overcame her, then she forced her eyes open, her gaze fevered. ''No we aren't. It's all right,'' she managed to whisper.

His breathing was suddenly erratic. ''I'll be careful, Sue. I promise.''

She twisted her head against his restraining hands, a sudden irrational panic sweeping over her. ''Don't. God, don't be careful. I need to feel you in me, I need—''

But he never gave her a chance to finish. Her words shattered his control and he pulled her to him, his kiss hot and demanding as he ground his body against hers. He made a low agonized sound as she responded and her mouth went slack beneath his, yielding him everything. There was no turning back.

Nearly out of her mind with desire, Susan mutely watched as he stripped off their clothing, pulled her down on the bed and dragged her beneath him. His weight on top of her, his mouth moving almost savagely against hers, his arms crushing her, were impelling a frantic need in her that only he could assuage, and she wrapped her legs around him, drawing him into her. He shuddered, fighting for control, struggling for tenderness, but the moment she moved beneath him, the struggle was lost, and their bodies were caught in a driving rhythm.

And there was a resounding crack of thunder overhead as the storm finally broke and the rain came down, soaking a parched earth, cloaking the sounds of the climax of another storm.

CHAPTER TEN

THE WIND LASHED THE RAIN against the windows, whipping the branches of a tree against the house as the storm hit with all its fury. But inside, all that remained of the storm of passion was a heavy, sated afterglow.

Filled with a dreamy lassitude, Susan slowly stroked Jason's naked back, quietly savoring the intimacy of their united bodies and the weight of him upon her. It was a long time before either of them had the strength or desire to move, but finally Jason stirred, and bracing his arms on either side of her head, he raised his shoulders and gazed down at her. He smiled softly, knowingly, then slowly stroked her cheek as he kissed away the tears that glimmered in her eyelashes. "God, but I do love you, Susan Lynton," he whispered.

His gently spoken declaration moved her beyond words, and her eyes brimmed anew as she gazed up at him, loving him so much that she felt as if she couldn't contain it all. She smoothed her hand up the back of his neck, relishing the silky texture of his hair as she slowly ran her fingers through it. "I didn't think I was ever going to wring that out of you," she responded softly.

The Chisholm dimple appeared and an irresistible gleam sparkled in his eyes. "I'd say you wrung it out of me very...forcefully," he responded, his voice even huskier than before.

His suggestive comment caught her by surprise, and she gave a shout of laughter, a telltale flush creeping up her cheeks. "Jason Chisholm, you surprise me."

He grinned down at her. "I surprise myself."

Susan laughed and looped her arms around his back, then whispered provocatively, "Well, you were certainly well worth the wait."

The laughter faced from his eyes, and his expression grew solemn and intense as he slowly combed his fingers through her tousled hair. "So were you."

He gazed down at her for a moment, then lowered his head and kissed her, his mouth pliant and moist against hers. Susan tightened her arms around his shoulders, losing herself in the infinite gentleness of his caress. It was a long, softly searching kiss that filled Susan with a satisfied warmth.

Jason exhaled softly and raised his head, a hint of reluctance in his eyes. Without saying anything, he started to ease his weight from her. Susan tightened her hold, her voice like velvet as she whispered, "Don't go."

He smoothed back wisps of her hair, his eyes smoky, his expression tender. "I'm too heavy, Susan."

She smiled as she caressed the back of his neck. "I can manage."

His eyes lightened as he laughed, then he lowered his head and gave her a quick kiss. "So you keep telling me."

Her mood grew serious as she gazed up at him. "I wish you'd start believing it."

He slid his fingers under her head, the heels of his hands resting against her jaw as he watched her. He didn't say anything for the longest time, then finally he spoke, his voice quiet. "Doesn't the age difference bother you even a little?"

Susan smiled and shook her head. "Not even a little. I like being with you. I like what you are and what you do and how you think. You give me a sense of rightness I've never had before, and I want to hang on to that."

"But it won't be just the two of us," he quietly pointed out. "I'd feel so damned guilty loading you down with so much."

A sparkle of mischief appeared in her eyes as she suddenly grinned. "Now see, there's where my age *is* an advantage. I'm old enough to handle the responsibility, but I'm young enough to adapt." Her teasing look became more serious as she gently stroked his cheek. "And I *can* adapt, Jase." She smoothed her fingers across his mouth, her expression becoming even more earnest. "And I know you're worried about having more kids. But I honestly think that's something we can deal with later. I may decide I *don't* want to start a second family, you may decide that you *do*. But I know it's something we can work out. We can work anything out as long as we're open with each other."

His hold on her face tightened as he held her gaze, his eyes kindling with emotion. His voice wasn't quite steady when he whispered, "You shook me up so damned bad the first time I saw you. I never expected to have anybody affect me the way you did, and there you were, so full of vitality, with the wind in your hair and eyes that seemed to swallow me up. And I knew if I allowed one crack in my defenses, I was in big trouble."

Susan blinked back tears and lightly touched his mouth. "Why?" she asked softly.

He swallowed hard and looked away, his face lined with strain. "Because I knew I could end up needing you more than I ever dreamed of needing anything or anyone. Because you could become my White Dove."

Catching his face, she forced him to turn his head and look at her. Tears slipped down her temples and into her hair as she gazed up at him, her heart in her eyes. "Then you know exactly how I feel about you, Jason Chisholm."

He roughly whispered her name as he slipped his arms around her, his feelings overpowering him as he found her mouth with a fierce kiss, the urgency of their common need sweeping them into another storm—a storm filled with a savage passion and the ultimate tenderness.

Night settled in and the rain continued to fall, cloaking the countryside in an enveloping hush. There was something about the sound of rain on the roof that added to the sense of seclusion Jason and Susan shared, and they lay together, sequestered in silence and semidarkness. The bedding was a tumble around them, and Jason was lying on his back with Susan cradled half on top of him, her head on his shoulder, one long leg draped across his. He stared into the dark twilight of her room as he slowly stroked her back, listening to the soft rain against the house.

"Jason?"

"Hmm?"

"Are you hungry?"

He laughed and hugged her. "Why do you ask?"

"Because your stomach's growling."

"Just ignore it."

Susan eased out of his hold and reached over to turn on the light by her bed. She squinted slightly as she looked down at him. "Are you hungry?" she repeated in her no-nonsense tone.

"Yes."

She gave him a narrow look. "I thought you said you had supper."

Smoothing his hand up her torso, he grinned up at her, a disarming gleam in his eyes. "I lied."

Susan laughed and gave him a playful push. "Serves you right." Placing her hand beside his head, she leaned over and kissed him, then smiled into his eyes. "If you can haul your lazy body out of my bed, I'll make you something to eat."

He ran his hand slowly up her back, his gaze warm and intimate. "I don't think I have enough strength left to move."

Her eyes were dancing as she asked, "Who are you trying to kid?"

Jason laughed as he rested his arm across her hips. "Let's face it, right now I hardly have enough energy to breathe."

With a light, lingering touch, Susan ran her hand across his abdomen, keenly aware of the hard, well-defined muscles and the athletic build of a man in prime condition. Unable to resist tormenting him just a little, she said, her sparkle of amusement turning to one of sheer mischief, "For a man your age, you've certainly shown considerable stamina."

He was laughing as he caught her and effortlessly rolled her beneath him. "Lord, you do ask for it, don't you?"

She grinned and draped her arms around his neck. "Only sometimes."

The laughter in his eyes softened as he gazed down at her, his expression becoming intent, as if he were trying to absorb every detail of her. His voice was low as he said softly, "Will you marry me?"

His question was so unexpected that it stopped her cold, and she stared up at him, almost disbelieving.

The laugh lines around his eyes creased as he gave her a crooked smile. "Well, will you?"

Her heart was hammering as an incredible feeling of anticipation surged in her. Her voice seemed to come from a long way off when she was finally able to speak. "Are you sure?"

His expression was soft and intimate. "Just say yes, Susan."

She stared up at him an instant longer, then hugged him fiercely, laughing and crying at the same time. "Yes! God, yes."

He tightened his arms around her, his face pressed against her neck. "I'll do my damnedest to make you happy."

Susan closed her eyes, her joy giving her new strength as she clung to him, her voice shaky. "You can't possibly make me any happier than I am right now."

He took a deep unsteady breath then eased away from her, his eyes dark and serious, his expression revealing a profound vulnerability. "I don't want you to ever regret this, Sue," he whispered, his voice rough with emotion. "I don't think I could handle that."

She touched his mouth with her fingertips, her eyes glistening with happiness. "Never, Jason," she promised softly. "You're stuck with me for the rest of your life."

There was an inflexible set to his face, as though he were struggling for control, and the muscle in his jaw flexed as he inhaled sharply, then covered her mouth with his. There was such a wealth of feeling and tenderness in that kiss that it brought new tears to Susan's eyes, and they slipped out from beneath her lashes. With immeasurable gentleness, Jason twined his fingers in her hair. As if surfacing from a long, deep dive, he hauled in a ragged breath as he slowly withdrew.

He gave her another soft, fleeting kiss, then reluctantly raised his head and gazed down at her. "So, Susan Lynton," he murmured softly, "the die is cast."

There was something about the way he said it that made her smile. "You don't need to make it sound as though you're going to jail, you know," she said in a slightly chastising tone.

He grinned and a tormenting gleam appeared in his eyes. "I guess I'm going to find out if Tyler called it right—about you being a handful to train."

"Tread lightly, Jason," she warned. "Or you could find yourself in a pile of trouble."

As if unable to resist, he kissed her again. "I already am."

"You tell such lies."

He gave a low throaty laugh as he lightly brushed his lips against hers. "When it serves a purpose."

She caught his head and made him meet her gaze. "Speaking of lying... Since you lied about having supper, I suppose you expect me to make you something to eat."

"More or less."

She laughed and pushed him away. "No wonder you're an only child."

Rolling onto his back, Jason grinned and laced his hands behind his head as he attentively watched Susan swing her long legs over the edge of the bed and slip into the beach cover-up she'd worn the night he'd told her about Michael. "An outfit like that should never be allowed past the bedroom door," he murmured huskily, the light in his eyes more than just amusement.

Susan belted it tightly around her waist as she gave him a pointed look. "You're too tired to move, remember?"

Turning on his side, he propped his head on his hand, his eyes flashing. "If you persist in wearing that, exhaustion could become a nearly permanent condition."

Laughing softly, she dropped his jeans on the bed beside him, then bent over and gave him a quick kiss. "I'll remember that. Maybe I'll get six more just like it."

He caught her head, his mouth moving with tormenting lightness against hers. "Why don't you say to hell with supper and come back to bed?" he whispered gruffly.

The familiar flutter of excitement unfolded in her chest, making it hard to breathe, and her voice wasn't quite steady as she murmured, "And have you complaining that I don't feed you?"

"Be nice, Susan."

"I'm trying to be."

"You're not trying hard enough."

That made her laugh, and she kissed him firmly then pulled away. There was a wicked gleam in her eyes as she slanted a deliberately provocative look down at him. "Well, well, Jason. Maybe older *is* better."

He grinned and gave her a firm slap on her bottom. "Don't get sassy."

"Watch it, Jason," she warned, then smoothed her hand across his muscled shoulder. "Come on. I'll make you an omelet and you can tell me about the horse sale."

Susan prepared his meal, then sat kitty-corner across the table from him, her chin in her hand as she watched him eat. It was an ordinary scene, but there was something very intimate about sharing a late supper on a rainy night, knowing they were completely alone in the big old house.

Jason had put on only his jeans, and his darkly tanned

kin was the color of bronze under the kitchen light, and
Susan could not resist the sudden need to touch him. She
lowly smoothed her hand up his bare arm and across his
houlder, her voice a little husky as she asked, "Would you
ike another coffee?"

Jason pushed his plate away, then slid his chair back from
he table. "No, I don't want another coffee," he answered,
is own voice gruff as he caught her around the waist and
ulled her onto his lap. She turned, straddling his legs with
ers, her heart pounding frantically as he brushed back the
abric of her cover-up. "What I want is to take you back to
ed."

Looping her arms around his neck, Susan closed her eyes
nd tipped her head back as he slowly ran his hand up her
pine, pressing her against him. The touch was galvanizing
s he gently traced the hollow of her throat with his moist
nouth, sending a current of ice and fire through her veins,
nd she made a low sound as she grasped his head, holding
im tightly to her. Desire caught them in its undertow, pull-
ng them into a vortex of intoxicating sensations as he con-
inued to explore her skin thirstily, throwing her mind into
senseless spin. And she was aware of nothing but his lips
gainst her flesh—

"Daddy!"

Jason jerked upright and Susan's eyes flew open, her ex-
ression frozen as cold horror shot through her. She clutched
he front of her housecoat as Jason roughly hoisted her to
er feet and jerked his arms away.

Patricia was standing in the doorway, her body rigid, a
ook of repulsion on her ashen face. It was evident that she'd
een far too much, and was both humiliated and revolted.

Susan wanted to die. But she somehow managed to blurt
ut, her voice sharp with alarm, "Patricia! What are you
oing here?"

Patricia looked at her with cold eyes, her face taut with
isgust. "Mrs. Donaldson decided not to go tomorrow be-

cause of the rain. So I asked Mr. Donaldson to bring me home so *you* wouldn't be alone."

Jason brushed past Susan and caught his daughter by the shoulders, his manner desperate. "It's not what it seems, Patricia. Let me explain—"

Patricia twisted out of her father's hands, tears of disillusionment glittering in her eyes. "Don't touch me, Daddy!" she choked out. "I'm not a baby! You don't have to explain anything! You talk about principles and morals, and what's right and what's wrong, and you're no better than one of your horses." She turned and confronted Susan, her whole body shaking. "What's the matter, Susan? Are you in season?"

Her nearly hysterical outburst stunned them, and for one awful moment, Susan thought she was going to be sick. It didn't take a genius to realize that Patricia's innocence had been violated by what she saw as a crude display of sexual promiscuity, but what made it a thousand times worse was that it had been violated by two people whom she had trusted. Guilt and humiliation hit Susan with a numbing force.

Her face was as white as Patricia's, and she was trembling just as badly when she went over to the girl. She was about to touch her hair, but realizing physical contact would simply repel the child more, she reluctantly withdrew her hand and folded her arms tightly in front of her. "I'm so sorry, Patricia," she whispered brokenly. "We can't make any excuses for ourselves, but it's not like you think. I care a lot about your dad."

Patricia finally looked up at her, her eyes flashing with condemnation, her face wet with angry tears. "Oh, come off it, Susan. All you care about is that he's a man! You're as bad as my mother!" And on a choked sob, she turned and fled from the room.

Jason jerked as though he'd been shot, the full meaning of her words stunning him, and he riveted his eyes on Susan, his face gray from sickening comprehension. For one brief

econd, they stared at each other, horrified. Jason swore and
losed his eyes in a grimace of repugnance as he slammed
is hand against the doorframe. He swore again, his ex-
ression filled with self-recrimination as he turned and went
fter his daughter.

Susan weakly sank into a chair, clutching her arms around
er abdomen as the full impact hit her, leaving her trembling
o violently it was impossible to stand. Knowing what Pa-
icia had witnessed when she walked through that door
ade Susan's whole body go hot with mortification. But
hat made it even more sordid was that Patricia had evi-
ently stumbled on something like this once before with her
other. It disgusted Susan beyond words to be cast in the
ame mold as Eileen, but she deserved it. Lord, did she
eserve it.

It was a long time before Susan moved, and when she
id, she was chilled by the aftermath of shock. She moved
iffly as she stood up, and still clutching her housecoat
ound her, crept to her room. With shaking hands, she
ripped off the garment with a shudder of disgust and
ulled on some clothes, then went numbly back to the
itchen. The initial shock was wearing off, and she sat back
own at the table. Resting her elbows on the top, she closed
er eyes and covered her face with her hands, but try as she
ight, she could not will the trembling to stop.

She was still sitting like that when Jason came into the
tchen, and she raised her head when she heard him enter.
e looked as if he had aged twenty years. "What did she
y?"

He came over and sat down, his expression bleak. "She's
etty upset."

Susan gave him a grim smile. "By the sounds of it, she
s every right to be."

He stared at her a minute then looked down, his face
ddenly like granite. "Yes, she does."

"Did she tell you about her mother?" Jason didn't answer and Susan watched him closely, her expression intent. "Jason?"

Finally he raised his head and looked at her, his voice very controlled. "Apparently she'd caught her mother twice with a man." He added bitterly, "Actually, with two different men, for God's sake. And the kid wasn't even seven years old."

"Why didn't she ever say anything about it before?"

Self-disgust made his voice harsh. "Because she knew what her mother did was wrong and she didn't want to upset me."

Susan looked away, feeling more horrible with each passing minute. There was a heavy silence, then Jason spoke, his voice expressionless. "I tried to reason with her, to explain how I felt about you, but she wouldn't listen. I told her we planned on getting married, but in her eyes, that didn't change anything."

A huge knot tightened her insides as Susan riveted her attention on him. "What did she say?"

Jason avoided her eyes. "Not much."

She got a funny churning feeling in the pit of her stomach as she pressed him. "What did she say, Jason?"

He stared at her for what seemed like a never-ending length of time, then forced a grim smile. "She said it should be an interesting breeding program."

For the second time that night, Susan thought she was going to be sick, and she groaned in despair as she stood up and abruptly turned away. It was becoming more revolting with each passing moment, and they had nobody to blame but themselves.

Feeling suddenly cold, she tightly folded her arms across her chest, her face ashen as she went to stand in front of the window. Her reflection confronted her in the darkened panes, and she shuddered and turned away. Her voice was expressionless when she finally spoke. "I can understand how she feels. I would've felt exactly the same way if I' caught my father and someone I really looked up to in the same...explicit situation.''

Jason didn't raise his head. ''It isn't your fault. I should have known better,'' he said flatly.

Susan stared at his rigid profile, a feeling of dread uncoiling in her. She was not imagining it; there was a sudden remoteness about him, as though he had completely withdrawn from her. Her heart was in her throat as she said softly, ''Jason?''

He refused to look at her. ''What?''

''Maybe I should go talk to her.''

''She doesn't want to talk to anybody.''

''Look at me, Jason,'' she pleaded softly.

She saw the muscles in his jaw work, then he roughly shoved the chair away from the table and stood up, self-contempt etched in every line in his face. His voice was low and seething as he spat out, ''For God's sake, Susan, she can't stand the sight of either one of us.'' His self-contempt turned to fury, and he flung the chair across the room, his eyes flashing in disgust. ''What in hell kind of parent am I? My God, it was like walking in on some damned X-rated movie!''

A cold sinking sensation made her shiver again, and Susan stared at him. She knew, with a chilling certainty, that whatever hopes and dreams she and Jason might have shared had been shot to smithereens the minute that child walked in the door. A jarring silence stretched out between them, and Susan closed her eyes, fighting to control the panicky feeling that gripped her as the inescapable reality hit home. She had only one choice before her, and the inevitability of that choice terrified her. How could she ever follow through? But she did, and her voice was devoid of all emotion when she finally spoke. ''I think it would be best if I went back to Ottawa.''

There was a long agonizing silence, then there was the sound of the chair being picked up. She knew if he came within two feet of her, she'd fall apart, and she turned to face him. But he was not anywhere near her. He was standing by the door leading into the hallway, his back to her, his head bent. His right arm was braced against the frame, and there was a rigid set to his shoulders. His hand curled into a white-knuckled fist as he spoke, his voice expressionless. "We'll make arrangements tomorrow." And with that, he straightened and resolutely walked away, severing whatever remaining hope Susan might have had.

It was finished. And there was nothing she could do about it.

IT WAS STILL DRIZZLING the following morning, the sky heavy and overcast. Susan had been unable to sleep after the disturbing episode with Patricia, and by nine o'clock in the morning, she was functioning in a gray vacuum. She hadn't seen Jason, but when she went into the kitchen after her shower, she found a note on the table saying he'd gone to pick up Lucy, who was still at the Donaldsons'. She went through the motions of making a pot of coffee, then started to make a list of groceries, but wadded it up and threw it in the garbage when she realized she wouldn't be around to get them.

She was sitting at the kitchen table with her head in her hands when there was a sound behind her, and she turned. Patricia was standing there, her body stiff, her pale face pinched from too much crying and too little sleep. Susan experienced the bitter taste of self-contempt for hurting her for mortifying her the way she had.

She clasped her hands tightly together, her face suddenly drawn as she met the girl's unwavering stare. "Good morning, Patricia."

"Where did Dad go?"

She thought she caught a hint of panic in the girl's voice and she frowned slightly as she handed her the note. "He' gone to pick up Lucy."

The stiffness in Patricia seemed to dissolve, and there wa no question about the flash of relief in her eyes. A horribl thought crossed Susan's mind, leaving her feeling slightly ill. "You said something to your mother once, didn't you Trish?" she asked quietly. Patricia didn't respond, but Susan could tell by the way the girl flinched that she was right. "Just because you said something to your mother and she left, doesn't mean the same thing's going to happen with your dad, Patricia," she explained gently. "He'd never ever leave you, no matter what."

Patricia abruptly turned away, but Susan saw her wipe her eyes, and there was an unyielding set to her shoulders as she walked into the porch. Without even asking, Susan knew the girl was going to stand at that door, keeping an anxious vigil until her father came back home.

Jason returned about a half hour later, and Susan went to the door when she heard his truck pull up outside. Lucy came dancing into the porch ahead of him, chattering away about her sleep over. As they entered, Susan caught a glimpse of Patricia's face, and her heart went out to the child. She was so white and so scared.

Jason kept the screen door from slamming behind him as he focused his full attention on his elder daughter, his eyes tormented by guilt. Patricia tried to say something then covered her face with her hands, and with his own face twisted with remorse, he cradled her head against his chest. Taking Lucy by the hand, Susan tried to fight down a suffocating tightness as she numbly led the little girl into the kitchen.

It was several moments later when he finally appeared in the doorway, Patricia shadowing him. "Clayton and Walter pulled in just as I was leaving," he said, his tone hollow. "I thought I'd better let you know I've talked to him already."

Susan nodded and looked away. Jason stared at her for a second, his expression inflexible, then he turned and followed Patricia into the main house.

Susan made Lucy a batch of play dough, and the littlest Chisholm stayed at the kitchen table playing with her toy dishes, talking under her breath to a host of imaginary companions. She was so involved that she didn't even look up when her Uncle Clayton came into the room a few minutes later.

He looked at Susan, then glanced at the child, a frown creasing his face as he swung his attention back to Susan. "Would you mind," he said quietly, "telling me what in hell is going on?"

Susan continued to unload the dishwasher, deliberately avoiding his gaze. "What did Jason tell you?"

"Not a damned thing, except that you'd be leaving within the next few days."

Susan sidestepped his obvious concern. "Isn't that what you wanted?"

He came over to her and caught her by the shoulder, forcing her to look at him. "It isn't when you look the way you do. What in hell happened?"

She shrugged and looked away. "Let's just say that Jason and I both decided it would be best if I left as soon as possible." Schooling her face into an impassive expression, she finally turned to face him. "Can you find someone to take over for me?"

His frown deepened as he stared at her, trying to read her expression. He sighed and nodded. "Yes, I can. In fact, I spoke to Mrs. Cook a while ago to see if she'd consider giving Mattie a hand after you left."

"Will you see if she can come now?"

He nodded. "If that's what you want."

She finished putting away the cutlery then ran her fingernail along a crack in the drawer as she continued, her face taut, "I need you to give me a cover, Clayton," she said, her voice strained. "I want everybody to think that something urgent has come up and you need me back in Ottawa right away."

He was watching her intently, his eyes narrowed in speculation. A few moments passed before he capitulated. "I'll take care of it," he answered in businesslike tones. "No one will be the wiser. When do you want to leave?"

"First thing Monday morning."

His frowned deepened. "Today's Saturday. Is that going to give you enough time?"

She nodded.

He sighed and dragged his hand across his face in a weary gesture. "Okay. If that's what you want."

Susan thanked him with a lifeless smile. Clayton cupped his hand along her face and gave her head a little shake. "I never wanted to see you get hurt, Sue. I hope you believe that."

She turned away and folded her arms in front of her. "I know that."

He continued to study her for a moment, his eyes dark with compassion, then he patted her on the back. "I'll take care of the details right now."

Susan stood rigidly in front of the sink until she heard him leave, then bracing herself for the coming ordeal, she went into the main house and slowly climbed the stairs to Patricia's room.

The teenager was lying on her bed, staring at the ceiling when Susan entered. She took one look at Susan and turned her back on her, her voice choked with tears. "I suppose you're here to tell me how much you want to be my new mother."

Susan stared down at her, her expression stark. "No, Patricia," she answered quietly, "I'm not. But I am here to tell you that your dad and I decided it would be best if I left."

There was a tense silence, and Patricia finally turned to look at her, a strange expression in her eyes. There was a tenor of uncertainty in her voice, as though she didn't quite believe what Susan had said. "You're leaving?"

"Yes. Monday."

Patricia picked up a stuffed animal and began twisting the ribbon around its neck. "Last night Daddy said you were going to get married."

Susan's face remained impassive. "We've changed our minds."

"Are you going to tell everybody it's because of me?"

The pain in Susan's chest was intensifying, and her voice broke. "It isn't because of you. There are things you don't know about. And besides, I have to go back to work." She stared out the window, trying to will away the blur of tears, hating herself for hurting this child the way she had, wanting desperately to make things right. "Don't blame your dad for what happened, Trish," she added softly. "It wasn't his fault. It was mine." Knowing she was going to lose control any minute, she turned toward the door. "But I do want you to know that I'm going to miss you a lot," she whispered, then left the room, quietly closing the door behind her. Shutting her eyes against the hurt, she clenched her teeth as tears spilled over, then choking back the aching need to cry, she slipped soundlessly down the stairs, desperate to get to the sanctuary of her room.

And behind the closed door, Patricia threw herself face-down on the bed and buried her head in her pillow, trying valiantly to muffle her sobs.

SEPARATED BY AN EVER-WIDENING GULF of guilt and shame, Jason and Susan carefully avoided each other for the rest of the day. The ball tournament was canceled because of rain, and by supper the boys were home. It was then, with everyone gathered around the table, that Clayton announced that something urgent had come up and Susan was going to have to go back to Ottawa. The dismayed reaction made things considerably worse, and the strain became unendurable. But it wasn't until that night, when Clayton heard back from Mrs. Cook, that Susan finally had to face Jason alone.

She found him in his bedroom, sitting at a huge desk, a clutter of papers spread out before him, a calculator by his elbow. She paused at the door and leaned against the jamb, dreading this confrontation. "Jason?"

He hesitated for a split second, then inhaling slowly, he

looked up. Susan felt as though every speck of color had drained from her face, and she found it almost impossible to speak. "Clayton went over to see Mrs. Cook about taking over the housekeeping. She'll take the job."

He looked away, the muscle in his jaw twitching. "Did he tell her when he wanted her to start?"

"She's coming tomorrow. With Mattie gone, I thought I'd better show her around before I leave Monday."

There was a strained silence as he toyed with a box of paper clips. "You don't have to leave that fast."

Susan was struggling to swallow the painful lump in her throat, and her voice was nearly inaudible when she answered, "I thought it would be best."

He didn't say anything. He just sat there, refusing to look at her, his face like stone.

She swallowed again. "Don't let this happen, Jason. Tell me not to go."

He shuddered and turned away, his shoulders rigid as he buried his head in his hands, his voice a ragged whisper. "God, I can't…"

Susan stared at his back, filled with an agony that seemed to consume her, and for an instant she almost hated him. Fighting for composure, she straightened and walked away, feeling as though half of her had just died.

Sunday was a nightmare from start to finish. Mattie phone and Susan had little choice but to tell her she was leaving. The older woman was so upset about her unexpected departure that finally Clayton had to talk to her. And the boys were impossible. They blamed Susan's leaving on their Uncle Clayton, and Todd was sullen while Michael was out-and-out obnoxious. Lucy, true to her dramatic flare, was a study of absolute misery. Patricia, on the other hand, avoided Susan as though she had the plague. And by mid-afternoon, Susan was beginning to wonder if Monday morning would ever come.

But it did. And the first rays of dawn seeped into Susan's bedroom, casting slivers of light across the quilt. The bed had not been slept in, and two large suitcases lay open upon it, their contents neatly packed. Susan stood staring out the window, watching the vivid colors of the sunrise, her exhaustion numbing her. Now if only it would last, that enveloping numbness. If only it would last.

But when it finally came time to say goodbye, it was the hardest thing she'd ever had to do. She managed, somehow, to get through breakfast without coming undone, but it became especially difficult when it was time for the kids to leave for school. They had fifteen minutes to make it to the road to catch the school bus, and Michael was suddenly in a panic because his father wasn't there to say goodbye to Susan.

Struggling to find the right words, Susan put her arms around his shoulders and hugged him against her. But she didn't know what to say to him. How could she tell this brokenhearted little boy that his father had left at dawn, and wouldn't be back until he was certain that his uncle's executive assistant was gone? She finally crouched in front of him and took his face in her hands. "Hey, Michael, don't worry about it," she said, forcing a smile. "Grown-ups find it really hard to say goodbye."

He was manfully fighting tears. "I don't like it much, either," he whispered, his voice breaking. "I thought you'd stay for the whole summer."

Aware that the four men seated at the table were silently watching, she hung on to her smile as she wiped his tears away. "I thought so, too, but I have to go. I promise I'll write, and I promise I'll get Pete to send you some autographed pictures. And you be sure to write and tell me what's going on here, okay?" The ache in her chest was so intense she couldn't even swallow, and she frantically blinked back tears as she gave him a quick hug and stood up. "Come on. I'll walk you up the lane to meet the bus."

He hung his head and mumbled into his chest as he quickly dragged is hand across his eyes. "Then all the kids on the bus will be watching."

Susan leaned down and kissed him on the temple, her own voice breaking. "Then we'll just say goodbye here."

He slipped his arms around her neck, his wiry body trembling with suppressed sobs. "I'm going to miss you, Susan," he whispered against her neck.

Sinking to her knees, she closed her eyes and crushed him to her, the pain tearing her apart. "I'm going to miss you too, Mikey. So very much."

Without looking at her, he twisted out of her embrace, and with one deep ragged sob, turned and ran out of the house. Todd touched Susan on the shoulder, his face set in the same rigidly controlled lines as his father's. "I'll look after him today, Susan. I will." He, too, slipped his arms around her neck and gave her a hard hug. "It's going to seem so funny without you here," he whispered, and Susan pressed her face against his shoulder, fighting to contain the awful pressure of tears that was choking her. The boy touched her hair, then reluctantly eased out of her embrace. "You'd better say goodbye, Lucy, or we'll miss the bus," he said, his voice quavering.

Lucy slipped into Susan's arms, her expressive face very serious. She laid her small chubby hand on the woman's wet cheek, her eyes dark with sympathy. "Don't cry, Susan," she said softly. "You aren't going to be really gone, 'cause we're going to keep you in our hearts." She gave her a swift kiss, then reluctantly submitted to Todd's tug. It wasn't until they were at the door of the porch that the little one finally gave into tears, and holding on to her brother's hand, turned to take one last glance before she disappeared.

Struggling to contain the emotions that were cutting through her crumbling defenses, Susan slowly stood up, her vision so blurred she could barely see. It wasn't until she turned that she realized Patricia was still standing in the shadows of the porch, her face ashen.

Acting on pure instinct, Susan went over to the girl, and with trembling hands she smoothed down her hair, then kissed her softly on the forehead. "You take good care of your dad,'' she whispered as she gave the teenager a quick hug. She drew in a deep, shaky breath, then gave Patricia a gentle nudge on the shoulder. ''You'd better go, Trish. I hear the school bus coming.'' Brushing away the tears with the back of her hand, she turned away as the screen door slammed shut. Susan went to stand before the kitchen window and watched the four Chisholm children disappear around the hedge, feeling as though she had just lost everything that could ever possibly matter in her life.

CHAPTER ELEVEN

SUSAN SURVIVED her first weeks back in Ottawa through sheer determination. She managed to keep up a carefully maintained front at work, especially after Clayton returned, but the effort cost her a heavy price, and the more she tried to let on nothing was wrong, the more alone she felt, until she fell victim to a kind of desolation from which there was no escape. It was an ordeal to go to work, it was an ordeal to come home, and she didn't want to do anything except to torment herself with old memories. She was aware that Clayton watched her with a growing concern, but nothing really mattered anymore. She was too weighed down by the never-ending emptiness in her life.

The boys and Lucy wrote faithfully, and those letters were her lifeline. The only time there was any lightness in her existence was when she'd arrive home from work, tired beyond words, to find a letter in her mailbox with an Alberta postmark. And for a brief space of time, she'd be back at the Double Diamond, listening to Michael relate about how funny Dudley looked when he tried to chase a flock of birds flying overhead and ran into the corner of the garage, or having Todd confide in her that the Chisholm and Redding boys were holding clandestine rodeos in the back pasture, trying to ride some of Jason's rank steers. And how Lucy had scared her grandmother half to death when Mattie caught little Miss Chisholm pretending to be a circus star on old Riley. And how Patricia had lost more weight and was starting to look like a "real" grown-up, and how Grandma was feeling better.

Susan was so anxious for news, she'd practically devour every word in those letters, though there was precious little about Jason, even in the two Mattie had written. After reading and rereading it, she'd put the latest one with the others in her desk, feeling even more alone than before.

It was the first week in August before she finally received one from Walter. It was laboriously printed on lined paper, carefully detailing what was blooming in the flower beds and solemnly promising he would send some of his Oriental poppie seeds for her mother's garden. There was something unbearably touching about his letter, and she finally broke down and wept, knowing full well what a labor of love it was. Like an enormous wave, her loneliness swept over her with a devastating intensity, and she felt as though the ache in her chest were tearing her in two as she carefully refolded the pages. She had not only lost Jase, she had lost them all, and nothing on earth could ever fill that awful emptiness.

Her face marked by her distress, Susan put the envelope with the others, then went to her room and changed into a pair of shorts. She was just hanging up the outfit she'd worn to work when there was a knock at her door. Sighing heavily she closed the closet door and went to answer it. Because of the security system, it had to be someone from within the apartment complex, which meant it was probably another cheery attempt to drag her out to some stupid pool party. And if it was, she'd scream. She really would.

But it was not one of her neighbors. It was, in fact, Tyler Redding. Sagging against the door, she stared at him, unable to believe her own eyes.

He took off his cowboy hat, his eyes gleaming with a rakish sparkle as he gave her one of his utterly disarming grins. "If I promise to take you out for dinner, will you at least invite me in?"

"How did you get in?" she managed to squeak out as she dazedly let him enter.

His grin broadened. "I sweet-talked a little filly into unlocking the door for me."

Susan finally smiled. "One of these days, you're going to sweet-talk your way into a pile of trouble."

He shrugged with amusement. "So you keep telling me." He turned and carefully set his hat on the table in the hall, then raised his head and looked at her, his expression serious. "I was pretty damned mad when I found out you'd left without even saying goodbye, Sue," he said quietly.

Her expression instantly changed, and she looked away as she tightly clasped her arms in front of her. There was a tense silence, and when she finally spoke, her voice was strained and very low. "I left in rather a hurry."

"I'll say."

His tone was somewhat caustic, and still feeling raw from Walter's letter, she was horrified to find herself on the verge of tears. She started to turn away, but he caught her arm and held her firm. "What happened, Susan?"

She shrugged and tried to pull back, but Tyler ignored her and gathered her into a comforting embrace. One ragged sob escaped her before she could press her face against his shoulder, and he tightened his hold on her as she fought to contain the surge of unhappiness that was threatening to break loose. "Why don't you just tell me what went wrong," he said gently, "and maybe we can put it right. You're miserable and Jason looks bloody awful. The kids talk about you constantly, and as far as Mattie's concerned, Mrs. Cook can't do a damned thing right." He caught her under the chin and forced her to meet his gaze, a determined tone in his voice. "Nobody's happy about this, Sue, and I bloody well intend on finding out why."

Sighing heavily, she pulled out his arms and wiped her face with the back of her hand. "You're going to have to talk to Jason, Tyler."

Annoyance edged his voice. "Do you think I haven't tried? Hell, I doubt if he's said more than ten words to me since you left." He exhaled sharply, then went on, his tone more subdued. "What happened, and why is it such a secret?"

"Tyler, I can't—"

Without giving her a chance to finish, he caught her hand and pulled her over to the sofa. "Sit down, Susan," he said, his tone firm. "It's time we talked." She did as he ordered, her eyes focused on his face as he sat down beside her. He slouched down as he hooked the heel of one boot on the edge of her coffee table, then crossed his other leg on top. He frowned in contemplation then turned to look at her. "I guess I idolized Jason Chisholm for most of my life. He was a top-notch athlete, there wasn't a horse around he couldn't handle, yet he was enough of a hell-raiser to be glamorous to us younger kids."

Tyler folded his arms across his chest and stared thoughtfully at the toes of his boots. "I guess maybe I feel I owe him, and not just because I consider him a friend. I got mixed up in a couple of stupid scrapes when I was seventeen, and it was Jase who bailed me out—without one word to my parents." Tyler finally looked at her, his expression grave. "He's hurting pretty damned bad right now, and I'd like to do something to change that, if I could."

Susan gave him a wry smile. "You didn't have to come all the way to Ottawa to day that, Tyler. You could have phoned."

He grinned lopsidedly. "I had to go to Toronto on business, so I decided on the spur of the moment to make a little side trip."

"Some side trip."

"I wanted to give you hell face-to-face for taking off like you did."

"It seemed like a good idea at the time."

"Why?"

Susan sighed and met his gaze. "I don't think it's my place to say anything, Tyler. I really don't."

He reached out and caught her hand, his voice quiet. "Susan, I would never do or say anything to breach a confidence. If you tell me something, these ears are as far as it's going to go. If I can find out what in hell happened, maybe I can do something to straighten things out.''

She stared at him, considering his offer, then she looked down as she began absently pleating the cuff on her shorts. "Everything fell apart the Friday night you and Jase came back from the horse sale.''

"What happened?''

She hesitated for a second before going on. "It ended up with just the girls and me at home. The boys had gone to Lethbridge for that ball tournament, and Clayton and Walter had decided to go fishing. Then Betty Donaldson phoned and wanted Patricia to baby-sit. She was going to take her kids to Drumheller the next day so she invited Lucy to go, as well. They were going to sleep over.''

Resting his hand against his mouth, Tyler squinted thoughtfully. "So you were alone when Jase got back.''

"Yes.''

"And?''

She turned her head away, her jaw clamped.

Tyler watched her, a hint of a smile in his eye. "I'm a big boy, Susan,'' he interjected dryly. "You don't have to draw me a detailed picture. Just tell me what went wrong.''

Without looking at him, Susan wearily rested her head against the back of the sofa. "The Donaldsons decided not to go to Drumheller when the storm hit, so Patricia had Jack bring her home that night because she didn't want me to be there alone.''

He winced, then dragged his hand down his face. "And she walked in on you.''

"Yes.''

"Did it upset her?''

"Very much. And she had every right to be. Apparently she'd caught her mother twice in…similar situations, but she'd never said anything because she didn't want to upset her dad. Needless to say, she was very distraught and dis-llusioned.'' She hesitated, then went on, her voice very low. "She said I was no better than her mother.''

Tyler swore, his face creased with concern. "So you thought you'd better leave."

"Yes."

"What did Jason say?"

There was a hint of bitterness in her voice. "Not much."

"And that hurt you pretty badly, didn't it?" She didn't answer, and Tyler gave her hand a reassuring little shake. "I know this may not be what you need to hear, Sue, but he's driving himself into the ground. You look into his eyes, and there's no life there anymore. It's like watching him die in degrees."

She swallowed against the aching tightness in her throat, then spoke, her voice unsteady. "He never even said goodbye when I left, Tyler. That hurt like hell."

"Maybe that was the only way he could deal with your leaving," he countered softly. "I spent that week with him, Sue. And I'd bet my life that if it hadn't been one of his kids involved, things would have been different."

Susan exhaled and raked back her hair. "But it *was* one of his kids, Tyler," she answered wearily.

"Does it have to be left like that? What if you talked to Trish?"

Susan gave him a lifeless smile. "You don't know how this has affected her. I doubt very much if she'd even be caught in the same room with me."

He frowned and slowly shook his head. "Maybe Trish's feelings have been taken too much into consideration."

"You mean ignore how she feels?" Susan firmly shook her head. "I could never ask Jase to make that kind of choice, even if I wanted to. I could never live with myself, especially when she was so revolted by—when she was so upset."

The expression on Tyler's face became more grave. "I was really that bad?"

"It was really that bad."

Tyler frowned, a deeply contemplative look in his eyes.

'Why do I get this feeling there's a rift between you and Jase?'' he asked quietly.

She shrugged and looked away. "I don't know if you'd call it a rift. We both felt really sick about what happened, and Patricia's reaction made it even worse. Jase was having a hard enough time dealing with our age difference as it was, and when a relationship becomes tainted by that kind of guilt, it creates quite a chasm."

He stared at her for a moment, then added astutely, "Add that to Jase's strong moral standards, and that makes it even worse. Especially when he felt you were getting the short end of the stick."

Susan managed a wry smile. "Well, nobody has to worry about that anymore."

He reached out and touched her hair. "I'm really sorry, Sue," he said quietly.

She turned away, her tone impassive. "So am I."

There was a brief silence, and Tyler sighed heavily and straightened up, then flashed her his bad-boy smile. "I think we should scrap dinner. Let's go out and get falling-down drunk and raise a little hell instead."

The way he said it brought a glint of humor to her eyes, and she gave him a crooked grin. "That's the best offer I've had in days."

Susan had seriously doubted if she could ever laugh again, but after one night on the town with Tyler Redding, she made a rather startling discovery: life could be worth living, in spite of how empty she felt. He ended up staying two days, providing Susan with a desperately needed respite from her loneliness and giving her the courage to face her future.

Summer passed into autumn, then the blaze of autumn faded into the bleak, leaden days that heralded winter, and Susan immersed herself in her job. But the challenge had worn thin, and she discovered that her job, no matter how fascinating it was, was no longer of primary importance to her. Which meant she had to work at it that much harder.

In the mid part of October, Clayton became responsible for the development of an international economic policy, and because of his involvement with other countries, he ended up spending a good portion of his time out of the country. With him gone so much, Susan's work load increased, and she put in longer and longer hours at the office.

The first snowfall of the season came in early November. It was a Saturday, and Susan had gone into the office to finish compiling some information Clayton would need when he came back. She was sitting at her desk, the dull sky turning heavy, when the first thick flakes started to fall. Sticking her hands in the pockets of her skirt, she went to the window and rested her shoulder against the frame as she solemnly watched them spiral down. The snow slowly blanketed the grounds, and as she continued to watch, an almost frightening feeling of isolation swept over her. She was so alone.

Trying to shrug it off as a simple case of feeling sorry for herself, she went back to her desk and stacked the folders she'd been working with. Another day alone in the office was what she did *not* need. She had just put on her coat and was about to turn off her desk lamp when the phone rang, its jangle reverberating shrilly in the still room.

Susan glanced at her watch, then reached across her desk and picked it up. "Susan Lynton," she answered crisply.

"Lord, woman, I've been trying to track you down for the past hour. Don't you ever go home?"

Her eyes widened with surprise. "Tyler?"

"Damn right. What in hell are you still doing at work?"

She grinned as she straightened some papers in her Out basket. "Crossword puzzles, what do you think?" She shifted the phone to her other hand as she checked her watch again. "Don't tell me you've made another side trip."

"No." There was a brief pause before he went on. "There's been some trouble at the Double Diamond."

A terrible sinking sensation made her stomach lurch, and

Susan tightened her hold on the receiver. "What happened?"

"Michael's appendix ruptured this morning. He finally came out of surgery about an hour ago."

Susan fumbled for the chair at the corner of her desk, then weakly sank into it. "How is he?"

"He's doing as well as can be expected. They're pumping him full of antibiotics, so hopefully there won't be any complications." There was a strained pause. "He's been asking for you, Sue. He's running a hell of a fever and is feeling really rotten. He could sure in hell do with a hug right now."

Her hand was trembling as she wiped away the tears with her fingertips, then swallowed hard. "Hang on a minute, Tyler. Let me check the flight schedules. Maybe I can get out of here this afternoon." She laid the phone down and went to the credenza to check the file she had on flight information. She double-checked the schedules, then went back to her desk and picked up the phone. "There's a flight out of here in a couple of hours that'll get me into Calgary about eight tonight, your time."

"Sounds good. Why don't you phone for reservations then call me back. I'll meet you in Calgary."

"I should be back to you within twenty minutes." She swallowed again, her voice breaking, "Tyler, I wonder if this is a good idea...."

"Save it, Sue," he interjected brusquely. "Don't talk, don't think, don't worry, just get on that damned plane. We'll talk about it when you get here."

Her eyes blurred but she managed a smile. "Yes, sir."

She could almost see him grin. "Hang in there, woman. We'll get this sorted out yet."

Tyler was leaning against one of the video game machines by the escalator when Susan came through the gate, and he grinned as he came toward her. "That's what I like. A woman who takes orders." She made a face at him, and his grin broadened as he took her carryon from her then

draped his arm around her shoulders. The amusement went
out of his eyes as he glanced down at her. "I'm glad you
came, Sue."

She exhaled sharply, her uncertainty compounding. "I
don't know, Tyler. I think this might be a monumental mistake."

She was still thinking that when they arrived at the High
River Hospital.

Tyler, being Tyler, totally dismissed her concern about
coming in after the posted times for visiting hours, and as
they approached the nursing station, he gave the nurse behind the counter his most disarming smile. "Ma'am, this
lady just flew in from Ottawa to see Michael Chisholm,"
he said in his lazy drawl, as he turned on the charm full
power. "Do you think we could sneak in for just a minute...just to let him know she's here?"

It was all Susan could do to keep a straight face as a very
businesslike middle-aged woman turned to a helpless female
before her very eyes. "I don't see why not," she responded
a little breathlessly. "Providing you don't stay too long."

"Thank you, ma'am," he said, politely touching the brim
of his hat, then draped his arm around Susan's shoulders
and propelled her down the corridor.

She glanced up at him, her eyes alight. "You're truly
impossible, do you know that?"

He grinned and steered her through an open door
"Damned right."

The curtain was partially drawn around the far bed, and
Susan's stomach did a sickening dive when she rounded the
foot of it and found Jason hunched over in a chair, his hands
clasped between his knees, the muted light from above the
bed casting his features in dark shadows. But before he even
realized they were there, and before either she or Tyler had
a chance to speak, Michael opened his eyes and saw her
"Susan?" He swallowed hard and wet his dry lips. "Is it
really you, Susan?"

Dropping her coat on the other chair, she slipped between

he curtain and the bed, then bent over and kissed him.
"Yes, it's me Mikey. I came as fast as I could."

He stared at her for a minute, then his eyes filled with
tears as he put his arms around her neck and pressed his
face against her shoulder. "I feel awful, Sue. And I was
scared. I wanted you to come so bad."

Struggling to fight back the tears that blurred her own
vision, Susan slipped her arms around his shoulders and
carefully hugged him. She fought to keep it light. "Tyler
said you could sure do with a hug, so I thought I'd better
bring you one."

A sob escaped him, then he relaxed his hold and looked
at her. He dragged his hand across his face and gave her a
wobbly smile. "He should've told you to bring some ice
cream, too."

She laughed as she straightened up and ruffled his hair.
"You never change, do you?" Taking the boy's small hand
in hers, she took a shaky breath and steeled herself as she
turned to face Jason. "Hello, Jason."

He had risen to his feet, his body rigid with shock, and
he stared at her, the muscles in his neck standing out in
thick cords as he clenched and unclenched his hands. An
expression closely resembling pain flashed across his face,
and his hands hardened into white-knuckled fists. "I...hello,
Susan."

Susan glanced at Tyler, desperately needing help in dealing with this very unexpected and awkward confrontation.
He was leaning against the wall, his arms folded in front of
him, intently watching her and Jason, apparently oblivious
to her unspoken plea for help. There was a contemplative
look on his face as he met her gaze, then he straightened
up and turned toward Jason. "I'll leave Susan's luggage
here, Jase, and maybe you can run her over to the motel
later. I've got some things to do yet, so I have to hit the
road."

Susan's eyes widened as panic gripped her. He couldn't
leave her alone with Jason. He couldn't!

Jason nodded stiffly, the pulse in his temple suddenly evident. "I'll do that."

Tyler nodded at Susan, then gave Michael's foot a little shake. "You hang in there, kid. We'll see you tomorrow."

Michael's voice was slightly unsteady. "Thanks for bringing Susan, Tyler."

He grinned and winked. "You're welcome, sport." With that, he touched the brim of his hat and disappeared into the corridor. And Susan felt as though he had just abandoned her.

The only way she got through the next half hour was by blocking out everything except the pale little boy lying in the bed. He had tubes in his nose and an IV in his hand and was enduring the discomfort with stoic silence, his hand still grasping hers. Susan sat on the edge of his bed, her back to his father, as she gently combed his tangled hair back from his face. He answered her softly spoken questions with a nod or a shake of his head, his grip almost desperate, and Susan ached to cuddle him, to comfort him. He was so little, and he hurt so much.

The nurse brought some medication, and a short time later his eyes began to grow heavy and his grasp slackened. He gave her a sleepy smile. "You can go now, if you want."

She leaned over and kissed his cheek. "Okay, but I'll be back first thing in the morning."

He nodded and gave her hand one final squeeze. "I love you, Susan," he whispered thickly.

Susan's vision blurred and she had to swallow hard as she returned the pressure, her voice breaking treacherously. "I love you, too, Mikey." She kissed him again and tucked the blankets around his shoulders. "You have a good sleep and I'll be back tomorrow."

Jason picked up his coat and hat, then stooped over and kissed his son, giving him a reassuring smile as he straightened. "If you want me to come in the night, tell the nurse, Mike. I've left instructions I'm to be called whenever you want, okay?"

Michael smiled at his dad. "Okay." A glint appeared in his eyes. "And maybe *you* can bring some ice cream."

Jason gave him a wry smile. "I don't think so. Not for a day or two."

Michael shrugged, his eyes drifting shut. "Darn." He sighed and nestled down. "Good night, Dad. Night, Susan." Susan smoothed her hand across the covers and gave his hand a final squeeze before she picked up her coat and carryon and slipped out of the room.

The drive to the motel was completed in virtual silence. Susan stared rigidly out the window, so aware of the man beside her that she felt as though she were going to come unstrung at any minute. At his slightest movement, she'd tense, and her heart would start hammering frantically in her chest.

Susan prayed that he would simply drop her off and leave. But he didn't. There was a stiff-lipped determination about him as he carried her luggage into the lobby and followed her to the desk.

Susan's hand wasn't quite steady as she filled out the registration form. "Will you leave this open, please? I don't know how long I'll be staying."

The desk clerk nodded. "Certainly. And how will you be paying?"

Before she had a chance to answer, Jason tossed a credit card on the counter. "By VISA," he answered curtly. The clerk glanced from one to the other, then shrugged and picked up Jason's card, ran it through the machine and silently gave him the bill to sign. Susan didn't even try to argue. She didn't dare. There was so much pain unfolding in her chest that she knew if she unclenched her teeth, she'd break down in front of him, and that was the very last thing she wanted to have happen.

She kept her mind blank as she followed him up a flight of stairs and along the corridor. He checked the number on the key, stopped and unlocked the door, and waited for her to precede him. Susan turned on the light, then took off her coat and dropped it on the bed, reluctant to face him.

"Susan?"

Clenching her jaws together, she clasped her hands tightly in front of her and reluctantly turned toward him. He was standing a few feet inside the door with his hands in the pockets of his sheepskin jacket, his head lowered, the brim of his Stetson shadowing his face. As she turned, he lifted his head and stared at her, a chiseled set to his face. The muscle in his jaw jumped and he abruptly looked away, his mouth compressing into a grim line.

Susan clasped her hands tighter as she fought back the sudden sting of tears. He had obviously lost weight, his face was thin and haggard, and a bleak, hopeless expression haunted his eyes. The ache unfolding in her became more intense; the look in his eyes was like a knife in her heart.

He tried to say something, then closed his mouth and swallowed hard, then tried again. "He woke up from anesthetic asking for you." His voice broke and he turned away again, and Susan saw him drag his hand across his face.

Tears slipped relentlessly down her cheeks as she gazed at him, wanting to stop his agony, not knowing how, her own despair tearing her apart. As he started toward the door, her ability to think was shattered by a rending pain, and she felt as if she were suffocating as he reached out and opened it. If he left...she didn't know how she could stand it if he left....

"Don't go, Jason."

He froze, then slowly turned, his expression carved by anguish as his gaze riveted on her.

Fresh tears spilled down her cheeks, and her voice was a tortured whisper. "God, please don't go."

For one, brief terrifying moment, he stood poised to leave, then dragging in a lungfull of air, he pushed the door shut.

Susan wasn't prepared for the eruption of pent-up emo

tion when he touched her, and a deep, racking sob was wrung from her as he caught her against him in a crushing embrace. Jason's expression twisted into a grimace as he roughly pressed her face into his neck, his hold fierce. A shudder coursed through him, his voice hoarse and shaking as he choked out, "Susan—Lord, but I thought I'd never see you again."

Driven by desperation, Susan twisted her head free from his hold, searching for his mouth, and a low tormented sound was torn from him as the searing contact unleashed a frantic hunger. He groaned again, his embrace becoming almost brutal as her breath caught on a ragged sob, and he ground his mouth against hers, his control completely shattered. Fueled by months of unrelenting loneliness and pain, their desperation escalated into a mindless frenzy that left no room for conscious thought, propelling them into a consuming passion. And the only thing Susan was aware of was the granite hardness of his body locked against hers and the crushing strength of his arms.

Like a drowning man battling for breath, Jason roughly grasped her head and tore his mouth away, his face contorted as he fought to haul air into his laboring lungs. His chest was heaving when he finally looked at her, his eyes black and fired with desire.

The pulse in his neck was erratic and his fingers were trembling as he gently touched her lips. He swallowed hard, then thrust his fingers deep into her hair. His eyes were mesmerizing as he caressed her scalp, then slowly, so slowly, he lowered his head, his touch immeasurably tender as he brushed his mouth against hers.

That soft, lingering kiss drove the strength out of her, enervating her with a thick, pulsating weakness, and her eyes drifted shut as she swayed against him, hypnotized by the magic of his touch. His hands tightened against her temples as he lightly moved his mouth back and forth across hers, slowly savoring her warmth, softly trying to soothe her raw emotions. He inhaled jaggedly as he shuddered again, his obvious struggle for control igniting a wild clamor that demanded more. With a soft moan, she caught the back of his head, the gentlness turning into a fierce and escalating need as the kiss deepened and became hot and searching.

Like a man struggling for the last thin thread of control, Jason crushed her to him, his hold unbreakable as he roughly dragged his mouth away and clamped her head against his shoulder. He was fighting for every breath as he buried his face in her hair, his body rigid. Several seconds passed before he was able to speak. "Susan.... God, I want you so badly—I can't think." He kissed her on the temple, then tightened his hold as he cradled the back of her head, his fingers tangled in her hair. "Sue—love—I need to hold you for a minute."

Closing her eyes, Susan took a deep steadying breath, then kissed him on the neck, her own voice trembling. "Please stay. I don't think I could stand it if you didn't stay."

He kissed her once more. "I will," he whispered gruffly. "All night." A vehement surge of emotion coursed through him, and he gritted his teeth as he sharply sucked in his breath. "God, but I've missed you." It didn't seem possible he could hold her any more securely, but his arms tightened further as he pressed his face into her neck, his heart pounding against hers. He held her like that for a moment, then raised his head and gazed down at her, an air of reluctance about him. "I have to phone the hospital and the ranch," he murmured, his tone low. "I have to let them know where I am in case anything happens."

There was a sober look in his eyes, almost as though he felt guilty, and Susan realized he hated having to put the needs of his family first. She smiled softly. "I know you do. And there's no need to feel guilty about it."

He closed his eyes as he tried to swallow. "But I do," he whispered. "It's not fair to you."

She struggled with a new swell of emotion as she moved to kiss the soft skin of his neck. "It's not important, Jason."

She inhaled deeply, savoring the masculine fragrance of him, then raised her head and looked at him. "I don't care what you have to do first," she whispered huskily, "just as long as you can spend the night with me."

His eyes darkened and his hand tightened in her hair, but he didn't say anything as he gazed down at her. He traced her jaw with his fingertips, then softly brushed his lips against the corner of her mouth, his control rigid. He sighed and reluctantly raised his head, then eased his hold on her.

Susan reached up and removed his cowboy hat and dropped it on the end of the bed, then slowly combed her fingers through his hair. A heady excitement began to unfold in her as she slipped her hands through the silky strands, then across his shoulders, slowly stripping the sheepskin jacket from him. The muscles in his back tensed as he watched her, his eyes kindling, his body disciplined against the sensations she was arousing in him. His jaw flexed and his nostrils flared as the jacket dropped unheeded to the floor, and she slowly smoothed her hands back up his arms.

His eyes darkened, then drifted shut as he breathed her name in a hoarse whisper. She touched his mouth with her trembling fingers, then blinking back tears, eased away from him. He caught her head, his eyes smoldering as he tried to draw her to him.

But she resisted, pressing her fingers against his lips. "Don't, Jason," she whispered brokenly. "If you touch me again, I won't be able to stop." She managed an unsteady smile as she caressed his cheek. "Make your phone calls. Then there's nothing to stop us."

He clenched his teeth, his whole body rigid, then sucking in a deep breath, he gave her one hard kiss and turned away, the tension between them nearly overwhelming. With his back still to her, he rolled his shoulders and reached for the phone. And with her heart racing, Susan pulled her sweater off over her head as she headed to the bathroom.

When she came out, Jason was still on the phone, standing with his back to her, absently tracing patterns on the phone book with the room key. He turned, his expression altering, and he didn't move a muscle as she came across the room. She had left on her ivory camisole and bikini briefs, the cut of the panties accentuating her long legs, the lace bodice revealing a tantalizing amount of flesh. He stared at her, his hold on the phone turning into a white-knuckled grip, then he closed his eyes and turned away, his chest heaving as he asked for the nursing station where Michael was.

Susan felt as if she were in a dream as she crossed the room, and resting her face against his back, slipped her arms around his waist. Jason tensed as though she had just branded him, then he turned to face her, their bodies lightly brushing together. He had taken off his boots, and the sameness in height made her blood rush, knowing how well their bodies meshed together. She resisted the pressure of his hand on her back as he silently urged her against him. She gazed at him, her eyes hypnotizing him with an unspoken promise as she undid the snaps on his cuffs, then began to slowly undo the ones down the front of his shirt.

He caught her hand when she reached the bottom one, his grip crushing as he stilled her movements and spoke into the phone. His voice was husky and very unsteady as he gave the nurse on duty instructions on where he could be reached and the number of the motel room. There was a brief silence, then he turned away and replaced the receiver. His face was carved by tension, his eyes as black as onyx when he finally turned back to Susan.

Her voice was nearly as unsteady as his when she whispered, "Have you talked to Mattie?"

He eased his hold on her hand, his expression unsmiling. "Yes. I gave her the room number here."

She stared up at him, a charge building between them as their gazes locked. She never took her eyes off his face as she withdrew her fingers from his grasp and slipped her hands across his shoulders and down his arms, stripping his shirt from him. A pulsating warmth spread through her body as she stared into his smoldering eyes, her hands trembling as she let them slip down his hard abdomen to his waist, where she undid the buckle of his belt, then slowly pulled his zipper down. He remained motionless, and she smoothed her hands down his hips, peeling the fabric away. But the minute she touched his swollen flesh, he reacted, and with a low, ragged groan, he pulled her roughly into his arms, their hips fusing together with a desperate surge.

He locked one arm around her buttocks, the other hand buried in her hair as he sought her lips, driving her into a mindless ecstasy as he moved against her, his body hard and thrusting, his mouth plundering hers. A fever of desire scorched through her, and Susan lost touch with all reality as she responded to him.

Jason rasped out her name as he roughly stripped the silky garments from her, his need finally raging out of control. Then he crushed her against him and dragged her down on the bed, their bodies fusing together from shoulder to thigh. He fought the frenzy of need that possessed him, struggling to regain some gentleness, but their passion was fed by desperation, their desire by urgency, and Susan cried out her need as she raised her hips to meet his powerful thrust. Whatever chance Jason had to temper the blaze was gone, and he entered her, his body driving powerfully against hers, their desire breaking around them, carrying them to incredible heights. The release was explosive, welding them together in the white-hot eruption.

CHAPTER TWELVE

THE SOUND OF A KEY in the lock dragged Susan from a deep sleep, and she slowly opened her eyes. Jason, wearing his hat and sheepskin jacket, came in and quietly closed the door, a dusting of snow clinging to the suede of his jacket. The room was still cast in early morning darkness, and the light from the bathroom framed him in the indirect rectangle of brightness. He was carrying two bags; one he tossed carelessly on the desk, the other one he continued to hold, and the smell of coffee permeated her groggy senses.

Sweeping her hair back from her face, she raised up on one elbow. "Good morning," she murmured, her voice husky with sleep.

He turned to look at her, an intimate warmth lighting up his eyes as he gave her a smile. He came over to the bed, bracing his hand on the pillow as he bent down to kiss her, his mouth soft and warm, and tasting faintly of coffee. "Good morning," he murmured against her lips. "I thought I could sneak back in without waking you."

Slipping her arms around him, she nuzzled her face against his neck. "I'm glad you did."

There was the rustle of paper as he set the bag down on the nightstand, then he slid his arms around her and kissed her again, the fragrance of cold air still clinging to him. "So am I," he answered, his voice a little gruff.

She tightened her arms around him. "Why don't you come back to bed?"

She felt him smile against her temple as he smoothed his hand up her naked back. "I brought you a coffee and Danish."

"I'd rather have you."

He laughed, his voice low and husky. "Don't be a torment, Susan. I had a hard enough time getting out of bed the first time."

Susan gave him one last kiss then reluctantly pulled out of his arms and sat up. She stretched lazily and smiled up at him. "You didn't have to make a special trip out for this, you know."

"I know, but I needed to pick up a razor and a few other things anyway, and I thought you'd be ready for a coffee."

"I am."

Jason tossed his hat on the foot of the bed then took off his jacket. Stacking the pillows against the headboard, he stretched out on the bed beside her, cradling her against the curve of his shoulder. He pulled the spread free and carefully tucked it around her bare shoulders before reaching for the bag.

Resting her head on his chest, she snuggled against him. "I can't believe I didn't wake up when you got up."

"You were dead to the world. You didn't move a muscle."

That didn't really surprise her. The vehemence of their stormy lovemaking had left her completely spent, her body drugged by a heavy sated sensation, and she had fallen asleep in his arms almost immediately. She took the steaming Styrofoam cup he handed her, then looked up at him. "How did you sleep?"

His jaw was rough with a heavy growth of beard, but even so, there was a softer look about his face, as though he, too, had been relieved of some very grating tension. He took the lid off his own cup of coffee, then gazed down at her, a desolate expression in his eyes. "That was the first decent night's rest I've had since you left."

The way he said it made her throat ache, and she watched him, her expression becoming more grave. She saw him try to swallow, and closing her eyes she brushed her lips against his rigid jaw, her voice unsteady as she whispered, "I know nothing's really changed because of last night, Jason. We made a mess of things, and we're going to have to live with that." She raised her head and looked at him, her face solemn. "But at least we can face each other now, and we've put some of the guilt behind us."

He avoided looking at her as he broke away a chip of plastic on the rim of his cup. "And what are you left with, Susan? The odd clandestine weekend, maybe a rare week together?" He finally raised his eyes and looked at her, his expression bleak. "I can't ask that of you."

She somehow managed an unsteady smile. "It's better than nothing, Jase. Anything is better than the agony of not seeing you at all."

His face looked as though it were hacked out of stone as he set his cup on the table, then silently removed hers from her hand and set it beside his. Drawing in a deep, ragged breath, he slipped both arms around her and gathered her against him as he turned toward her, his hold almost savage. His voice was hoarse as he whispered against her hair, "God, Sue, I thought I was going to go out of my mind after you left. And each day seemed more empty and unbearable than the one before. I don't think I can face that kind of loneliness again."

Holding him tightly, she slipped her hand up his neck until her fingers were buried in his thick hair. She closed her eyes, her lashes matting wetly together as she pressed her face against his, her voice unsteady. "I don't think I can, either, Jase. I need you in my life, even if it's only for an occasional weekend."

He inhaled sharply. "I wish I could give you more, Susan," he whispered, his voice thick with emotion. "I hate making you take second place like this."

She closed her eyes tighter, her voice breaking as tears slipped down. "I know you do."

"I'm so sorry."

"I know that, too." She stroked his head, overwhelmed by all the incredible feelings she had for him. "I love you so much, Jason Chisholm and that's all that matters."

He shuddered and pressed his mouth against the hollow

in her throat, his stubble of beard rough and abrasive, his face wet against her skin. She swallowed hard and continued to stroke his head, waiting for the strangling pressure in her chest to ease. Finally the contraction abated, and she smiled, her voice laced with humor as she whispered huskily, "Who knows, I might make a much better mistress than I did a cook."

That wrung a shaky laugh out of him, and he raised his head and gazed down at her. "A mistress sounds a damned sight more expensive than a cook."

She grinned and kissed him on the end of the nose. "And more interesting."

There was a mesmerizing quality to his lopsided smile. "*Definitely* more interesting."

Her expression sobered and her breath caught as she murmured, "Come back to bed, Jason."

He raised up on one elbow and lightly kissed the whisker burn on her shoulder. "I should shave first," he answered, his voice gruff.

She cupped her hands along his jaw and raised his head. "Later."

He stared at her a minute, the pulse in his neck throbbing, then he drew her head down, his mouth moist and hungry against hers as he answered, "Later."

IT WAS MUCH, MUCH LATER when they finally arrived at the hospital. In fact, it was going on ten o'clock. Their consummation the night before had been savage and driven by desperation, but that morning it had been the exact opposite—slow, sweet, and so tender that Susan felt as if every nerve in her body was dissolving in one glorious sensation after another.

But this time, it had been Jason who had drifted off to sleep, his breath warm against her breast, his arm draped across her abdomen, his leg wedged between hers. Susan lay awake, idly caressing his hair as she listened to his deep, even breathing, savored every second she had with him, knowing moments like this were going to have to sustain her through many long and lonely nights.

They had breakfasted on cold coffee and slightly dried out Danish, and by the time they left the motel, Jason Chisholm looked rested, relaxed and completely revitalized.

They found Michael partially sitting up in bed wearing clean pajamas, his face having a freshly scrubbed look. He greeted them with a broad smile. "Hi. I didn't think you guys were ever coming." He took the bag that Susan handed him and grinned up at her. "Did you bring me ice cream?"

She bit back a smile. "I most certainly did not. I brought you a coloring book with little pigs and bunnies in it and a box of crayons."

Michael gave her a dubious look as he set the bag down and started to unfold the top. "You didn't, did you? You're just kidding, right?"

"I never kid about pigs and bunnies, Michael."

He narrowed his eyes and grimaced as he slowly opened the bag. His expression froze for a split second, then his eyes lit up. "A Walkman! You got me a Walkman radio!" He looked up at his father, his eyes wide with happy disbelief. "She brought me a Walkman, Dad. Boy, my very own!" He lifted the small portable radio and cassette deck out of the package, and hurriedly plugged in the headset, then clamped it on his head. He turned it on, a look of sheer ecstasy glazing his eyes as he tuned in to his favorite radio station.

Jason glanced at Susan, his eyes glinting. "I think he just found seventh heaven."

Susan laughed as she took off her coat and laid it on the foot of the bed. "I wouldn't laugh about it if I were you. Just wait until you find out what it's going to cost you to keep him in batteries."

The gleam intensified as he unbuttoned his jacket and gave her a slow, seductive smile. "Two major new expenses in one day—could be critical," he murmured softly.

She gave him a loaded look, and he grinned, and without thinking, he reached toward her. Susan knew that he had been about to brush back her hair, but he caught himself before he touched her. The muscle in his jaw jumped as he clamped his mouth shut, ramming his hands in the pockets of his jeans. A grim look darkened his eyes, and a knot formed in Susan's throat. She wanted to touch him in the worst way, to physically reassure him that it was all right, but she dragged up a smile instead, her voice very low and husky as she murmured, "Didn't your mother ever teach you not to touch when you were little?"

He stared at her for a few seconds, his jaw rigid, then his expression relaxed and he smiled. "That's so long ago, I can't remember."

"Try."

He laughed, his gaze like a warm caress, and she smiled back, her eyes soft with love. She saw him catch his breath, and fighting down the sudden flutter of excitement, she tore her eyes away and sat down beside his son. Catching the headphones, she pried them away from Michael's ears. "Look, kid, if you're just going to lie there looking like a contented cow, I may as well go back to the motel."

Michael grimaced and sheepishly shut off the radio. "I sure like it, Susan. Thanks a lot."

"You're welcome. How are you feeling?"

He shrugged. "I felt yucky this morning. Really hot and barfy, and my stomach hurt. But they gave me something and I feel okay now." He glanced at his dad. "Aren't you gonna take your jacket off, Dad?"

Jason shook his head. "I'm not staying, Mike. I promised that since it was Sunday, I'd bring everybody in to see you, so I'd better leave soon."

Michael looked at Susan. "Are you going, too?"

"No, I'll stay with you."

He stared at her, a strange, thoughtful expression on his face. "Aren't you going to go to the ranch at all?"

She managed to keep her voice level. "Probably not."

He glanced from his father to Susan, then back to his father. "Oh," he said as he suddenly looked down at his hands.

It took considerable discipline not to look at Jason, and trying to let on nothing was wrong, Susan began tidying up the clutter on the bed. Jase's voice was carefully regulated as he spoke. "I guess I'll take off, Michael. I should be back in an hour or so, okay?"

"Okay."

Susan did not look up as Jason left the room. She hadn't been quite prepared for this—the strain of becoming a secret lover. Or the guilt about deceiving the kids. She hadn't been prepared for that at all.

Michael's temperature climbed sharply again, and by the time his father returned with the others, the boy was flushed, his eyes glassy, and Susan could tell by the set of his mouth that he was in considerable pain. His extreme pallor was accentuated by the scalding-hot fever spots on his cheeks, and she gently sponged him off, trying to ease the heat that radiated from him. She was bending over him, wiping his drawn little face when she heard the Chisholm family coming down the hallway. Michael looked up at her, his eyes glazed with pain, an unspoken entreaty in them.

She brushed back his sweat-dampened hair as she said quietly, "Don't worry, love. If you don't feel up to it, they won't stay long."

He licked his dry lips as he slipped his hand into hers. "I don't feel like talking, Susan."

She smiled and tightened her hand around his. "Then you don't have to."

There was a nervous flutter in her stomach as she drew in a deep breath, bracing herself for a face-to-face confrontation with Patricia. But it was only Mattie, Todd and Lucy who came through the door, and Susan felt a twist of pain as she recognized the silent snub. But Mattie's face creased with a wide smile and she opened her arms in welcome. "Well, Susan, this is the best surprise I've had in some time."

Fighting the sudden sting of tears, Susan hugged Jason's mother, her voice uneven. "It's so good to see you, Mattie."

The older woman hugged her tightly, then patted her

back. "And it's good to have you back, my dear. You were sorely missed."

Susan quickly blotted her eyes then pulled away. She glanced down at the two children, only she didn't have to look down quite as far as she used to. "Todd! Look how you've grown. I can't believe it. And look at Lucy!" She crouched and hugged the little girl to her. "And I see the tooth fairy's been to visit."

Lucy hugged her hard then gave her a gap-tooth smile as she lisped, "Yeth. And she left me five whole dollars, but Daddy thaid she left so much because both teeth came out at once and she only had to make one trip."

Susan laughed, her eyes sparkling with a mixture of amusement and affection as she smoothed down Lucy's mop of curls. She hugged her once more, then looped her arm around Todd's hips and looked up at him. "And how about you, Tiger? What's new with you?"

He leaned against her as he slipped his arm around her neck. "Not much. Me and Mikey are playing hockey already." He grinned down at her, his eyes bright with mischief. "Have you ever played hockey, Susan?"

"Not a chance," she said with a grin as she stood up and ruffled his hair. She managed to keep her smile in place as she asked the question she knew she had to ask. "Where's Patricia?"

"Oh, she had a whole bunch of homework and couldn't come," Todd answered as he went over to the bed and touched his brother's hand. "How are you, Mikey? Are you feeling pretty yucky?"

Michael licked his lips, his eyes glazed. "A little."

Todd touched the Walkman laying beside him. "Hey, a Walkman. Where did you get a Walkman?"

"Susan brought it for me."

"Hey! Neato! Can I listen to it?"

Michael nodded then glanced at Susan. Mattie read the look. She leaned over him and brushed back his hair. "Would you like a drink, dear?"

"Yes, please, Grandma," he answered weakly.

Mattie supported his shoulders as she gave him a sip of water, then gently laid him back down. "How about if Susan takes Todd and Lucy out to the waiting room for a visit, and I'll stay here with you. Would that be all right?"

He nodded again, and Susan and Mattie exchanged a look, then the younger woman caught Lucy's hand. "Come on, Princess. Let's go find a place where we can talk."

Todd slid the headphones back on, the faint sound of music emitting from them as he looked up at Susan. "Dad had to take Walter uptown to get some stuff. He said they'd be back in about half an hour and he'd take us all for lunch."

Thinking about the one cold cup of coffee and the Danish that had been her breakfast, Susan grinned and started out of the room. "He'd better not be much longer than that, or I might be forced to gnaw on somebody's leg."

Lucy grinned up at her. "You can have mine, Thusan. Duffy thays I look sweet enough to eat."

Susan slanted a dry look down at the little girl. "And Duffy certainly should know."

The visitors' lounge at the end of the hallway was empty, and Susan sat down on the settee and put her feet up on the magazine table in front of her. With unaffected ease Todd slouched down beside her, his weight resting against her side as he bobbed his head in time to the Walkman's music. Lucy climbed up on the other side, then turned on her knees and faced her as Susan slipped her arm around her. "I'm glad you're back, Thusan. I really missed you, you know."

Susan tried to ignore the funny ache in her chest. "I missed you, too, Pumpkin." She gave her a little hug and smiled at her, then draped her arms around both children's shoulders. "Now tell me what's happening in your life."

She lost all track of time as she listened, asked questions and laughed a great deal, and it wasn't until she heard someone coming down the hallway wearing boots that she realized how long they'd been there. She glanced at her watch and swung her legs down. "Hey, guys, that sounds like your father coming. Maybe now we can go eat."

Only it wasn't Jason who came into the sun room. It was Tyler Redding. And he had Patricia with him.

Susan's stomach lurched, and she slowly disengaged herself from the other two and stood up, the animation draining from her face as she stared at Jason's daughter. The unexpectedness of seeing the girl welded her to the ground, and she pressed her hands tightly against her thighs, not knowing what to do, not knowing what to say.

Tyler, however, had no such reservations. He strode over to the settee and grasped Todd and Lucy by the hands. "Come on, kids, we're going for a walk so Patricia and Susan can talk."

Todd grabbed the Walkman before it slid out of his lap, then gave Tyler a confused look. "But, Tyler, Dad said—"

"No buts," Tyler responded firmly. "We're going for a walk." And with that, he marched them out of the room with such speed that Lucy's feet barely touched the ground.

Susan drew in a slow measured breath, then turned to squarely face the girl. She was barely recognizable as the same person Susan had first seen at the Double Diamond. She had lost all the extra weight, she had her hair styled in another new cut, and she wore her clothes with a sense of style that she'd not possessed before. She had turned into a truly beautiful young lady. And Susan wanted to cry.

She took another shaky breath, then addressed Jason's elder daughter. "Hello, Patricia. I'm glad you were able to come."

There was a slightly belligerent set to the girl's chin as she stared at Susan. "Are you?"

Susan stared back at her, her solemn expression marked by an underlying bleakness. "Yes, I am. Whether you want to believe it or not, it didn't seem quite right without you here."

The girl bent her head as she traced a line on the floor with her toe. "Well, I don't believe it."

Susan folded her arms in front of her as she looked away, trying to hold back tears. "Well, it's true. I've thought about you a lot these past few months."

"Then why did you leave?" she retorted, her voice laced with resentment. "If you cared about us so much how could you leave like that?"

Susan turned her head and looked at the girl, hurt by that accusation. "You said I was just like your mother, Patricia, and knowing you felt like that, I didn't think I had any other choice but to leave."

"That's just what my mother did. Leave. It was the easy way out."

Susan turned to the window and rested her shoulder against the frame as she stared blindly out at the street. "It wasn't the easy way out, Patricia. That was the hardest thing I've ever had to do in my entire life—to walk away from you kids and your father. But it seemed like it was the only thing I *could* do, under the circumstances. I felt so awful about what had happened...about you."

Susan sighed and turned back to face the girl. Patricia was standing with her dark head bent, her hands stuffed in the pockets of her coat, and as she gazed at her, Patricia wiped her cheek with the heel of her hand, and Susan realized she was crying.

Feeling utterly helpless, Susan went to her, hesitated, then gently stroked her hair. "Oh, Patricia," she whispered softly, "you don't know how much I hated myself for doing that to you. You should have never seen what you did."

A choked sob escaped from the teenager and she roughly rammed her hands back in her pockets, her voice breaking. "Were you and Dad really going to get married, or was that just a line?"

Susan sighed. "Yes, we were."

Patricia finally raised her head and looked at Susan, her eyes brimming with tears. "Why? Why would you want to get married with all us kids and everything?"

Her own vision blurring, Susan took the girl's face in her hands, her voice strained. "Because I love you, Patricia. I love every one of you, especially your father. Those few weeks on the Double Diamond were the best—the very best. And I thought I was going to shrivel up and die when I went back to Ottawa, because I was leaving behind everything that mattered.''

Tears slipped down the girl's cheeks as she stared at Susan, then her face crumpled, and with a low sob, she launched herself into Susan's arms. "Oh, Susan. I felt so awful, and so confused—and so embarrassed.''

Closing her eyes, Susan gathered the girl against her, rocking her as though she were a very small child, and finally her own tears slipped down her face. "I know, love. I know. And I felt so badly for you." She quickly wiped her face with the back of her hand, then tightened her hold as Patricia's body shook with heavy sobs. "Don't cry, love," she whispered unevenly. "It's all behind us now. So don't cry.''

There was a movement in the hall, and Susan looked up just as Jason strode into the room, his face lined with anxiety, his taut expression forewarning what he expected to find. He saw them and stopped, his momentum abruptly arrested by the unexpectedness of the scene before him. He stared at them, his jaw clenched, a tense, worried look in his eyes.

Trying to swallow the ache in her throat, Susan stroked Patricia's head then whispered softly, "Your father's here, Trish." She could feel the girl make a massive effort to stop weeping, but there was too much pent-up misery, and finally Trish gave up trying and raised her head and looked at him, silently pleading with him to understand. "Daddy…I'm so sorry, Daddy.''

Jason only hesitated a split second, then he crossed the room in two strides, catching them both in a fiercely protective embrace. He tightened his hold around his daughter, his voice thick with emotion as he whispered, "I'm sorry, too, Trish. You should have never had to deal with something like that.''

Several moments passed before anyone moved, then Patricia pressed her face against his jacket in an attempt to blot her tears. She finally raised her head and looked up at him, her gaze clear and steady. "It wasn't that, Dad. How

I acted had more to do with my mother than it did you and Susan." She looked down, her embarrassment apparent. "And then I was upset with Susan because she left. I thought she'd taken the easy way out."

Jason brushed back a curl that was clinging to her temple, his expression somber. "But it wasn't the easy way out, Trish. She did it because she thought it was best for you."

Patricia raised her head and looked at him, then glanced at Susan before she focused on him again. "I know that now."

Jason gave her a reassuring smile and pressed her head against his chest. "What made you change your mind about coming here?"

There was a brief silence, then she gave a muffled little laugh before she looked up. She shrugged sheepishly. "Well, I didn't exactly change my mind. Tyler more or less dragged me here. He said if I had something to say, I'd better say it to Susan's face." She glanced at Susan, a blush creeping up her cheeks, an impish sparkle lighting her eyes. "I think he should be your maid of honor, Susan. I think he deserves it."

Susan and Jason exchanged a tense look, then Susan stared down at Patricia, her expression uncertain. "Patricia, are you certain that's what you want?"

"Do you mean do I want Tyler to be your maid of honor, or do I want you and Dad to get married?" Patricia flashed the disarming, if slightly unsteady, Chisholm smile. "Well, it doesn't matter—it's yes to both." Her expression grew serious as she gazed up at Susan, and fresh tears gathered along her lashes. She swallowed hard, then whispered, "Remember when you told me that I couldn't give up the things that were really important to me because someone made me feel guilty? Remember?" She brushed away the tears as she drew in a tremulous breath. "You aren't, are you? You aren't giving up the things that matter to you? You *are* coming home, aren't you, Susan?" The tears slipped down and her mouth began to tremble. "We really need you to come home."

Her own vision distorted by tears, Susan looked at Jason. He was watching her, his face immobilized by emotion, as though he were afraid her answer would be the wrong one. He gently touched her face, his gaze locked on hers. Reading the answer in her brimming eyes, he smiled softly before he brushed his mouth against hers, his voice gruff as he said, "Of course she's coming home."

THE PAGES ON THE CALENDAR had turned nearly full circle, and the distinctive fragrance of early autumn drifted in through the open kitchen window, bringing with it the pungent smell of burning leaves. Susan inhaled deeply as she propped her head on her hand and gazed through the glass. The long shadows of late afternoon slanted across the backyard, the sun setting the windbreak of trees ablaze, the smoke from Walter's bonfire curling up in the clear, still air. It had been such a beautiful fall. The weather had been perfect and the autumn colors were enough to take her breath away.

She glanced at the postcard, which was propped against a vase holding a mixed bouquet of flowers from the garden. It had just arrived that day, and it was from Mattie. Jason's mother had finally been given a clean bill of health from her doctor, and Clayton, being Clayton, had celebrated the good news by arranging a trip to Spain for the two of them. They had left four weeks ago and, by the sounds of it, were having a marvelous time.

Susan sighed contentedly and picked up the sewing she had been working on. It was a new jacket of Walter's that needed the sleeves shortened, and she arranged the garment in her lap and began stitching.

"Susan, do you know where the atlas is?"

Susan looked up at Patricia. "Isn't it on the bottom shelf of the bookcase, next to that big book on birds?"

"Oh, maybe. I'll go check." She turned to leave the room, neatly sidestepping her little sister as she came flying in. "Wait till you see what Walter's bringing you," she bubbled. "You're going to love it, Susan. You are." She hugged herself then scrambled up on a chair. "What are you doing?"

"I'm fixing Walter's jacket."

"Oh." Lucy glanced out the window, then hopped off the chair and went dancing out to the porch, calling out loudly, "I'll hold the door open for you, Walter."

A few minutes later, Walter came into the kitchen, carrying a huge plant pot filled with an enormous clump of carnations he had dug out of the garden. The scent filled the room, and Susan's eyes lit up with delight. "Oh, Walter, how lovely."

He gave her his slow smile. "I thought you'd like them in the house. It's going to freeze soon."

Her expression was one of pure pleasure as she moved some papers so he could set the pot on the end of the counter. "That was such a nice thing to do," she said softly. "They're so beautiful and I hate the thought of the frost getting them."

He gently straightened some of the blossoms, then slowly nodded. "They should bloom inside until Christmas."

Susan squeezed his arm. "You're going to spoil me, Walter, giving me carnations up until Christmas."

He chuckled and shook his head. "You won't spoil, Susan. Not you."

She gave him a quick kiss on the cheek, then indicated the jacket that was laying on the end of the table. "Why don't you try that on so I can check the sleeve length, and I'll see if I can find you a piece of pie."

He grinned. "Sounds fine."

Lucy had her face buried in the enormous arrangement of carnations. "It smells just like heaven, doesn't it, Susan. Don't you think heaven smells that way?"

Susan's eyes were sparkling as she answered the little girl. "I'm sure it does, Lucy."

Patricia had just entered the kitchen, and she rolled her eyes skyward in a hopeless expression as she set her book down on the end of the table. "Sometimes I wonder about her."

Susan laughed. "Don't despair, Trish. Someday that imagination of hers will make us all rich."

There was an impish gleam in Patricia's eyes. "Or make us all crazy."

Susan was kneeling on the floor by Walter, straight pins in her mouth, adjusting his left sleeve when the back door slammed open and the boys came boiling in, followed closely by Tyler Redding and Jason. Susan made the adjustment, then taking the pins out of her mouth, she grinned up at them. "Well, Tyler Redding. Where did you come from?"

Jason chuckled as he dropped several parcels on the counter, then took off his hat. "He's like a stray dog, Sue. He shows up whenever he's hungry." He came over and stooped down to give her a kiss, his grin broadening. "So what's to eat?" he asked, his eyes drifting to the pie sitting on the counter.

She gave him a narrow look, and Tyler chuckled. "He's a sneaky devil, Susan. He's using me for cover, you know. He's the one who's eyeing the pie, not me." He cast it a quick glance, then tipped his head in appreciation. "Although it does look damned good."

Biting back a smile, Susan sighed in resignation. "Patricia, would you please cut some pie for these two big bottomless pits?"

Michael leaned against her as she picked up some loose pins that she'd accidentally scattered on the floor. His grin was pure Chisholm. "What about us little bottomless pits?" he asked, turning on the charm. "Can we have some, too?"

She smiled back at him. "Yes, you can have some, too."

Todd was rummaging through the parcels as Susan stood up and set the scissors and pins on the counter. He glanced up at her. "We got my new jeans, Susan, but the saleslady couldn't find the right length so they're too long. But I told her my mom would shorten 'em for me."

It happened again. An incredible, warm flutter unfolded in Susan's abdomen, making her breath catch. It always affected her that way—turning her insides to warm mush—

when one of the kids called her "Mom." She'd experience such a rush of love that it would nearly suffocate her. She inhaled slowly before she looked up. Jason was leaning against the counter, his thumbs hooked in his belt loops, watching her with a steady gaze. He smiled softly, knowingly, then reached out and drew her against him so her back rested against his chest, then slipped his arms around her waist. He dropped a kiss on her temple, then murmured, "I can't believe how fast the time has gone—another two months and we'll have been married a year."

She laughed and tipped her head back to look at him, a tormenting gleam in her eyes. "I suppose when you're older, the time goes by quicker."

He grinned and narrowed his eyes. "Watch it, woman." He drew her closer, his cheek pressed against her hair. "What are you thinking right now?" he asked softly.

She watched the kids gather around the table as Patricia cut the pie, she watched Tyler inspect the leather tooling Walter had brought in to work on, she savored the warmth and security of this man's arms around her, and she smiled. "I was thinking how completely happy I am."

He tightened his arms around her, his voice husky as he brushed his lips against her hair. "Then that's all that matters." And it was.

Harlequin Romance®

Delightful
Affectionate
Romantic
Emotional

Tender
Original

Daring
Riveting
Enchanting
Adventurous
Moving

Harlequin Romance®—
capturing the world you dream of...

HARLEQUIN®
Makes any time special®

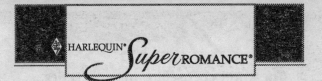

HARLEQUIN®
INTRIGUE

WE'LL LEAVE YOU BREATHLESS!

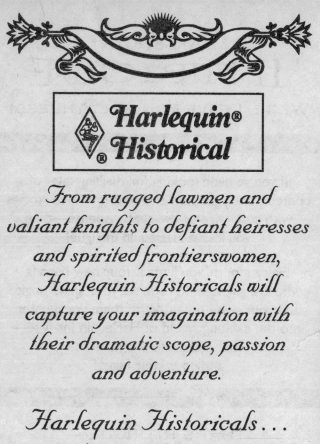

Harlequin® Historical

From rugged lawmen and valiant knights to defiant heiresses and spirited frontierswomen, Harlequin Historicals will capture your imagination with their dramatic scope, passion and adventure.

Harlequin Historicals...
they're too good to miss!